MW01595027

MAIN STREET PRESIDENT

PRESIDENT HENRY F. SCHRICKER'S 1945 WORLD WAR II DECISIONS

DICK ELAM

Registered with the Library of Congress

ISBN Paperback — 979-8-9920036-1-1
ISBN eBook — 979-8-9920036-0-4

Edited by — Kelly Colby
Cover Painting by — Mitch Markovitz
Cover design by – Deena Rae; E-BookBuilders
Book interior design by – Deena Rae; E-BookBuilders, adaptation for ebook

For information contact:

Dick Elam Books
464 S. County Road 4837
Winnsboro, TX 75494
dickelambooks@gmail.com

File version: 202408024.018

BOOK LIST

Anne Bonny's Wake, 2016

Pappy, A Musical in Two Acts, Dick Elam and Ron Yates, 2024

DEDICATION

In memory of Louise Rubbi Williams

For the invitation to visit Knox, Indiana where this novel

began. For providing a listening ear, honest and valued

feedback, ongoing support, the writing 'perch' and so

much more.

MAIN STREET PRESIDENT

DICK ELAM HEARD THE BELLS ringing on the newspaper's Associated Press Printer. The "Flash" bulletin read the U.S. dropped the second atomic bomb on Nagasaki. The lanky Texan was 17 years old, Editor of his high school newspaper, working part time at the Abilene Reporter-News.

Main Street President, Elam's second novel, focuses on the final days of WWII. Henry Schricker is the fictional Vice President, not Harry Truman. The novel begins when FDR dies. In the turbulent days following the death of President Roosevelt, the 'accidental president' Henry Schricker, former governor of Indiana, immediately faces one of the most consequential decisions in history. This man of faith must now be the one who decides to drop an atomic bomb and destroy the Japanese Islands. President Schricker's story tracks the actual historical events of 1945. How he makes decisions, how the Schricker family adjusts to those events comprises the fiction.

These events could have actually happened because the author learned that FDR sent an emissary to ask Governor Schricker if he would consider campaigning as vice-president in 1944. Would World War II decisions made in 1945 been different?

ACKNOWLEDGMENTS

WRITING THE ACKNOWLEDGMENTS FOR *MAIN Street President* on behalf of my late father Dick Elam presents a special challenge. I can no longer ask the clarifying questions that brought forth my dad's enlightening and usually humorous answers. Using his emails, notes, and my memories of many conversations, I've tried to ensure recognition of each who made contributions to this book. In some places, semi-educated guesses fill the gaps of information. There may be those who go unmentioned, not with intent just oversight. I ask your understanding.

Main Street President exists because Louise Williams suggested that Dick spend the hot Texas summer at her Knox, Indiana home. One day Dick asked about the two-story 'museum' located on the Main Street of Knox. Told "that's the Schricker House where our twice-elected Governor lived and died. He might have been FDR's successor instead of Harry Truman." Intrigued, Dick found that FDR had asked Governor Henry Schricker to run as his Vice-President in 1944. However Schricker declined, choosing to finish his term as governor. The answer inspired Dick to ask, 'What if?' In his alternate historical fiction, Schricker accepts the Democratic nominee for vice-president and, upon Roosevelt's death, becomes President. The reader experiences the momentous decisions the President must make in 1945 as World War II draws to a close.

To family—Cynthia, Michaela, Kelson, Brenda, Margo, Rick, Malia. You heard his thoughts and read his drafts, after which you listened to updates of his thoughts. Many, many times. Your patience and willingness to listen supported his pursuit of this dream.

Support during Dick's time in Indiana came from the Starke County Historical Society, The Starke County Community Foundation and the people associated with the Shricker House Museum. Ron Vendl, Peg Brettin, Russ Blais, Venita Cunningham, Melba Shilling and Deborah Katz, thank you for providing ongoing access to the Schricker House and Indiana research information.

Dick discovered many supporting talents in Knox, Indiana. Savannah Gohr—your expertise and patience in the world of word processing saved the day on many occasions. Mike Reimbold, I still hear my dad saying, "I'll just call Mike." Thank you for sharing your publishing experience, and assistance with logistics and computer issues. Finally, Mitch Markovitz, Sagamore of the Wabash, you beautifully captured Dick's vision for a cover painting of the Schricker House on Main Street.

To the Early Reader and Advisor group: You listened to his ideas, read draft manuscripts, provided your thoughts and insights, and, above all, encouraged him. Jeffrey Higgins, Richard Schnakenberg, Diana Hayes, Tom Kraycirik, Julie Morgan, Jim Bryant, David Powell, Elise McGinnis, Richard Morgan, Emily Clarke-Pearson, Roland Waddell.

A special call-out to Dick's former students at UT and UNC who accepted his 'extra credit' assignment. Dick took fatherly pride in your post-graduate accomplishments and didn't hesitate to take some credit for your success. He treasured your precise feedback, analysis and suggestions. Somewhere during your exchanges, you became the teacher and he the learner.

Tom Young, thank you for your detailed assessments of Dick's writing, and your flying expertise to calculate appropriate 1945 story lines. What a joy to watch two authors share their friendship and love of writing.

And "blessed are the #$%^&** editors"—Dr. Tim Boswell and Christine Eastus. With his lifelong newspaper editing experience, Dick believed that his writing might not require editor review; however, when the editing work was complete, he always extolled their work, talent, and perspectives. Christine, suspect you're keeping him honest upstairs.

This book reached publication through the efforts and support of Sandy Lawrence, the publicist who acquired many roles over the four years she worked with Dick. Aimee Ravichandran, Kelly Colby, and Deena Rae provided the skills and talents that this woman needed to 'help me publish my dad's book'. Always with an abundance of patience and explanations. Thank you.

Finally, to Daddy. In your words, 'You done good.' Your voice guided me as we finalized this manuscript. Therefore, you'll find very few inactive verbs, reduced use of commas, a small amount of fat boiled out of your copy, and some format changes. Your story and vision remains which we'll share with others. I am grateful I could be a part of this work.

With love,
Sheryl Elam Pappa

AUTHOR NOTES

No man ever steps in the same river twice. For it's not the same river and he's not the same man.

—Heraclitus

He is the best man who, when making his plans, fears and reflects on everything that can happen to him, but in the moment of action is bold.

—Herodotus

HERODOTUS'S EFFECTIVE ATTEMPT TO DRAW moral lessons from the study of great events formed the basis of the Greek and Roman historiographical tradition which he is held to have established. Herodotus believed that the universe is ruled by Fate and Chance, and that nothing is stable in human affairs. Moral choice is still important, however, since arrogance (Hubris) brings down upon itself the retribution of the gods (Nemesis).

MAIN STREET PRESIDENT

PROLOGUE

Resident Henry Schricker waited for Secretary of State Byrnes, and Secretary of War Stimson to take sips from their coffee. The president had finished his two cups of coffee that followed his usual 6 o'clock wake-up.

"We must decide how to use the nuclear power we now possess."

Byrnes and Stimson put their cups on the table. Nodded. They understood the momentous decision that President Schricker had to make.

Henry's next words sounded more like a prayer.

"We want the Japanese to surrender. We don't want an invasion or a starvation blockade. That would kill many more people, their people as well as ours."

President Schricker scanned the two faces before he spoke.

"The moment for our historical decision has arrived. Let's pray we know best how to end this war—and not destroy civilization."

CHAPTER 1

THE SUN WAS SETTING ON Japan.

Inside the bottom of the Japanese merchant ship, the fire heated the rivets, furnishing welcomed warmth but giving off little light.

Their guards hadn't detected Lee and Gregg drilling over-sized rivet holes. The American prisoners of war hoped an inspector wouldn't notice that they'd stuffed mud into the holes before they riveted the ship's iron plates. When the merchant ship launched, seawater would wash away the mud and the rivet hole would leak.

Lee hoped he would live long enough to hear their sabotage worked.

Both prisoners waved a hand at the Japanese guard and pointed at the empty sack. He understood. They needed more rivets. The guard nodded, descended, took the empty bag, and climbed the ladder.

Gregg leaned against the interior hull. "It's Friday here. But it's Thursday back in Illinois. Fourteen hours on the other side of the dateline. Wish we were going to work at a shipyard there. We'd be using rivet guns, not hammers."

The emaciated Marine rubbed his hands against the thin cloth around his shoulders. "The way I figure the dateline difference, I'd be sitting down to eat some ham and eggs. I can count on one hand every egg I've eaten since 'Dugout Doug' left Corregidor."

"Lee, why don't you like MacArthur? Remember President Roosevelt ordered Mac to leave Corregidor."

"Gregg, I bought that. President still Commander-in-Chief, and my family voted for FDR, but if we—"

Their guard yelled, "Work! Work!" as he climbed back down the ladder, the bag of rivets across his shoulder.

"No talk! No talk!" the fat guard yelled. Itchy had learned some American city names. "We bomb you, *Nu Yark*. We bomb you, *Wasz-in-ton*."

The guard handed them the bag of rivets. With his other hand, Itchy waved a baseball bat-sized wooden cudgel. Lee knew Itchy brandished a lethal weapon. Another Corregidor captive didn't survive the blow. Lee helped bury Marvin four days ago.

Two young Japanese soldiers, maybe sixteen or seventeen year olds, looked down and watched. They carried World War I rifles strapped over their shoulders. Their frozen faces suggested they didn't understand, or care, what Itchy was trying to say.

Guards weren't really needed. For every American POW who tried to escape, the Japanese would kill two inmates.

And escape to where? Swim across the bay to Tokyo? he thought. *If Tokyo Rose's radio sweet talk was true, you would swim to Hawaii to escape. And she reminded them often that Pearl Harbor was still a cemetery. The Japanese furnished prisoners a radio tuned to her propaganda, delivered between American music.*

Itchy wasn't as subtle as Tokyo Rose. Yesterday, the fat guard had chanted, "We bomb bat-ships. We bomb Mack-ar-tur."

But Lee had seen fires burning near their shipyard. "We bomb Yok-o-hama" he wanted to chant back.

When their guard took a break, Lee and Gregg also quit working.

Gregg whispered, "Lee, you heard our cook say this morning that MacArthur was sending our troops to die, but that tells me that Mac has returned to the Philippines."

Lee smirked. "Oh, yeah. 'I shall return' over our dead bodies."

"Lee, you still don't like the man. What's really bothering you about MacArthur?"

Before answering, Lee made sure Itchy hadn't returned. "Two days before Dugout Doug left Corregidor, I met him in a tunnel. I'd been sitting three days behind a machine gun. Sometimes sleeping, sometimes firing at Jap planes."

Lee picked up his drill when he saw one of the young guards peer down into the ship's hull. When he was gone, Lee resumed whispering behind his open hand. "My jaw was swollen from a wisdom tooth that was killing me. My buddies called another Marine out of the tunnel to replace me. They insisted I go to the infirmary."

The other young guard appeared above. Lee coughed loudly into his hand. Gregg gave his head a deferential bow, which seemed to satisfy the guard who went away.

Lee continued, "Inside the tunnel, going to sick bay, I met the General and saluted. And MacArthur barked, 'Soldier, you need a shave. Change your uniform.' And he walked on. I didn't know, or I would have asked Mac if he was hurrying to catch his submarine. And, probably, I would have got court-martialed."

Gregg only nodded, because he saw Itchy wave his wooden club toward the merchant ship ladder.

The two prisoners hurried to climb. At the top of the ladder, Lee felt the chilling wind.

Enough daylight remained for Lee to see smoke still rose from Tokyo across the bay. Last night they'd heard the air raid sirens. While they shivered on their cots, they heard bombs explode. When Itchy marched the prisoners to breakfast, Lee estimated at least a dozen distant Tokyo fires.

Now, Itchy assembled his prisoners of war on the dock, waved his club, and pointed to their barracks. With little head movement, Lee scanned the Yokohama harbor.

Blackened damage appeared everywhere, except for the bamboo huts that comprised their POW quarters. Two days ago, the only day in the year when American POWs were bussed to the Red Cross Building for medical checkups, the Army Air Corps had bombed near the shipyard where they slaved everyday.

Forget the Jap's propaganda, Lee thought. *Somebody watches over us. Washington bombed? Not likely when we're bombing Yokohama.*

Lee and Gregg swung their arms, as they marched. They had learned to survive by showing no emotion. They lowered their heads but raised their shoulders as they walked the dock.

Often, Gregg reached across to steady himself by resting a hand on Lee's hip. His right leg wasn't getting any better.

Two more prisoners climbed out of the freighter hull and fell in line. The Americans marched to the dining area. Lined up to eat stale rice and wilted cabbage served by a talkative cook.

Makoto, the one-eyed cook, spoke pidgin English and taunted prisoners who passed his food table. But when large American bombers started dropping fire bombs across the bay, he had greeted each prisoner with a scowl and sarcastic words from his limited English category. Unlike Itchy, Makoto knew enough English to serve a small amount of banter as the men passed in the chow line.

Today, Makoto beamed. It was a bad sign that he knew something the Americans didn't. Makoto made sure Itchy wasn't looking before the cook whispered.

Lee watched fellow prisoners ahead of him whisper from one member back to another. Then Jones, in front of Lee passed on the message: "FDR dead. Henry Schricker, now president."

Lee watched until Itchy looked away, then passed the news back to Gregg.

Gregg's face clouded. When the guard wasn't looking, Gregg passed the news down the line.

Then whispered his question to Lee, "Who's Henry Schricker?"

Lee shook his head and shrugged his shoulders. The line moved forward, and Lee held out his plate to receive Makoto's three spoons of rice and something that looked like cabbage.

At the table, the men filled their cups, passing the water jug from one end to the other. Lee drank three cups of water. Water helped fill his stomach. When—Lee didn't want to think if—they were free, he vowed to drink three beers a meal. He had only been back home to Illinois twice after he graduated from high school and joined the Marines, back when Franklin Roosevelt was nominated to run for a third term.

And, now, Lee worried that Makoto probably spoke true.

"Schrick-er. Hen-ry Schrick-er?" It had been three years since Lee had heard an American newscast, and he never heard "Schricker" mentioned. Maybe FDR was not only dead, but so was Vice President Wallace. Maybe the new President had been the Speaker?

As they marched to their barrack, Lee whispered to the prisoner behind him. "Pete, you know this Henry Schricker?"

Pete whispered back. "Maybe? I'm from Indiana. We've got a politician by that name."

Itchy heard someone talking. He yelled, "No talk! No Talk!"

When Itchy turned his head, Pete whispered, "Some Democrat. My folks voted against him for governor. Before Pearl Harbor. President Schricker? No way. He's a Kraut. A German Hoosier."

Sirens sounded.

Lee smiled. American bombers were coming, sent by a command from Washington, D.C. *Thanks to you, Mr. President. I may get back home before I die.*

Henry—Mr. President Henry Schricker —bomb 'em back to hell.

CHAPTER 2

Vice-President Schricker and his wife held hands. Henry offered thanks to the Lord for their breakfast. Maude pursed her lips, blew Henry a kiss, and poured him a cup of coffee.

"Henry, I was able to buy eggs yesterday. But no ham or bacon. Both gone by the time I shopped. As usual, no butter, but I colored the oleo. That's your news from this 'home front.' What news does our vice president have to report?"

"Well, Mom, as Gabriel Heater said on the radio last night, there's good news. Just like General Eisenhower predicted at the Cabinet meeting eleven days ago, Patton and Patch have their tanks advancing in France.

"When I stopped by Sam Rayburn's office yesterday afternoon—the old Texan always ends the day in Congress with what he calls a 're-adjustment party'—I heard that Ike said Stalin informed him that Berlin was of little importance. But then, Sam heard Harry Hopkins was in Moscow talking to Stalin, and we would get better info when he returned."

Maude thought, *Henry tells me more than I want to know. Don't know if old folksy Harry Hopkins helped or hurt us when he talked Henry into running for vice president. Now I wonder if Rayburn serves my teetotaler husband a root beer?*

Henry took another sip of coffee. "Who believes Russian news reports? Everyone knows the Soviet's main objective is Berlin. One senator said that April one, the day we invaded Okinawa, will be remembered as a key day in military history. Now we're flying escort planes from Okinawa. We're bombing Tokyo, only 360 miles north of Okinawa. I didn't add my two cents that we're paying a terrible price."

Maude patted Henry's arm. "Thanks for updating your loving kitchen cabinet member. Any Indiana news? Your stenographer Rathel Odum still keeps up with our mail that comes to the Senate, doesn't she?"

Henry blushed, reached inside his hanging jacket, and handed two envelopes to Maude.

"Uh huh, I forgot to give you these two letters from back home in Knox. Read them. One's from Israel Mishkovsky. He dictated to his daughter. The other one came from Almo Smith. Almo sounds like he has run out of Kaintucks he can move to Starke County. Ordnance plant must have hired all the women they need to load shells."

"Henry, it's good the folks back home still remember you. In Washington you can get lost in Franklin Roosevelt's shadow."

"Doesn't bother me, Maude. The president plays one cabinet member against another to make the decisions he wants. I think he's happy for me to just bang the gavel in the Senate. Works for me. When the orations begin, I read the newspaper clippings that Miss Odum thinks I need to read."

Maude brightened. "You remind me that most people who buy a newspaper read Ernie Pyle. You left for the Senate yesterday before I read Ernie. Saved the page. He's writing about the Okinawa regiment where they were fighting." *She quoted, "Didn't look at all unlike Indiana in late summer when things have started to turn dry and brown, except the fields were much smaller. The wheat, which looks just like ours, is dead ripe in the fields now—"*

A knock on the apartment door interrupted. Henry pushed back his chair, stood and put on his jacket. "Bet every farmer in Starke County can identify with what Ernie's describing.

"That knock will be my guys taking me to the Capitol. As we drive to the Capitol George Drescher, my Secret Service escort, keeps the driver Tom Gohr and me updated on how our baseball team is doing in spring training.

"I'll see you for supper, after the Senate quits orating about water rights this afternoon." Henry leaned across the table and kissed Maude's cheek.

❧ —— ❧

THURSDAY, APRIL 12, 5:47 P.M. (EASTERN WAR TIME), WARM SPRINGS, GEORGIA

International News Service Flash!
President Franklin Delano Roosevelt has died.

❧ —— ❧

DIAMOND HEAD, HONOLULU

THE CHIEF PETTY OFFICER HELD the door open for two lieutenants. They advanced toward the large screen on the wall, stood in front of the admiral, braced, and saluted. He returned their salutes.

"At ease, gentlemen." The admiral motioned the junior officers to come alongside where he stood. The large picture screen, now blank white, framed the three men. They faced a room of 46 officers who sat behind tables covered with briefing portfolios.

The admiral swept his eyes across the seated men. "I want to introduce the two newest—and, as you old devils can see, the youngest members of our planning team." The admiral looked at the two names he had inked onto his left palm—a memory trick that got him through the Naval Academy.

"Lieutenant Jerome Pryor."

Jerry braced.

"And Lieutenant Alvin See."

Al braced.

"As you planners were briefed earlier this month, these two men have volunteered or Kaufman 'volunteered' for them." The admiral chuckled. "Mr. See, Mr. Pryor, I was a Firstie at Annapolis when Captain Kaufman was one of the plebes I commanded. Kaufman was a charger then. Made our Academy swim team in his first year."

The admiral changed to a somber tone. "Also, I know much about what my Plebe Kaufman did after he graduated. Gentlemen,

Kaufman was not commissioned upon graduation. He had poor eyesight, and I think that was used as a reason. So Kaufman went to England. Volunteered for the London bomb squad. And helped the Limeys defuse unexploded bombs the Germans dropped. After Pearl Harbor, Kaufman returned, was commissioned, and, given his learning experience thanks to unexploded Nazi bombs, was tasked to form what we now call UDT, underwater demolition team.

"Or as Mr. See and Mr. Pryor are usually called, frogmen. Welcome aboard our invasion planning group. Much of our precise timing when we invade the Japanese homeland will depend upon your early reconnaissance.

"As you need to know, we have targeted the southern part of Kyushu to establish our first beachhead."

The admiral paused. "I'm sure you know that what you hear here, stays here."

Al and Jerry nodded understanding.

"We also want you to know that we do not represent the final word. Our invasion proposals will be considered by our commanding officers, approved, then submitted to the president for final approval.

Al almost laughed. Final approval after MacArthur approves. MacArthur would let the president know that his personal approval was mandatory.

The admiral continued, "Although you are junior to officers here, please, do not hold back any opinions you might think pertinent to our—"

Slam! The door hit the wall.

The frowning chief petty officer didn't wait for permission. He marched toward the admiral. The chief handed the admiral a piece of paper then dropped his head.

The admiral read, frowned, then spoke.

"Men, President Roosevelt has died."

WASHINGTON, D.C., WHITE HOUSE, CABINET ROOM

ELEANOR ROOSEVELT MET VICE PRESIDENT Henry Schricker when he entered the Cabinet room.

A calm Eleanor said, "Henry, the president is dead."

Henry took her hands. He looked past her to solemn members of the Cabinet. Then looked into her eyes. "Mrs. Roosevelt, is there anything we can do for you?"

Eleanor closed her eyes, took a deep breath, then opened her eyes. She replied, "Is there anything we can do for *you*? For you are the one in trouble now."

Finally the last of the cabinet members arrived, followed by Maude. Henry's driver, Tom Gohr, escorted her to Schricker's side.

Henry looked at his wristwatch: 7:09 p.m. He placed his hand on the Gideon Bible that someone found in the White House. *I have been vice president for 82 days. During that time I have seen little of President Franklin Roosevelt or Secretary of State Edward Stettinius who stood with other members of the Cabinet. Stettinius and Roosevelt have spent most of February meeting with Churchill and Stalin at Yalta.*

Maude stood at his side as Secretary of Agriculture Henry Wallace, who had served as Vice President for eight years, administered the oath to Henry Fredrick Schricker, the 33rd President of the United States.

President Henry Schricker addressed the cabinet members. "Gentlemen, and Mrs. Perkins, although I have attended most cabinet meetings this year, I have much to learn about previous presidential decisions. I will depend upon each of you."

As he looked around the room Henry noticed Secretary of War Stimson, Treasury Secretary Morgenthau, and Labor Secretary Perkins held eye contact. Others dropped their heads. *He understood. They don't want to show their innermost thoughts. Their concerns. Probably, their misgivings.*

Agriculture Secretary Wallace looked at the ceiling. Henry wondered how often the former vice president thought he might have been President, might have been addressing this cabinet.

Henry continued, "I can tell you that my years as lieutenant governor and four years as governor have taught me the need for delegation, the wisdom to let able people do what they know best, and to keep my office door open to you. You, who have faithfully served President Roosevelt, can help me try to fill some of the void that his death leaves."

The new president made eye contact with those cabinet members who hadn't dropped their heads.

"Mrs. Roosevelt will be consulted about funeral arrangements before she flies to Georgia in the president's plane."

Henry paused. He thought, not the time to use the 'Sacred Cow' nickname for the president's airplane.

"As soon as I hear of the arrangements for the"—Henry almost said the president, but caught his words—"burial of our beloved Franklin Roosevelt, I will have staff contact you with details."

The cabinet members assembled a line. Each one passed silently in front of President Henry Frederick Schricker. Each shook the president's hand. Some covered Henry's hand with their second hand.

Secretary of War Henry Stimson waited so he could leave last. He looked around the empty cabinet room, except for Maude who waited near the door.

Stimson spoke quietly. "Mr. President, I need to talk you privately, about an immense project underway—a project looking to the development of a weapon of almost unbelievable power."

⁓ — ⁓

LONDON, 10 DOWNING STREET

PRIME MINISTER CHURCHILL POINTED THE unlit cigar toward his military aide. "Richard, surely, he knows about our code breaker, but do you know if the Americans have briefed Schricker on our largest secret?"

Churchill thrust his empty hand into his robe pocket, while he waited for an answer.

Captain Pim shook his head to signify no, but also to keep himself awake. "I don't, Prime Minister." He held his notepad and pencil at the ready.

Churchill growled. "Well, we need to know if Schricker knows about all of our mutual projects. Stimson would know. Let's see if we can reach their secretary of war or General Grove, before I place my Trans-Atlantic courtesy call."

Pim wrote down Churchill's phone call requests.

"Damn, Richard, I think Schricker's a teetotaler. What will happen when Uncle Joe wants us to down the hatch when he proffers vodka?"

WASHINGTON, D.C., WHITE HOUSE, SIDE ENTRANCE

MAUDE TOOK HENRY'S EXTENDED ARM. They walked out of the lighted hallway into the fading outside light.

The two uniformed guards on each side of the portico saluted. President Henry Schricker returned the salute. Two Secret Service men stepped forward and escorted Henry and Maude to the automobile.

Tom Gohr opened the car door. Henry waited for Maude, then entered and sat beside her.

"Tom, thank you for driving Maude over here. It's a short walk from Blair House, but I expect we're now to ride armor-proofed."

"Yes, sir. And you can also expect to see a black, bullet-proof limousine ahead and behind filled with secret service detail."

"Well, Tom, in the last four months, I've got accustomed to riding up and down Pennsylvania Avenue and chatting with you. I would like you to continue driving me."

"Thank you"—Tom looked back and smiled—"Mr. President, but—"

"Tom, you're going to tell me that some senior person is supposed to drive the president. Well, this president's first request is that you continue to drive us. Pass it on to your boss. I expect there's a good chance my request will be honored."

"Thank you, sir."

"Mrs. Schricker and I will still live at Blair House until Mrs. Roosevelt arranges her move. Until then, I'm glad we live near the White House. You may not have a passenger every morning. The Secret Service boys may have to get used to my usual early morning walk to work."

DIAMOND HEAD, HONOLULU, CANNON CLUB

THE SUN STILL HUNG ABOVE the ocean when Al and Jerry walked out of the tunnel, turned, and set a course to the officer's club.

Al avoided eye contact with the three-star general and two other braided officers drinking at a corner table. He knew he wasn't expected to salute while in the club, but better to wait until tomorrow to meet others in their planning group. He followed Jerry to the bar. Both ordered a beer.

"Sad day, Navy," the bartender said as he served.

Both nodded. They let the beers sit on the counter. The newspaper deserted on the bar caught their attention, the Honolulu newspaper *Extra*.

Jerry spoke first. "I read some stuff here I didn't hear when he was running for vice president. Schricker has some military experience. Infantry. But not much. Come on, 1916. Captain in the Indiana state militia. Al, there may be some who doubt our new Hoosier president knows enough to critique the plan underway to invade Japan."

"My best guess, Jerry, is that MacArthur, Leahy, and Marshall will make the big impression. Secretary Stimson wielded lots of influence with FDR. Probably will get serious attention when he counsels President …" Al hesitated. It was going to take some practice saying President Schricker after 13 years of President Roosevelt. "Schricker."

Jerry nodded. Japs wouldn't surrender, which would result in a fight to the death. Kamakazi planes against US ships. After they landed on that beach sand, the troops would need flamethrowers to close their bunkers and grunts to clear their tunnels. It would be Iwo Jima all over again.

"Well, Al, if you want my innermost thought, I hope all this invasion planning isn't needed. When we whip the Nazis, the Russians will declare war against the Japanese and Hirohito surrenders."

"I'll drink to that, Jerry, but I'm afraid you and I will be swimming ashore to a Kyushu beach before the end of the year."

The admiral from the corner approached. Al and Jerry braced. "At ease, gentlemen. Mind if I join you Kaufman boys for a drink?"

Jerry beat Al to the answer. "Honored, sir. Please do."

The admiral nodded toward the bartender who was already mixing his drink. "Well, then, let me get my windjammer and let's sit at a table."

Al looked over his shoulder and saw the bartender swirl his long spoon inside the admiral's glass of orange juice. Probably vodka, he thought. Better than the raw alcohol and juice the crew served aboard the submarine that had taken Jerry and Al to swim ashore at Iwo Jima.

Al and Jerry waited until the admiral sat. They raised their mugs when he raised his drink. The admiral clinked his glass against their mugs then drank.

"Lieutenant Pryor, Lieutenant See, let's keep this conversation off the record. Between us. Want to ask you about Captain Kaufman. What you tell me won't go beyond this table."

Al and Jerry nodded understanding.

The admiral leaned toward them. "Every man in this Navy is proud of what you frogmen do. I'm particularly impressed with the stories about your work cutting nets protecting enemy harbors. Plus all the demolition work you do on underwater obstacles."

Al began to wonder "*Where is this going?*"

The admiral came to his point. "I'm sure you two know about the court martial. May even know the frogman who left the 'Kilroy' sign."

Al thought, *Do we ever.* But he kept a poker face.

The admiral didn't wait for an answer. "What was your frogman thinking? Give him this. Brave guy. Swam onto the beach ahead of the invasion. Like you two have volunteered to do. But unrolling his little sign that read, 'Kilroy was Here—UDT,' and leaving it on the beach was just plain stupid, don't you think?"

The admiral waited for confirmation.

Al confirmed, "Yes, sir. Jerry and I went through officer training with the guy. We appreciated his ability. But Captain Kaufman was right on when he court-martialed him."

Although many frogmen thought Kaufman was too harsh, Al thought. But he knew what the admiral wanted to hear.

"Damn right, Lieutenant See. If one of the enemy patrols had found the sign, the landing would have been compromised. Right?"

"Yes, sir."

❧ — ❧

WASHINGTON, D.C., BLAIR HOUSE

HENRY TURNED OFF THE BEDSIDE lamp and sunk his head into his pillow.

Maude turned toward him. "Henry, Margaret called while you were downstairs telling the Blair House staff we wouldn't move until Eleanor left the White House. Margaret said, 'Tell Pop to hang in there. Some Knox militia coming for him to command.'"

Henry put his hand on Maude's shoulder. "Margaret's coming here? Good. You're going to need helping hands."

"Oh, Henry, I think I knew that the day we won the election. After the White House inauguration ceremony, Mrs. Roosevelt hinted that when we won the war, the president planned to resign and move to Hyde Park. I gathered all their children knew his intention."

Henry squeezed her shoulder. "President Roosevelt said something similar last summer when we dined outside the White House. I thought the purpose of our outside lunch was to take campaign photographs of two Democrats sweating in shirtsleeves. But Franklin also hinted of important—most important he'd said—military projects underway that I would hear about. If we got elected.

"Also, Maude, I'm pretty sure I wasn't Roosevelt's first choice as running mate. If Hopkins had been in better health, Franklin would have preferred him. The president, as usual, played one faction against the other. And then settled on this governor of Indiana."

Maude interrupted. "Because you're a good campaigner, honey." She thought, but didn't add, *You were the candidate who got more Indiana votes than Roosevelt when FDR ran for the third term.*

Henry squeezed her shoulder. "Thanks, honey, but I remember too well when I lost my first campaign, running for district clerk. Taught me a thing or two. Today, after Wallace swore me in, I thought I have only met privately with Franklin twice. I couldn't miss his failing physical condition. When he delivered his back-from-Yalta speech to Congress, I sat behind him, alongside Speaker Rayburn, and watched the president struggle with ten pounds of steel on his legs. Last time I saw him at a cabinet meeting, he was a weary man leaving for Warm Springs."

Maude put an arm over his shoulder, kissed his cheek, and snuggled.

"You need to see what's important from my side of the bed. I've been married to a publisher, a lawyer, a banker, a governor, but never before to the President of the United States. What's still important to me are your letters I reread most every night when I was a lonely schoolmarm homesteading in North Dakota.

"Now, we're going to move into a larger house, meet a world of people, but I'm not forgetting how much I still love that great guy, the man I first saw striding down the railroad tracks on his way from Hamlet to a lawyer's office on Main Street, Knox."

CHAPTER 3

H ENRY LOOKED IN THE MIRROR. He pulled out the stray nose hair in his sharp nose and straightened his tie.

He stuck the small *Constitution* in his jacket's inside pocket. He remembered today was Thomas Jefferson's birthday. Then he placed his *Gideon New Testament* in the other inside coat pocket.

Henry noticed his coat looked a bit worn. Maud said time had come to buy a couple new business suits. Maybe with a president's salary of $75,000, they could also afford a new white fedora hat.

As he left the bedroom, Maude called to him. "Henry, Margaret's on the phone." Maude handed him the phone.

"Hi, Hon."

"Hello, Mr. President. Henry and George send congratulations, praying for you. My two little brothers asked, and your baby girl wants to know, can we still call you Pop?"

The president chuckled. "You betcha, Baby Girl."

"Hah. When do I get to grow up? Anyway, Mom said you're getting ready to walk over to the White House for your first day in the Oval Office. Get going. We Robbins are taxpayers paying you. Before you put Mom back on the phone, I want you to know that Lewis and I are figuring out how to get your baby girl there by train. I'm traveling light. My public health officer husband will ship the rest of my clothes before they deploy him in a couple of weeks.

"Hey, Mr. President, you think you're the only one making big decisions?" She didn't wait for an answer. "Love you, Pop."

Henry sounded a bit choked up. "Love you, Baby Girl."

Two Secret Service men waited downstairs. "Mr. President, we're taking you the back way. Too many people out front waiting to see you."

Henry thanked them.

When he stepped out of the Blair House, Associated Press reporter Vaccaro waited at the rear entrance. Henry tipped his hat to the reporter he had come to know in the Senate press room.

"Come on, Tony, walk the back way to work with me."

When they arrived, a dozen reporters waited outside the White House. Henry touched the brim of hat and addressed them. "Boys, I know you need something for the afternoon editions. Say the president asked the nation and all our allies to pray for him."

Henry waved his hand, walked on, stopped, then turned. "And tell your proofreader to check the spelling. There are two C's in Schricker."

───

WHITE HOUSE, OVAL OFFICE

ROOSEVELT'S CHIEF OF STAFF, ADMIRAL William Leahy, welcomed the president.

"Thank you, Admiral. Really good to see you. I've watched your excellent service to President Roosevelt. Glad you're here for this rookie's first day."

"Kind of you, Mr. President. Allow me to brief you on what's transpired so far this morning. Several members of the press have already called. They want details about Henry Schricker's first working day. They were reminded, nicely, of our usual procedure. We will tell them what you want us to tell them."

Henry chuckled. "Same operating procedure we used at the Capitol in Indianapolis. If the papers assigned a new person to cover the statehouse, I had to remind him, or sometimes her, I was once an editor and publisher and didn't want them to scoop me."

Henry walked to the center of the room, taking note of all the ship pictures on the wall. Then he walked behind the large desk in front of the window. Admiral Leahy motioned toward the chair. Henry lowered himself into it, leaned back then forward, finally running a hand across the desk.

"Mr. President, this is a memorable day in many ways. Today was Thomas Jefferson's birthday."

Henry chuckled. "Well, Admiral, I hope by my birthday we have defeated the Nazis and have the Japanese suing for peace." Henry ran his fingers across the old Resolute desk, tapping a few bars of *Over There* as if he were playing a piano.

"As you may have read during the election campaign, I was born on August 30." Though the campaign press releases hadn't included that his parents came from Bavaria, since the campaign wanted to avoid any Republican smear about favoritism to Germans.

Leahy grinned. "You're a Yankee Doodle Dandy, sir."

"Great song, Admiral. My father was a self-trained musician. He sold groceries in Indiana and made enough money to buy a second-hand piano. He learned and played all of Cohen's music. Taught me. Not sure my children fully appreciate my piano playing. I often used to wake them up in the morning playing peppy tunes."

Henry took his small New Testament Bible out of his coat pocket and put it in the top, right drawer. "Thanks for sorting the letters on my desk. What's your system?"

The admiral pointed to three piles. "We open, notice the return address, and separate by the supposed importance of the letter. We put what looks urgent in the right stack. Letters that look like your personal interest in the middle. What we can't classify from sender or location to the left."

The president gave a thumbs up, then reached into his pants pocket and pulled out a fistful of printer's type wrapped in black tape. He recounted to Leahy how he made the paperweight in his newspaper publishing days. Henry turned the paperweight so Leahy could see the reversed letters that would print *Abide with Me*.

"Helps me remember what's important. If we had a piano here, I could play that hymn for you."

When he swiveled in the chair, Henry noticed his legs didn't center under the desk top. About ten inches of an enclosed box reduced his legroom. Atop the box Henry saw two buttons.

Henry pointed and asked, "Admiral Leahy, what are these buttons?"

"Oh, those. The buttons connect to an enclosed wire recorder. President Roosevelt had the device installed so he could push the left button if he wanted to secretly record who sat across from him."

President Schricker put his hands atop the desk and frowned. "Please see that the recording device and the covering woodwork are removed."

Leahy braced.

The president noticed. "No condemnation intended, but I was a lawyer before I was a banker or a governor. I would never record a client, or anyone with whom I talked. Which leads me to another concern, I will need a confidential secretary. I'm open to your recommendation."

Leahy nodded. "Will consider, then bring you names of several people. Matthew Connelly comes first to mind. Or how about your present Senate secretary?"

Henry nodded. "Rathel Odum has served me well while I was President of the Senate, but I think we should reassign her to help my wife Maude with her correspondence."

Leahy responded, "Good idea. Just today we received a half dozen letters addressed to your wife at the White House."

Henry worried over the burden now put upon his wife. "Thanks. I will deliver them to Maude. We'll not move into the White House before Mrs. Roosevelt decides to depart. Let's not hurry her. Besides, I enjoy the short walk from Blair House. In Indiana, I was accustomed to walking to work."

Leahy nodded. "I remember during the campaign last year, your advance man told the press that when you were a young man, you walked seven miles each day and read for the law, then you were admitted to the Indiana bar. Correct?"

Henry returned the smile. "True. And that's when I saw my Maude. She was milking the cow her family kept outside town. We waved to each other. I noted the time she usually milked and scheduled myself to walk the railroad track from Hamlet to Knox about the same time every day."

"Good story, Mr. President."

"Thanks, but I'm keeping you from your tasks. Any other things I need to know at this time?"

Leahy braced. "No, sir. By your leave, I'll take care of needed assignments." He saluted.

Schricker returned the salute. "Admiral Leahy, I appreciate your salute, but your new president never ranked higher than captain in the Starke County regiment of the Indiana state militia. Treat me like a civilian, if you don't mind."

Leahy smiled. "If I might remind, Mr. President, you have now been promoted from Captain to Commander-in-Chief. I may be the first to salute you, but I won't be the last."

Schricker chuckled. "I'll need some help getting use to that. I would much appreciate it if you would continue as the President's Chief of Staff."

"Of course, I will. I'm honored you asked. Here's your schedule of appointments for today. As before, I try to limit visits to fifteen minutes. I will come to the door after thirteen minutes and announce your next appointment awaits, unless you want a different procedure."

Henry made his thumbs-up sign.

Leahy continued, "I have scheduled a longer joint meeting with Secretary of State Stettinius, the Joint Chiefs of Staff, and the Secretaries of War and the Navy."

Henry nodded approval. "Admiral Leahy, we need to include you in that meeting. Can you give me a heads up on what to expect when I ask how long the war will last?"

"Yes, sir, I can tell you the answer President Roosevelt received when he asked that question before he left for Warm Springs. Joint Chiefs predicted six more months of war with Germany."

Leahy took a deep breath. "And eighteen months with Japan."

Henry broke eye contact with Leahy. Looked at the paperweight on his desk labeled *Abide With Me.*

Leahy waited until Henry looked back to him. "You will note under some of those names there are reminders of why they were here before. How President Roosevelt dealt with their requests."

Henry looked over the appointment schedule. He spoke Leahy's first name to break with formalities. "Bill, if you remember what they wanted, please note it. If you know what the president had already decided for any of the requests, just add a 'Y' for 'yes' and a 'N' for 'no'. When I became Governor of Indiana in 1940, I found quite a few people solicited help from me that the previous governor had turned down—often for a good reason."

"Can do. I can tell you that President Roosevelt turned down his good Hyde Park neighbor Secretary Morgenthau's requests more than once. He will be back at eleven. And I'll bet he will try, again, to get you to ratchet up controls on Germans when we defeat them."

Henry nodded, as he continued to read through the appointment schedule.

"Mr. President, not on my list of appointments is a personal request from Secretary of War Stimson. He asks for a lengthy appointment—an hour, maybe more."

Henry fixed his eyes on his chief of staff. "Secretary Simpson told me he would brief me on the awful power that might soon be placed in our hands. May I presume President Roosevelt's chief of staff knows to what Secretary Simpson refers?"

The chief of staff scowled. "Yes, I do. This is the biggest fool thing we have ever done. The bomb will never go off, and I speak as an expert in explosives. But I will schedule Secretary Stimson to lunch with you. Soonest. I think you should have been informed when you became vice president."

"Yes, schedule Secretary Simpson for lunch. Soon. And for today, I want to have late lunch with Speaker Rayburn at the Capitol. Tell Sam I want to discuss delivering a message to Congress as early as Monday."

Leahy looked surprised. "You may find some opposed to you speaking to Congress so soon."

"Probably some opposed. But tell Rayburn to invite others who need to hear I am coming, prepared to make a statement continuing policies of the late president. Congress and the nation need reassurance as soon as possible."

WHITE HOUSE, OVAL OFFICE

HENRY SET HIS GLASSES ATOP his nose and thought, *Our reading glasses may be one thing that Franklin Roosevelt and I have in common, along with a deep loyalty to the Democratic Party.*

President Henry F. Schricker signed the proclamation for President Franklin Delano Roosevelt's funeral to be a day of national mourning. Only his chief of staff witnessed.

"Admiral Leahy, you can tell the press this was my first official act."

"Yes, sir. And, now, your first official appointment is needed for federal land commissioner. If you follow previous protocol, you may want us to place a call and inform Secretary of Commerce Jones."

"Sure, get Jesse on my line. And ask Miss Odum to come on in."

Henry kept the phone call brief. " Secretary Jones, the president has appointed John Snyder to federal land commissioner."

Jones asked, "Did he make that appointment before he died?"

Schricker answered, "No, *the* president made it just now."

Henry waited for the message to sink in. "Jesse, my corresponding secretary for the past three months just arrived. I'm going to put her to work. Nice talking to you."

Rathel Odum entered as the president signed off. She waited, stenographer's pad and letters in one hand, a framed photo under her arm.

"Thank you for joining me here, Miss Odum."

"Thank you, Mr. President, for inviting me over from the Senate."

"I see you've brought my correspondence from the vice president's office. Give those to Admiral Leahy to separate. I'm guessing you've brought the photograph of my daughter when she christened the USS *Indiana*. Where over here do you think we should hang the picture?"

Rathel moved closer to Leahy's office door and held the framed picture against that wall. "Do we need a caption that says it's your daughter christening the USS *Indiana*?"

"I don't think so, Miss Odom. If anyone asks, I'll identify Margaret and brag on the crew of the *Indiana*. Bet Leahy will be happy when he sees the late Admiral Knox's picture on the Oval Office wall. That is Knox and me pictured behind her. A great day. Nearly a thousand Hoosiers came for the ceremony. A special train ran from Indianapolis. I'll ask Admiral Leahy to tell tour guides who's in the picture."

Henry paused. "It occurs to me, nobody has told me who's admitted here in wartime, but I'm sure there's already a visitor's policy in place."

Rathel smiled. "Yes, sir, there is. Admiral Leahy briefed me when you asked me to come over from the Senate."

"Well, Miss Odum, we both have to figure out what else we're supposed to do now we're here. For starters, I've got one letter that came to my Senate office that we need to answer first."

Henry pulled out the letter and handed the envelope to his stenographer. "You can send to the return Knox address on the envelope. Israel Mishkovsky is one of my oldest friends in Knox. He emigrated from Lithuania years ago and has prospered collecting scrap metal. And now his sons help him load one boxcar on his spur each week. And his letter told us that the Boy Scout troop I helped organize years ago collects scrap paper and cleans the courthouse each week.

"His daughter, Lee, wrote the letter for him. But she also made sure I knew she and her younger brother work weekends on the family farm outside town. She also reminded me she was one of the students this governor received in Indianapolis when she won an Indiana high school essay contest. If you're ready, Miss Odum, let's send my first letter from the White House."

She smiled, opened her stenographer pad, and poised her pencil.

Henry dictated, "Dear Israel and all your fine family, first paragraph, your daughter Lee wrote ..."

WHITE HOUSE, OVAL OFFICE

HENRY NOTICED HIS CHIEF OF staff wasn't smiling.

Leahy waited until Henry sat at his desk. "Mr. President, while you were at lunch, Stalin sent you a message that says, 'will cooperate.' He's sending Molotov to the United Nations meeting in San Francisco, but sending him here first. I'm afraid you'll find Molotov is not a very gracious person."

Henry smiled. "Good. Better we stand face-to-face and get over some of the hurdles the Russians have erected, especially their demands for Polish territory."

Leahy continued, "There was some good news. Last week the Soviets denounced their non-aggression pact with Japan. Also, James Byrnes is at the Shoreham Hotel waiting for your call."

Henry lightly slapped his desktop. "Very good. He's just the man I need to talk to. Let's get him here soon. I have questions about the Teheran and Yalta meetings with Stalin and Churchill. He counseled Roosevelt both times."

Leahy turned back before he exited. "I see your daughter's christening picture now on our wall. I'll let the admiral know. Knox will be happy he's in the Oval Room."

Henry raised his index finger. "Which reminds me, what's the possibility I can get some reports about how the USS *Indiana* performs in the South Pacific?"

"I'll pass the word. I know you haven't been to our map room, since it's a downstairs secret. President Roosevelt had us build him a copy of Churchill's 'War Room' in London. I'll see that you get a daily report from there. And include updates on the *Indiana*. As of now, she's probably off Okinawa."

Henry gave a thumbs-up gesture.

Leahy continued, "You probably also want us to keep up with the USS *Indianapolis*. I'm afraid there's bad news for her. A Kamikaze plane dropped a bomb from 25 feet above her deck. Nine men died instantly. Yet even with holes in her hull, she survived. She limped back to San Francisco, six thousand miles under her own power. Cruiser *Indianapolis* is in dry dock in Vallejo, California. That's her latest survival report."

Henry took a deep breath, knowing the ultimate responsibility for all our service men and women rested in his chair. "Bill, I presume you furnished President Roosevelt with significant daily military reports. Please continue that practice with me. Provide me with a brief sentence or two on current, not secret, developments that you can put on my desk."

"Will pass the word, Mr. President. Those reports come daily to the secret Map Room. I'll also work a visit to the Map Room into your schedule."

⚜ —— ⚜

LONDON, HOUSE OF COMMONS

A SOMBER WINSTON CHURCHILL ADDRESSED Parliament. The gallery overflowed.

"Thank you, members of Parliament, who have responded to this memorial meeting. Under the influence of heavy emotion, we grieve for the departure of the President of the United States, Franklin Delano Roosevelt."

Churchill bowed his head. He waited for the sighs to die before he placed hands on his lapels, raised his head, and pronounced each word slowly.

"What greater testament of friendship than this: He was there when we most needed him."

CHAPTER 4

PRESIDENT HENRY SCHRICKER CLASPED THE Kentuckian's outstretched hand. "Senator Barkley, thank you for coming to my office this early. I hope you'll accompany me to meet the train bearing President Roosevelt's body."

The Kentuckian nodded. "Honored, President Schricker."

"Thank you, Alvin, but I also wanted to see you early because I want you to consider undertaking some of the duties I had as vice president. You've got plenty of legislative experience. We need to hear from you at cabinet-level meetings and at meetings of the National Security Council. How about you become the first non-elected working vice president in United States history? With your outstanding talent for public speaking, you'll become my administration's principal spokesman.

"Before you say yes—we're not taking a no—Leahy has already commissioned a vice-presidential seal and flag from the army's heraldic branch. It will look good on the vice-presidential auto we're assigning to you."

Barkley beamed.

NEAR NASHVILLE, TENNESSEE, ON A TRAIN

Dear Lewis,

I am writing on the train. Intend to stay in Washington until Mrs. Roosevelt moves from the White House. Mom and Pop are attending the D.C. service for Roosevelt, then taking the train to Hyde Park for the burial ceremony. Then back in D.C. before Your Camp Follower gets to the Capitol.

Short note because we are almost in Nashville. Will post at the RR station. Miss you so much already.

Will call you when I get to the Blair House.

Love, Margaret

WASHINGTON, D.C., WHITE HOUSE, EAST ROOM

THE NEW PRESIDENT AND FIRST lady stood on the balcony beside the prior first lady, Eleanor Roosevelt.

Henry looked at his watch. Just past three and he already needed to wipe the sweat on his brow. He guessed the afternoon temperature was nearing ninety degrees.

They watched the approaching procession. The presidential train had brought Roosevelt in his coffin. Now the traditional six black-draped horses and the coffin came into view. He heard Eleanor breathe deeply. Then they went to the East Room for the funeral service.

In the room filled with flowers, the service began at 4 p.m.

Mrs. Roosevelt and the Roosevelt family sat in the front row, across the aisle from President Henry F. Schricker and Maude Schricker.

Behind the president, the cabinet members sat, as well as Supreme Court justices, labor leaders, agency heads, and other politicians. Also seated were diplomats from all the United Nations countries, including British Foreign Minister Anthony Eden and Russian Ambassador to the U.S. Andrei Gromyko.

Eleanor remained calm while others near her sobbed. She selected the hymn *Faith of Our Fathers* to begin the ceremony. And the minister ended with President Roosevelt's well-known words, "The only thing we have to fear is fear itself."

Time magazine would later report what President Schricker noticed when Harry Hopkins stood. The frail man looked like he was about to faint. Henry hoped Hopkins kept his strength. The new president needed Hopkins's strength.

On the train travelling to Hyde Park, Chief of Staff Leahy had arranged for the president and first lady to ride in a different car from the one occupied by Eleanor Roosevelt and Franklin Roosevelt's coffin.

Henry and Maude sat side by side with Maude close to the window to get the best light while Henry wrote on two yellow, legal pads. From scribbled memos, he transferred full sentences to the pad he had labeled "Words for Congress." When Henry finished a topic, he passed that legal pad to Maude who waited with fountain pen in hand correct any errors with blue ink.

Henry waited for Maude's appraisal. At one point he almost snickered as he thought, *I can see her now. Standing in the front of the classroom in that one-room North Dakota schoolhouse, running her blue chalk through the incorrect white words a farm boy wrote on the blackboard.*

SUNDAY, APRIL 15, HYDE PARK, NY

THEY ASSEMBLED INSIDE THE FOUR walls of the garden. Lilacs were in bloom, their aroma was fragrant. In the quiet birds chirped.

President Schricker, the new first lady, the Cabinet, General Marshall, Admiral King, James Farley, and Edward Flynn, congressmen and senators, family and friends stood near the gravesite.

The music swelled. Then the cannons fired. Black-draped horses appeared bringing the coffin. A hooded horse carried an empty saddle, stirrups reversed—traditional symbol of the fallen leader.

Henry placed a hand over his heart. The West Point Cadets in scarlet capes braced. Maude leaned against his side. The resolute Eleanor looked above the Reverend George Anthony when he committed the body and reminded the audience of "earth to earth, dust to dust."

When the West Point cadets raised their rifles and fired, FDR's faithful Scottish terrier Fala barked and repeated his bark again after the next two volleys.

Maude nudged Henry, as Eleanor waited for those who would shovel soil and cover the casket.

Henry took the first lady's arm, and they left the garden.

They waited for Harry Hopkins who walked with a cane, a newspaper folded under his other arm.

Henry raised his hand and motioned Hopkins to come nearer. "Harry, would you be so kind as to ride back to D.C. in the same railroad car with Mrs. Schricker and me?"

Hopkins raised a quizzical eyebrow, before he answered, "Of course. An honor."

Henry gave a quick wink. "More payback than an honor, Harry. Remember you recruited me for this job. 'Heavy' should hang over your head. This time I'm recruiting you to help me and Maude work on words to say to Congress. I've got a pretty good idea what I want to say about our nation's war effort. But I need some help choosing the right words for Joe Stalin to hear, the man you know better than anyone."

Hopkins straightened. "Of course, I will help, Mr. President. And Stalin may already have signaled more cooperation through a *New York Times* reporter in Moscow. How about this headline?"

SOVIET FLAGS SHOW MOURNING BORDER
TRIBUTES NEVER BEFORE PAID TO FOREIGNER
HONOR ROOSEVELT AS FRIEND OF PEACE

⚜ — ⚜

WASHINGTON, D.C., WHITE HOUSE, OVAL OFFICE

THE ADMIRAL STOOD IN FRONT of the president's desk. "Mr. President, I was surprised you called. I wasn't expecting you back in the Oval Office until tomorrow. Have you had a chance to sleep?"

"Yes. Dozed some on the train coming back from President Roosevelt's funeral. Little cat nap when we weren't working on tomorrow's speech for Congress and the nation. Harry Hopkins rode back with Maude and me. Gave me some good counsel."

"President Schricker, I admire your fortitude. You haven't taken much personal time since Franklin died."

"Thank you, Admiral. My daughter Mrs. Margaret Rollins, is arriving on a train tonight. Her husband, Lieutenant Rollins, put her on the train in Texas. She will be a great help to her mother. And to me."

Leahy nodded. "Yes, indeed."

"And Jimmy Byrnes and Sam Rosenman will be here soon to help me finish writing my speech to Congress. I've decided to expand the usual prayer ending. I'm going to repeat some words I have orated previously in Indiana. Figure those Hoosier senators and congressmen from Indiana won't remember, or will forgive me, for using some phrases I delivered as governor. But we don't have time for me to coin any new clichés."

CHAPTER 5

MONDAY, APRIL 16, WHITE HOUSE, OVAL OFFICE

A DMIRAL LEAHY WAS SORTING THE mail on the desk when Henry entered. "Mr. President, your escort delegation from Congress will arrive in forty-five minutes. And I have today's USS *Indiana* report. Actually the report is from yesterday because of the time difference between here and the Pacific. The USS *Indiana* is now steaming off Okinawa. She was called to General Quarters at 1310. Aircraft gunners shot down two oscars. Time: 1341-1345."

"Oscars?" Henry inquired.

Leahy chuckled. "You need to meet Lieutenant Will Rigdon soon. He may tell you more than you want to know about an oscar. It's a nickname for an enemy plane. They can give you more details when you visit to the Map Room."

NORTH OF KNOX, INDIANA, KINGSBURY ORDINANCE PLANT

THE ASSEMBLY LINE CONVEYOR STOPPED. Another shell casing to be filled with explosive stood in front of Maudie Wireman. Like the other women, she wore plant-issued coveralls. The required cloth that covered Maudie's hair accentuated her facial beauty. She was taller than others. And the required coveralls bulged at her breast.

As she loaded gunpowder, she shouted to make sure the girls heard in the second and third rows behind her.

"Girls, I'm Maudie. Maude Schricker is our new White House boss, and this here Maudie will be the first lady of you bunch of shell-loading hens."

A woman in the third row cackled. "You can't be first lady just because your name's Maudie. You're from Kaintuck. You're not a Hoosier."

Maudie rushed to reply. "Where do you get that stuff? I live in Knox, same as the Schrickers. And I ain't planning going back to them hills in Kentucky. I'm a Hoosier now."

Patty chimed in. "Maudie is a boosier, and she can't wait to get off this line and to O's bar in Knox."

"You ought to know, honey. Leave me a parking place on Main Street."

"Next to your jalopy with the A gasoline sticker?" Patty retorted. "You wrangled that goodie because you live twenty miles away, right?"

The foreman interrupted the banter. "Watch what you're doing, ladies. Keep filling the shells moving down the line. Don't yack and get us blown up."

Maudie thought, *What if we did explode this building? This sweat shop was built in woods where no one lives closer than ten miles. Just put down some new railroad track, build some new buildings, load more shells. Hire some more hillbillies.*

Maudie and Patty both stuck out their tongues at the man, laughed, then loaded another empty casing that passed down the line to the packers.

The foreman didn't smile. "War's not over. Gotta keep up the war effort." He shook his head as he walked outside.

"War effort? War effort?" Maudie growled. "His main war effort is trying to get those young gals mixing gunpowder a mile from here into his bed."

A third row voice crowed. "Tell 'em, Kaintuck woman. All we need to finish this war is to get your pretty mug on a poster, like Rosie the Riveter. How about Maudie the Shell Loader?"

Another woman chimed in. "How about Maudie the Mudder? You gonna mud wrestle this weekend, Maudie?"

The conveyor moved, delivering another shell casing.

Maudie loaded as she responded, "Not on your sweet behind, Sweetheart. But the promoter said I had the figure for it. Betcha a little mudcake on your cheeks might be uplifting."

A woman near the door yelled a warning. "Boss back!"

The middle-aged man limped into the assembly room. He pounded the floor with the cane he carried to remind others he was 4-F in the draft.

"Break for lunch, ladies." He pushed the switch that stopped the conveyor.

Maudie, Ethel, and Patty took their lunch boxes outside to sit at a picnic table under a large sycamore tree.

Ethel opened her lunch box, pulled out a small fruit jar, and held it up. "Either one of you girls want some canned peaches?"

Patty answered, "Hell, Ethel, I was hoping you had some Kaintuck moonshine you were going to spare, not peaches."

"How about you, Maudie, you're from Kaintuck hill moonshine country, what's in your fruit jar?"

Maudie answered, "Just some green beans. My Mom Nelise didn't let my dad or my four older brothers make any white lightning, but my sisters and me canned a bunch of things in these Ball fruit jars. Mostly vegetables from Mom's garden. What corn the boys helped Dad grow on the side of the hill, we ate and fed the shucks to the pigs. Now that we've moved to Knox, my older sister Mary has planted some sweet corn out her back door. Wish I could ship some corn to my Army brother Edward overseas."

Ethel slid her peach jar down the table to the other two women. "Maudie, sounds like we couldn't fight this war if it wasn't for your family."

Maudie frowned. "I'll take that for a compliment. For your information, Mary works the night shift here at KOP. My other sister, Maggie, works on the Willow Run airplane assembly line in Michigan."

Patty nodded. "Good for Mary. And Maggie. I don't have any family in service or working in a war plant. I was the baby my mother didn't expect at her age."

Maudie understood. "I'm the baby girl, also. Got four redheaded older brothers. Oldest is Ben. He farms south of Knox. His oldest,

Charles, now in the Navy. Only seventeen years old. Charlie lied about his age. His little brothers, Joe and Jack help my Brother Ben with his farm work now.

"My second oldest brother, Albert, enlisted for World War I, but Army sent him home 'cause he was only seventeen years old. Now working in Texas oilfields. Says he's helping win this war, because the Germans and Japan are running out of oil. Then, there's my brother Bill. He's deferred although he could easily pass a physical. Only college graduate in the family. Could have made a fine officer."

Maudie looked like she was about to cry. "Patty, I think I love my brother Bill maybe best of all. When he left for Beria College, I offered him my piggy bank so he would have spending money."

Patty teared a bit and tried to think of words to keep Maudie talking. "What did your brother Bill study at Beria?"

Maudie brightened. "Bill studied physics. Honor graduate. Bill had offers to student teach physics at several colleges. Earn a PhD. Then the war started. If you don't mind me getting this off my chest, Patty, Ethel, the family hasn't been very friendly with Bill since he moved his family to Tennessee."

Maudie paused. "Family thinks he's a draft dodger. He's fit for service, but he joined the plumber's union, and he's got a defense job, as Bill tells us, fitting pipes. Hell, he could have come north. Almo Smith recruited us from Kentucky. Almo could have found a college graduate in physics a real, important defense job."

Ethel put an arm around Maudie's shoulder. She hurried with a question. "Ah, Maudie, where is your brother working in Tennessee?"

Maudie choked back a sob. "Somewhere near Knoxville. Place that Bill's boy says they call Dogpatch Town in Oak Ridge."

WASHINGTON, D.C., U.S. CAPITOL BUILDING

HENRY DIDN'T SEE ANY MEMBER of Congress sitting on their hands, but they didn't clap as long as they did when Roosevelt spoke. *He's gone. Help me, Lord. Don't let me rush. I must remember to pause where Maude penned three dots to better help my listeners understand.*

"Mr. Speaker, members of the Cabinet, members of Congress, and my fellow American citizens. I have been called by fate to the high office of President of the United States. I humbly accept the prescribed obligation, and pledge my whole-hearted fidelity to the sacred trust that the untimely death of President Franklin Delano Roosevelt has thrust upon us.

"As one who's fully cognizant of his own frailties and the limitations of his own strength, I earnestly beseech the guiding hand of Almighty God, and the sympathetic understanding of a friendly people, to help us discharge this exacting and important duty. Without the assurance of His help and support, there could be little hope, if any, of fulfilling the tasks, making the decisions, or bringing the leadership needed today.

"It is comforting to know, however, that I need not tread these rugged paths alone. I welcome assurances of help already received. I call upon you—my fellow public servants, my fellow Americans—to help shoulder the burdens in this most trying time of our Republic.

"All of us are deeply grateful for Franklin Delano Roosevelt. He gave his fidelity, his guidance, and his life for our great country."

Congress rose and applauded.

"Franklin Delano Roosevelt leaves a great legacy. Today we stand united, risen to the height of our wartime powers. We have recovered strength from the Great Depression. All men and women who want jobs work. Industrialists have performed miracles and equipped our 12 million soldiers, sailors, and airmen. And armed our allies.

"Together, we are facing some of the most testing, and most difficult, problems in our country's history. The cost of government has risen to unprecedented and unpredictable heights. Our people buy War Bonds to help hasten the return of our men and women from this great conflict thrust upon us.

"Let us never forget those brave Americans who will not return."

Congress rose and applauded.

"We live in a grave and troublesome world war, perhaps the most depressing conflict in human history. Unfortunately, we find our free government is little more than a mockery in many nations of the world.

"The surprise and dastardly attack on Pearl Harbor caused these months of misery, these years of an unrelenting war. Our miraculous production and household sacrifices express our faith with our sons and daughters in the armed forces. I am confident we shall continue to keep faith with them."

"Our country is almost untouched by the destruction of war—no ruined cities, no splintered railroad networks, no pocked farmlands—that has marked so much of Europe, not to mention the devastated Far East.

"We can thank President Roosevelt for his preparedness and foresight, for his deep and sincere love of country, his love of fellow Americans, and his love for the people of the world."

Congress applauded.

"While this speech marks the beginning of a new presidency, it in no way reduces the ongoing loyalty and sacrifice we must all continue to contribute. All of us, my fellow Americans, share in common the search for peace and freedom that only Victory can provide. We grieve for those who, like President Roosevelt, have dedicated their lives to our survival. May they never be forgotten."

Congress rose and applauded.

"Allow me to repeat, in a bi-partisan spirit, the tribute rendered in the 1944 Democratic platform that honored President Franklin Delano Roosevelt:

> *"He stands before the nation and the world, the champion of human liberty and dignity. He has rescued our people from the ravages of economic disaster. His rare foresight and magnificent courage have saved our nation from the assault of international brigands and dictators. Fulfilling the ardent hope of his life, he has already laid the foundation of enduring peace for a troubled world and the well being of our nation. All mankind is his debtor. His life and services have been a great blessing to humanity."*

All, including Republicans, rose and applauded.

"Fellow Americans, we owe a great debt to Franklin Delano Roosevelt. None of us here would exchange our freedom for any other treasures, or inducements, that a partial victory would offer. As

President Roosevelt proclaimed, we fight for a return to freedom, for an unconditional victory.

"Join me, Americans all, in dedicating ourselves to a victory that will bring national freedom and security. We pray for speedy victory, because every day peace is delayed costs a terrible toll.

Congress applauded.

"I have only one purpose in this solemn hour. That purpose is to dedicate myself, wholly and completely, to the task of bringing freedom and liberty to share in the Peace of the World. With God helping our nation, you and I shall not fail."

Congress rose as one and applauded their new president.

TUESDAY, APRIL 17, BLAIR HOUSE

MARGARET POURED A SECOND CUP of coffee for Mom then Pop. She replaced the pot on the kitchen stove, returned, sat, sipped her coffee, then picked up the newspaper she had been reading.

Mom opened the honey jar, spooned out a teaspoon of honey, and passed the honey pot to Henry.

Margaret watched her parents complete their morning ritual. She thought about repeating what she had been told numerous mornings, *Honey helps ward off colds.* Instead she commented on the commentator.

"Hey, Mr. President, even David Lawrence said you made a fine speech. '*Fifteen minutes with multiple applause interruptions.*' You think, maybe, he doesn't know you're a Democrat?"

Henry chuckled. "Wait until you read tomorrow's Capitol Press reaction. Your pop holding his first presidential press conference today. If I know the boys, and a few girls, the gloves come off today."

WHITE HOUSE, MAP ROOM

ADMIRAL LEAHY TOOK A LAST look at the European map then turned toward the door. "Thanks for the quick briefing, Colonel Graham. I will bring the president here after the capitol press conference."

The colonel frowned when he saw Leahy was leaving. "Pardon, sir, but I have a question. How do I handle the 'For President Eyes Only' message received this morning? As you know, procedure has been only Admiral Brown or President Roosevelt's military aide, which I presume I still am, saw the Army ULTRA messages delivered to the Map Room. Do we now need General Marshall's approval to introduce ULTRA to President Schricker?"

"Colonel, you are going to be talking later today to all the highest authority you need. You should prepare Lieutenant Rigdon to brief him on both ULTRA and SIGINT and all other coded-message venues. Arrange for him to read all files collected here. The president may want to read those files in the late afternoon, some evenings. He wants to 'get up to snuff,' as he put it.

"Yesterday, I reported the U.S. Seventh Army took Nuremberg. I didn't have to tell the son of a German emigrant where Nuremberg is located. But the president remarked he was counting on your wall maps to orient him to Pacific locations.

"Also, I told him your daily report would include up-to-date information about the USS *Indiana*. In case you didn't know, President Schricker's daughter Margaret christened the *Indiana* three years ago."

The colonel braced. "Will do, Admiral. I have another question. You know my concerns about Wild Bill Donovan's Office of Strategic Services, the OSS, or the oh-so-social. He recruited his society friends of which some are known communists. Do you know if Roosevelt passed on to his vice president any of my OSS concerns?"

"Colonel Graham. I suggest you confine your briefings to President Schricker about intelligence gathering. Magic and SIGINT for openers as well as where the USS *Indiana* fights."

When Leahy left, the Army colonel laid the paper on the Navy lieutenant's desk. "It's a message for president's eyes only. Leahy will bring him down sometime after his press conference today. The admiral wants one of us to brief him on ULTRA and SIGINT. And,

Rigdon, you will like this detail. Brief Leahy's office daily with a written report on the *Indiana*. Schricker's daughter christened her, and I gather the Hoosiers think their state owns the battleship."

WHITE HOUSE, OVAL OFFICE

CHIEF-OF-STAFF LEAHY WINKED AND SMILED.

"Mr. President, we counted as they went in. We think you have three hundred reporters waiting for your first press conference. Largest group I ever remember. Here's a copy of the press rules that President Roosevelt imposed. Good Luck."

Leahy opened the door for the president.

Members of the press filled the room, shoulder to shoulder. Henry noted that some courtesy prevailed. The few women there had been afforded space in front of his desk.

"Gentlemen and Ladies of the Press, I appreciate the job you were sent here to do, but don't think any of you started reporting before I did, year 1908. If my *Starke County Democrat* had enjoyed your kind of circulation, I would be your publisher today."

A few half-chuckles from the three hundred reminded Henry that regal respect had never been a hallmark of the American press.

"Admiral Leahy, who has graciously accepted my request to continue serving as the President's Chief of Staff, gave me a copy of the press conference rules under which you have operated for over a decade. First, a little history. President Roosevelt's rules differ from those first promulgated for the Capitol press, by then President Calvin Coolidge. At the time, about fifteen reporters covered the White House. At his closed press conferences, President Coolidge required that reporters write their questions before he arrived. He reserved the right to answer the questions he chose.

"One day, the boys all submitted the same, identical written question. When President Coolidge arrived and opened the first written question, he didn't answer it. In silence, the president opened all the other identical questions. After Coolidge opened and silently read the last question, he invented his own question, pretended to read, and answered his own question. Then he said, 'Thank you, gentlemen,' and left the room."

Henry noted a few grinned but most frowned.

"Not to worry. For this president, the press conference wartime rules that President Roosevelt employed should work very well."

Schricker read from the paper Leahy had given him."Off-the-record kept as confidence. Background only, not attributed to the president unless given express permission to quote directly. And I will try to hold one press conference per week. Remember, I once owned and edited a newspaper, and I know you need a new lead." Henry noticed the frowns had turned to smiles. "Now, your questions."

"Mr. President, will you be going to San Francisco to greet the United Nations delegates?"

Schricker answered quickly, directly. "No. I have asked Eleanor Roosevelt to welcome the delegates."

"Mr. President, will you be meeting with Churchill and Stalin?"

"Not scheduled yet. I have talked with both by secured Trans-Atlantic telephone. Next?"

"Mr. President, *New York Times*, David Lilienthal's term as head of the Tennessee Valley Authority is soon to expire. Who do you see as a possible replacement for that important post?"

"I'm not ready to discuss appointments. Next question?"

"The *Washington Post* readers would like to know where you stand on race relations."

Henry thought, *The Washington Post wanted him to comment on racial segregation in the military, and segregation in defense plants. Really the* Post *wanted to know if he would continue the last president's refusal to say "no more segregation," words that would have lost southern Democrat votes.*

President Schricker opened his coat and put both hands in his jacket, the way he saw Lincoln portrayed in movies.

"The State of Indiana abolished slavery in 1804. All men are created equal in Indiana. And as the former Governor of Indiana, I live by those words that Jefferson wrote."

Henry noted most of the three hundred reporters scribbled on their note pads. "Can't see you, but will the reporters from the Indianapolis newspapers raise their hands?"

They did.

"Make sure the folks back home in Indiana get that quote."

Among the many chuckles, Henry heard a few guffaws.

"Mr. President, will you see Mr. Molotov before he goes to San Francisco?"

"Yes. He's going to stop and pay his respects to the President of the United States."

Henry thought, *Molotov should pay respects for all the lend-lose war goods our Merchant Marine has delivered.* That quip would please a few senators he knew, but he decided to pull that punch. "Thank you for coming."

The Press Corps applauded as the president walked into Leahy's office.

Leahy smiled. "You startled them. These people are used to attending charm school, but you didn't beat around the bush. You've been on the job for only five days, and I can see you made a great impression on this bunch. Well done, boss."

Henry smiled, but thought, *I've lived five years in those five days.*

CHAPTER 6

Maude held the *New York Times* up for Henry to read the headline. "Oh oh, what terrible news."

Ernie Pyle Is Killed on Ie Island; Foe Fired When All Seemed Safe

⚜——⚜

WHITE HOUSE, OVAL OFFICE

Henry crossed his hands over his chest while he stared out the window. Between tree limbs, he focused on the green lawn. When he swung back to his desk, Matthew Connelly, the secretary Leahy had recruited to take dictation for letters, was ready for service.

"Mr. Connelly, I deeply regret that one of the first letters you and I write goes to Ernie Pyle's parents and family. I'm sure there's more unfortunate letters ahead for us to write, but this one hurts deeply."

No need for formality, Henry thought, *not with the man handling your correspondence. He's here to free you to worry about other problems.*

"Matthew, I dictated when in the Indiana capitol. But when I was a small town newspaper editor, and publisher, I often wrote long hand. Sometimes, I set my own type or pulled some type to fit in the chase. You know that experience?"

"Indeed, I do, Mr. President. I was once a college newspaper editor. But I hope you will just want a typewritten copy, not something from a Linotype machine."

Henry thought, *Connelly knows about a Linotype machine? We'll get along fine.*

"I'll tell you when I want a typed draft. Not often. Just when I want to second guess myself. After my Maude read the news this morning, she reminded me she starts just about every day reading Ernie Pyle's columns. More like a personal report about her own two boys, she said, than a battlefield account. Maude added, 'What a loss,' and I thought that's just what all Ernie's readers are thinking."

Connelly kept his note pad and pencil in his lap, waiting to begin.

"Okay, Matthew, let's start. 'Dear Mr. and Mrs. Pyle, your son, Ernie Pyle, will always be remembered.' Back up. Need to remember more people."

The letter ended up looking something like:

Dear members of Ernie's family,

Your president joins you as we weep for the loss of our beloved Indiana Son, Ernie Pyle.

When I was governor, Ernie and I met in Indianapolis. We talked about newspapering, because I once put out a county weekly in Knox. We talked about how we were both born in small Hoosier towns, about the war in Europe ending, about the boys from Indiana, and the rest of the nation, that he wrote about.

Washington D.C. paid Ernie a great tribute when Congress passed a law to pay GIs for combat duty, just as the Air Corps pays additional for flight duty. His column from Italy last year inspired that action. Ernie's pen was powerful.

You will understand this simple tribute that my Indiana wife and children send as we mourn his death and cheer his dedication: Ernie Pyle, a great Hoosier, and even more, a Great American.

Henry F. Schricker
President of the United States of America

"Matthew, I'll need to see this letter. I may pen something after my signature. And, yes, I've got a dictating machine right here. I will try and use it for less sensitive letters we send. It will allow you to sleep through some of those late nights when I think of a letter we need to write."

I'll let you sleep, Matthew, when this job keeps me awake.

WHITE HOUSE, MAP ROOM

PRESIDENT SCHRICKER THANKED THE BRIEFING officer. "Lieutenant Rigdon, you have impressed me with your wide range of information and details compiled from both war zones. I'm impressed you're able to position the Japanese fleet twice a day. Tell me more about the SIGINT program that provides you this intelligence. Maybe you can prepare a briefing for early next week. Also, your up-to-date positioning of the USS *Indiana* is much appreciated. But you need to warn me what information stays here, and what I can pass along to my daughter, Margaret."

"No problem, Mr. President. Your daughter's ship, the USS *Indiana*, now underway from Pearl, headed to Midway. No security problem in that part of the Pacific. We sunk the Japanese carriers last seen in that part of the ocean."

"Thank you, Lieutenant Rigdon. And now, what report do you have from Okinawa?"

Rigdon frowned. "Not good. Very few Japanese military or their civilians have surrendered. Like on Iwo Jima, the natives are surrounded, but choose to die."

Henry didn't comment, but thought, *And we have yet to attack these fanatics on their homeland islands.*

BLAIR HOUSE

Maude asked, "How did your day go?"

Henry sunk his head deeper into his pillow. "Pretty overwhelming. Especially the 'For the President's eyes only' secrets. Also, J. Edgar Hoover say he 'feels compelled' to tell me about the 'other woman' in President Roosevelt's life. He says, everybody has heard she was there when Franklin died. Did you, Maude?"

"Yes, Henry. Even before he died. But I just tuned out that woman's gossip at a Perle Mestas' reception."

"Well, I didn't just tune him out. I let J. Edgar know that I didn't need FBI gossip information. But I can't do the same with for my eyes only messages. I usually go to a special war room and hear military or diplomatic secrets I can't tell even to you. First time, I ever kept any secrets from you."

"Oh, I don't think so. There was that wedding night when I first saw you without clothes."

Henry turned off the bedroom lamp.

FRIDAY, APRIL 20, WHITE HOUSE, EAST ROOM

Military, Cabinet members, and White House staff filled the East Room.

President Schricker kept his speech short. He applauded all those who had worked on the 7th Bond Tour. Then he presented the Navy medals to the three Iwo Jima Flag Raisers, Marines Bradley, Hayes, and Gagnon.

"All of America has seen the poster showing your platoon raising the flag on Mount Suribachi. I can tell you that our late President Franklin Roosevelt hung that picture in this White House.

"You have helped raise $24 billion for the US Treasury, more than any other bond tour, the largest borrowing from the American public in history. Now you go to the Capitol to raise the Iwo Jima flag. Your Senators and Congressmen wait to greet you. And this evening, Washington's baseball fans will greet you.

"Your Marine watchword Semper Fidelis, Always Faithful, resounds for all our service men and women who continue our struggle. God bless you, and our glorious nation."

⁓⁓—⁓⁓

WHITE HOUSE, OVAL OFFICE

THE SECRETARY OF TREASURY SAT in front of the president's desk. "I want to compliment you on the short speech you made this morning in the East Room, Mr. President. D.C. is not accustomed to anyone getting a presentation over that fast."

Henry chuckled. "This country banker is more impressed that you have raised $24 billion."

Morgenthau smiled. "Well, Henry, compliment Franklin Roosevelt. When you've got time, I need to tell you the story behind the bond drive."

"We'll take time. What's the story?"

"Franklin telephoned me two months before he died, and told me his first reaction when he saw newspapers everywhere running the Associated Press photo of the flag raising. Even printing and selling 'special editions' of the photo. Franklin said his first thought was that publishers across the country were profiting, again, off the war.

"Then he realized the flag-raising picture was creating an admiring public. He said, 'Hank, I've got it. The symbol for the seventh bond tour. Let's get those boys who raised the flag back here.' Franklin didn't waste any time. He put out a presidential order to bring them to D.C.

"Turns out, not only did he sense people loved the picture, but one of the Marines was of Indian blood, a Native American. Great for our politics."

Henry nodded approval.

"And I think Banker Schricker will be pleased. Your treasury boss also saw that we hung 15,000 posters in banks across the country. As any robber knows, that's where the money is."

The president leaned back in his chair. "Secretary Morgenthau, your efforts deserve a medal, also. By the way, there's another member of their Marine platoon I have yet to decorate."

Henry reached into his shirt pocket and brought out a note. "He's their platoon leader, Lieutenant Keith Wells. Before the ceremony, the Marines asked me to remember him. He was wounded when he led their charge at the base of the mountain before they fought through the tunnels and raised the flag.

"They told me he's in the Naval Hospital at Oakland. If the United Nations gets organized, I will go to San Francisco and congratulate the delegates. And maybe have time to personally visit Lieutenant Wells."

❧ —— ❧

KNOX, INDIANA, IN A HOTEL

JOHNATHAN KRACERIK MOVED THE LAMP and centered his portable typewriter on the hotel desk. He crushed his cigarette in the ash tray, rolled in a sheet of paper, interlaced his fingers. and popped his knuckles.

Johnathan shrugged his shoulders. He really didn't understand why his friend wanted, or needed, this information, but he could use the money. He hunched forward and typed.

Dear Oppy,

Per your instructions, in order to add to the Schricker '44 campaign info as requested, (see billing time) your loyal correspondent has spent three days on the road and two nights in a northern Indiana flea-bitten Knox hotel (invoice attached) a little south of U.S. 30, the so-called Lincoln Highway.

Some items concerning Schricker's innermost thoughts about war I found in a day spent (see invoice) reading his newspapers, back when he was editor and publisher of the Starke County Democrat, 1908 until 1918.

1. He's got a sense of fairness, even to having his newspaper competitor, the Starke County Republican, speak to his national guard unit H—of which he was the Captain, until he flunked 1916 physical when unit called to Mexican border.

2. Per your assignment request, did find he's got an opinion about declaring war: His 2.2.16 editorial:

H.F. Schricker, Editor and Publisher:

It does not seem to have occurred to some blatant congressmen and blasherskite newspapers that it requires an act of Congress to make war. President Wilson could not send the regular army into Mexico "at once," nor could he send it at all, without authority from the war making power. Colonel Roosevelt knows this, of course, but no one would suspect that he did from a reading of his recent statements.

3. Noted boiler-plate (that is type set in St. Louis and sent to Knox and other weeklies) story about Tesla that he ran. Being scientific, you would have enjoyed reading how Tesla, in 1918, said the next war would be fought by scientists with yet to be developed weapons.

4. Schricker wrote several paragraphs criticizing German airplanes bombing cities and hospitals. Said aerial attacks on civilians was no way to run a war.

And, Oppy, when Armistice signed, Schricker ran a picture of U.S. flag under his masthead. He was big Woodrow Wilson supporter. Quoted Wilson: "America asks nothing for herself but what she has a right to ask for humanity itself."

I asked some natives who happened to be standing nearby at the Bass Lake bar (see invoice) about Schricker. They remember him as a banker—first in Hamlet then in county seat Knox—without a glass eye. Said he was fair to farmers who needed loans to plant crops.

Bought some ice cream and talked to milk man who delivered to Schricker two-story house on Main Street (see invoice) and he praised Schricker's wife's gumption. She homesteaded acreage in North Dakota before she married Schricker. No hanky-panky found. No other women.

Schricker teaches adult Sunday School class. Plays the organ.

Started the Boy Scout troop here back before WWI. Clean and all those other Scout Laws. (I quit Scouts after I made 2nd Class.)

Lincoln Highway runs all the way to California, and I'll have my flivver on that road tomorrow. Estimated gas and hotel costs in advance (see invoice). Look forward to seeing you in Berkley next time you and I knock back a few of those good martinis your wife mixes.

Johnathan

P.S. Happy 41st birthday, Professor Oppenheimer. Nice sabbatical for you, basking out there in the New Mexico sun. Still chilly here in northern Indiana. For a present, reduce my invoice by a carton of cigarettes. JK

CHAPTER 7

"**H**ENRY, THIS ISN'T A VERY pleasant breakfast story to read to you before we go to church at Walter Reed. What's more, I'm no fan of Claire Booth Luce, as you know."

President Henry Schricker nodded in understanding. He remembered how unhappy sweet Maude had been when they'd left the movie theater in Indianapolis after watching *The Women*. "Too damn catty," Maude had said. It was one of the few times he remembered her using that strong a word.

"But this story makes me proud of her. Mrs. Luce and two other Republican Congressmen who went to Buchenwald Germany. Let me read you this paragraph from the A.P.

> *"Mrs. Luce spared herself none of the grisly spectacles. She said that she hoped the people of the United States would see motion-picture records that have been filmed there. She visited the basement crematorium where, in a white-walled room, thousands had been hanged from iron hooks."*

Maude paused, ran a finger under her nose, and sniffed before she continued reading.

> *"Her prisoner guide told her how the executioner had used clubs shaped like potato mashers to kill victims who did not die quickly enough in the noose.*

> *She saw the elevator that carried bodies upstairs to the furnaces. Outside the crematorium she saw a wagon stacked high with shriveled bodies. She did not remain long, saying, 'It's just too horrible.'"*

The president listened. His head leaned forward. One hand covered his chin. His elbow rested on the dining table.

> *"In the barracks she saw prisoners too weak to move from the tiered shelves on which they lay. Six had been forced to lie on shelves in a space big enough for three."*

"Oh, Henry, what a terrible thing for Mrs. Luce, any woman, anyone to see. I'll shorten the story. She saw a six-year-old boy, emaciated, kept there nearly three years. Picked up in Paris, because he was out after curfew. But before you leave, I've got to read you something else she said.

> *"No one wants to believe these things, but it's important people know they're true."*

Henry nodded assent.

"When she asked prisoners what should happen to Germans who committed these atrocities, she quotes them as saying the same they did to us. Though she replied that wasn't an answer, she did not amplify."

Henry took down the hand from his cheek and slapped it on the table. "Claire Booth didn't amplify because she knows under our Constitution, you are innocent until proven guilty. Luce didn't answer because she probably thought they didn't deserve a fair trial, but she knows a Congresswoman should never say that."

He pursed his lips. "But I've gotta believe there's a special place in hell for those who ran those concentration camps."

BETHESDA, MARYLAND, WALTER REED HOSPITAL

HENRY NOTED THE INSIGNIA ON the man's left sleeve: Infantry, First Army, Sergeant. The other sleeve hung down behind his bandaged shoulder and arm. He used his good left hand to move a paperweight that held back the turned pages.

The soldier wasn't tall, maybe five foot six or seven. About Henry's size. But gaunt, probably recovering from a steady diet of battlefield K-rations. Henry cupped a hand behind his ear to better hear the Sergeant.

"I read the verse from 1 John 4. *You, dear children, are from God and have overcome them, because the one who is in you is greater than the one who is in the world.* Let us pray."

The soldier's baritone voice resonated with authority. Henry thought, *That's a better closing than when last year I raised the volume on the organ while our Knox area Lutherans sang "Onward Christian Soldiers".*

After the closing prayer, the president and first lady walked forward from their seat at the rear of the church. Henry shook hands with everyone on the aisle seats, waved to those in wheelchairs near windows.

When the Schrickers stood in front of the sergeant, Henry offered his left hand and shook the soldier's good hand. "Well done on the scripture reading. What's your name, sergeant? Tell me about your home, when and where you got your wound? What's your future plans?"

"Henry Boren, sir. Springfield, Illinois. Battle of the Bulge. Day after Christmas. They have me back walking, but I don't think I will be playing golf anymore. Or typing as fast. Like you, Mr. President, I was a newspaper man. In Springfield, Illinois, before the war. But won't be returning to that job. I'm enrolling at Chicago University this fall. Thanks to the G.I. Bill."

Henry was impressed. "What will you study?"

"Ancient history, sir. Have already started reading about the Roman Republic. Learning some Greek language. God willing, let's pray you will become a peacetime president, and I'll become a history professor."

"Yes, Brother Boren, we will pray for that day. And for you."

As Tom Gohr started driving to Blair House, Henry spoke softly to Maude. "You know, I've been reminded again that I might have been wounded in World War I, if I had passed my physical exam at Fort Harrison. Maybe injured if I had gone with my boys to chase Pancho Villa on the Mexican border. If the medics had cleared me, I might have been sent over there."

Maude squeezed his arm. "And not come back to your young bride."

Schricker frowned. "Who knows? We lost one of the Shilling boys in my regiment. I remember composing the obituary for my newspaper. Schilling was trained to man a seven-inch gun. Didn't die in battle. The 1918 flu epidemic killed him. And a lot of other Yanks crowded unto troop ships between the U.S. and Europe."

Henry paused, as he remembered his Map Room briefing about the troops advancing in Europe. He reminded himself to inquire how they'd be transported from Europe to the Pacific. But did not need to mention that thought to Maude.

"Honey, there's much fighting left. But like the scripture Sergeant Boren read, we will overcome them.

⁘ —— ⁙

WEDNESDAY, APRIL 25, WASHINGTON, D.C., BLAIR HOUSE

MAUDE POURED HENRY A SECOND cup of coffee. "Mr. President, just want you to know, you are not the only one going to the White House today. Mrs. Roosevelt asked Margaret and me if she could take us on a tour, before she moves next week."

Margaret laid her newspaper on the table. "And, Pop, will I get to see the maps that spot the USS *Indiana*? The wall map that you keep telling me about?"

Henry took a sip of his coffee while he thought of an answer. "No, baby girl, maps in a military office are part of the White House where Eleanor won't take you. A bit off limits, as they say, for civilians."

Their frowns said they didn't find that funny. *Find a better exit line,* Henry thought. "I get most of my news sent to Admiral Leahy's office. One of his staff brought me the news you read this morning. I was told yesterday the British Royal Air Force bombed Hitler's mountain chalet, Berchtesgaden. No information that Hitler was there, or if he got the death the *Saturday Evening Post* has been asking us to pray for."

Henry drank the rest of his coffee. "Girls, think I need to start walking to the office pretty soon. Got a luncheon appointment with the secretary of war and a telephone call with Prime Minister Churchill."

WHITE HOUSE, OVAL OFFICE

"BUSY DAY SCHEDULED FOR YOU, Mr. President."

Chief-of-Staff Leahy handed the president his schedule and a newspaper clipping. "Thought you might want to see this column by Steven Drury, United Press, before you meet and lunch with Secretary Stimson. Bet Stimson has."

"Thanks, Bill. This morning, my Maude called my attention to his fancy words when she read the newspapers. She reminded me that Steven wrote some good copy when I presided over the Senate. The closer we get to defeating the Nazis, the more we hear about not sending anymore eighteen-year-olds overseas. Afraid the casualties we suffered on Iwo Jima, and now Okinawa, have some folks back home writing letters to their senators."

Henry scanned the schedule. "Also want to talk with Senator Barkley. See if you can get him on the phone. Ought to be simpler than my trip to the Pentagon this afternoon for the secured transatlantic connection with Churchill."

When he heard, "He's on the line now, sir," the president picked up his telephone.

"Senator Barkley, Henry Schricker here. I wanted to call you before my appointment with Secretary Stimson. Thank you for heading the delegation that General Eisenhower has assembled to witness the German concentration camps."

When Henry heard Barkley's reply, he chuckled. "Well Alvin, indeed your name is first on the list in the *New York Times* yesterday. I think the word's got to New York that you are our acting vice president. Well your president thinks you are doing more than an acting job. Let's talk about your delegation going to Europe. What did Ike's advance people tell you?"

Barkley replied, "Ike's briefing officer keeps saying 'unbelievable.' That's why we're taking more newsreel and press photographers, radio commentators, more photo print people. He said when people see newsreel pictures of the emaciated survivors, see the pictures of the death chambers, hear how many died, see a map showing where all the victims came from—all over Eastern Europe—how could anyone ever want this tragedy to happen again?"

"Alvin, everyone needs to hear your message. Just two days ago Rabbi Stephen Wise of the Zionist Council was here. He told me some horrible stories about what you will witness. Use those press outlets. Talk loud enough to make those delegates working on the United Nation charter hear you in San Francisco.

"By the way, I noticed Ike included Adler from the *New York Times* in your group. Butter him up a bit. We Democrats are going to need the *Times* on our side when the Congressional elections come next year."

⚜ — ⚜

WHITE HOUSE, SECRETARY OF WAR OFFICE

HENRY SHOOK HANDS WITH SECRETARY Stimson. "You know, I feel as if I should salute you. After all, you may not know, but you ordered my Starke County infantry brigade to the Mexican border in 1916."

Stimson smiled. "Matter-of-fact, President Schricker, I do know. Last year, before President Roosevelt decided to ask you to become his running mate, he asked my office to search your military record."

The Secretary of War opened his file folder and read aloud. "Manual of Military Training, 1914. Captain, Company H, First Indiana Infantry. Fitness report: outstanding. Honorable discharge, medical."

Henry laughed. "I wasn't strong, or big, enough to carry that ninety-six pounds of issued equipment. And by the way, President Roosevelt and I discussed you during our lunch last August. I teased him a bit about his Republican military secretary. President Roosevelt told me he welcomed Republicans in his cabinet, because you added bipartisan endorsement to his campaign for a fourth term."

Stimson nodded. "A most pragmatic politician. But I wish he had briefed you on this most serious information. Mr. President, may I proceed?"

When Henry nodded, Stimson took a typed manuscript from his briefcase. "I typed this manuscript earlier this morning. Alone. Excuse any of my typing mistakes."

With the aid of his reading glasses, Henry studied the manuscript. After he read the first page, Henry stared at Stimson. "Mr. Secretary, if you intend to shock me or grab my attention, I can guarantee you that in my ten years as an editor and publisher, I never wrote anything so compelling. Although Secretary Byrnes hinted to me that I had yet to hear about some 'secret' activity, I must admit I never envisioned anything of this magnitude."

Henry read the first paragraph aloud. "Within four months we shall in all probability have completed the most terrible weapon ever known in history, one bomb of which could destroy a whole city.

"I know you, and Admiral Leahy—I don't know who else—are aware that President Roosevelt never briefed me. Maybe he hinted. I remember one mid-August hot day last year—so hot we lunched outside. We took off our jackets and posed for a campaign photo. Our campaign managers spread the photograph everywhere. President Roosevelt hinted we were engaged in an armament development race with the Nazis. But, again, I didn't perceive we were trying to develop anything this powerful."

Henry returned to reading. When he finished reading, Schricker took a deep breath and exhaled, before he asked, "Who else knows about this?"

Stimson ran his thumb across his fingers as he answered. "The Joint Chiefs of Staff, Churchill and a few of his English scientists, the Interim Committee of fifteen experts I have organized, and General Grove and those people working under him on the Manhattan Project."

Henry frowned. "Manhattan is part of our largest city. How many people are working there on this project?"

Stimson shook his head. "I should have explained that 'Manhattan Project' is just a code name. There are three principal locations: a research facility in New Mexico, a production plant in Tennessee, and another production plant in Washington state. The project employs over four thousand scientists, equipment specialists, and support staff. Most work at a specific task, sworn to secrecy, but don't know the overall plan."

Henry waved both hands to signal Stimson to stop. Then spoke with a measured tone. "Secretary Stimson, are you telling me that our government has been paying all these people weekly? By contract? And that we've built buildings that are visible? And nobody—nobody?—in Congress has learned of or questioned these expenditures?"

Stimson waited, watched Henry drop his hands into his lap, then stared at him. "The answer is only one group that you presided over in the Senate knows. Senator Harry Truman's committee tracking wartime expenditures. He came to me over two years ago and asked about our large land purchases in the eastern part of Washington state, where our plant produces plutonium."

Henry waved his hands to interrupt. "Plutonium? I read that in your notes. Don't I need to know more? And what did you tell Harry Truman?"

"Mr. President, I told Senator Truman we were working on a secret wartime project."

"And what did Harry say?"

"Senator Truman said he would take my word that we needed to keep the project secret."

"What number was Harry asking you about?"

"Several million he saw that we had spent on land acquisition."

Henry blinked. "Mr. Secretary, just how much has General Grove spent so far on this project?"

"So far around $2 billion."

Henry took a deep breath and waited for Stimson to continue.

"I've taken the liberty of inviting General Grove to come to the White House—by a back door to avoid the press. By your leave, he is here to brief you on his Manhattan Project. We can go to a nearby office, unobserved, if you are ready, sir."

Henry exhaled before he answered, "Am I ever. Lead the way, Secretary Stimson.

꘎——꘎

WHITE HOUSE, SECRETARY OF WAR INTERIOR OFFICE

GENERAL GROVE STOOD, BRACED, AND saluted when President Schricker entered.

Henry returned the salute, added a formality that he doubted. "Pleased to meet you. Secretary Stimson tells me you will bring me up to date on the Manhattan Project—of which in twelve days as your Commander-in-Chief, I have never heard. Please, let's be seated."

Henry focused his attention on General Grove. "As Indiana's governor, I learned a great deal about munitions when Kingsbury built their ordinance plant near my home. Plant officials briefed our Kiwanis club on their safety procedures. Told us how powerful the shells were that workers, mainly women with hands trained to knit and sew, were loading. So powerful that they built assembly buildings a mile apart. But nothing I heard approached this magnitude.

"General Grove, Secretary Stimson tells me $2 billion have been spent, so far. That number would cause this one-time country banker to read the loan agreement more than once."

Henry reached into his coat pocket and held up Stimson's typed paper. "Secretary Stimson's summary makes me want to read more about nuclear physics. But your new president does not have the pleasure, nor the time, to visit a library."

Henry's thoughts went to *A Boys Life* spy story he had read about cyclotrons. He knew about novels by Wells and Huxley. *Maybe one of them had written about harnessing the sun's energy.*

"I did read many years ago that the atom could never be split. Are your scientists saying, so much for never?"

Grove nodded. "Yes."

Time to rethink reality, be positive, Henry thought. *If this project succeeds, I may have to pass out sixty or so medals—as Secretary Josephus Daniels did after we landed troops at Veracruz. A successful effort by our scientists would be as commendable as any successful military leadership.*

"Secretary Stimson, I trust you will continue to monitor the project. Please report what you think the president needs to know. And, yes, General Grove, I think it prudent that I reaffirm President Roosevelt's trust in your operation. I'm pleased to praise the work of your people, and let them know, General, that their President encourages them. Having said that, I must honestly say I am overwhelmed by the expenditures to date. And your projection of impending costs. Be assured, I also want to end the war. Yet I'm not prepared to subscribe to the 'at any cost' philosophy. However I do not know how to put a price on a life."

Stimson braced. "Mr. President, the overall objective of this nuclear project has always been to bring the war to a successful end more quickly. To save American lives."

"Of course. Thank you, General Grove. Thank you, Secretary Stimson. Would you be so kind as to join me for coffee at 10 o'clock tomorrow morning?"

"Yes, sir, I will see you at ten, tomorrow."

Both men rose and accepted a handshake from the president.

President Henry Schricker returned to the Oval Office, sat at his desk, put his elbows on the desk, covered his face with his hands, and closed his eyes.

PENTAGON

THE AMERICAN PRESIDENT AND THE British prime minister concluded all the diplomatic formalities. Then they discussed how to handle Himmler's offer to surrender to American and British forces, but not the Russian army that had surrounded Berlin.

Churchill agreed with Henry that there couldn't be a piecemeal surrender.

Henry said, "I will cable Stalin we resolve that the Nazis surrender to all three nations."

Churchill said, "I will back you up on this."

BLAIR HOUSE

HENRY HUNG HIS WHITE HAT on the rack, then turned and kissed his wife.

"Oh, Henry, what a great day. Instead of hearing Gabriel Heater start his radio report with 'there's bad news,' tonight he began his newscast with 'there's good news.' The Germans are almost defeated, talking surrender. Today must be one of your best days as president."

Henry forced a smile. "Maude, let's delay dinner long enough to hear Eleanor Roosevelt's speech on the radio. I think her words will serve better than my platitudes as she greets the United Nation delegates in San Francisco. Want you to tell me what you think."

Maude took off her apron. "Sure, honey. But I thought you said you were given an advance copy yesterday."

"I was. But our Illinois acquaintance, Adlai Stevenson, helped write her speech. And I'm thinking about asking Secretary of the Navy Forrestal to assign Adlai to my office as a speechwriter. I want you to listen and tell me if his Midwestern style fits this Hoosier."

Maude nodded. "I remember his speech supporting you as vice president at the nominating convention last summer. The cadence was similar to yours. What else can you tell me about your second week as boss?"

Henry sighed. "Bit complicated. Today reminded me of when I managed the little bank at Hamlet, back when we first met. When the robbers ruined the safe doors but didn't get the money. I took the currency and valuables home and slept with them until we got a new safe."

Maude wrinkled her nose at Henry. "I do remember when you told me. Added to our romance. Young girl thought you needed a more affectionate sleeping partner."

CHAPTER 8

CHIEF OF STAFF LEAHY POINTED toward the top of the president's desk. "I put the dispatch on the right hand pile of correspondence. That's the latest report from the Map Room. I expect the press boys and girls are going to want your comment."

"Thanks, Bill."

Henry swung his glasses in place and read.

> *Benito Mussolini, Il Duce, his mistress, and 16 of his Fascist henchmen executed at the village of Dongo on Lake Como. Bodies brought to Milan and thrown in the streets. Their bodies kicked and spat upon.*

Henry read and thought, *If I were a* Capitol Press *reporter I would want to get the president's reaction too.* "Admiral, I think you need to send in Mike Quinn, and I will put him to work."

The president's newly appointed press secretary took wide steps as he walked into the Oval Office. Henry remembered Quinn was listed as six foot, four inches tall when he played basketball for Valparaiso, the college where Henry studied business for a year. He'd met Quinn in Indianapolis. Back when Henry was the lieutenant governor, he avoided standing next to Quinn when a photographer was nearby. A photo would make them look like the cartoon characters, Mutt and Jeff.

"Welcome Mr. Quinn to your first assignment. Leahy suggested we issue a comment about Mussolini's death. I'm not going to say 'one down, one to go' although that's what I am thinking. Let's just say the president promised our troops would now press even harder to defeat the Nazis and Hitler.

"That said, Mike, what else do your press buddies want to know?"

Quinn read from his notepad. "First, your reaction to Congress extending the draft. Do you agree with Senator Sparkman from Alabama? Require eighteen year olds get six month's training before deploying to combat."

Henry snapped a reply. "Yes to extending the draft. For the second question, I remember the eighteen-year-old young men who served in my Indiana state militia group learned quickly and were strong saplings in our brigade." Also, I think we need to talk about Boy Scout training. Sleeping in the outdoors and doing your own cooking has prepared a bunch of our city boys for the rigors they will face. You could best make up a sentence about how sports train for combat. But, Quinn, don't make me sound like the British talking about their playing fields of Oxford. Next question?"

Quinn read from his notes. "Can you justify continued exemptions for farm workers. Are they more valuable than other defense jobs?"

Henry chuckled. "However I answer that question some of our press brethren will slip in I come from Indiana, a state big on taking care of farmers. How about the old 'an army marches on its stomach' cliché? Quinn, you were a Hoosier farm boy. Devise a good answer for me. Make it an indirect quote. Or give them an 'off-the-record' observation. They'll have fun with their own surmises. That dodge worked well for President Roosevelt. Also, hold off answering the press until Monday when I meet with the cabinet. I want them prepared when the press calls for their reaction."

The president's press secretary smiled. "I think the press will like your answers. I haven't forgotten, Mr. President, you were editing and publishing before I was born."

MONDAY APRIL 30, WHITE HOUSE

AT THE ENTRANCE HENRY MET Eleanor Roosevelt. She led a line of White House attendants exiting, all carrying memorabilia. "Good morning, Mr. President. As you can see, this old first lady is making room for your sweet first lady to store the many mementos that will soon come, unsolicited, to the White House."

Henry gazed over her shoulder at six, no, seven people carrying boxes. "And a good morning to you, Eleanor. Gracious me, where will you keep all these memories?"

"Good question, Henry. I'm sending this load to our Hyde Park home. For now, I'll move temporarily into a Morgenthau apartment here in Washington. Eventually, I'll help create a library for Franklin's many documents at Hyde Park."

Henry thought of all the ship pictures hanging in the Oval Office. "After they load these mementos, would you like to come to the Oval Office and tell my staff what mementos you want from there?"

Eleanor waved the attendants to go ahead before she answered. "Oh, no. Thank you, but I never enjoyed visiting the president's office. Always too official. I'll arrange with Admiral Leahy to gather Franklin's many nautical pictures—the ones you don't want to keep, of course. And tell your gracious Maude—and she is very gracious—I look forward to meeting with her and her daughter to tour this place."

Henry nodded. "I will tell them. But, you know, this old house is going to miss you."

Eleanor huffed. "Henry, after thirteen years, I doubt that. But what else can I do to help you?"

Henry decided now was a good time to ask. "Mrs. Roosevelt, things look good at the United Nations. If we can get Senate approval for the charter they are now completing, would you accept an appointment as our first delegate?"

"Of course. I would be honored to serve."

"And perhaps you could share your speechwriter, Adlai Stevenson, with me?"

"Yes, indeed. But Secretary Forrestal wasn't too pleased I took Adlai away from his Navy Department duties."

Henry smiled. "I've also detected some annoyance on the secretary's part. But I think the Navy long ago became accustomed to accepting presidential requests. But I must tell you, I doubt Adlai did much to improve your early drafts. Maude and I have been reading your newspaper columns for many years."

"Too kind, Mr. President. Too kind"

"It's you who are being very kind to take my Maude and our daughter on your White House tour."

Henry took her half-smile as gratitude, but also a show of remorse. He left for his day's appointments.

WHITE HOUSE, SOUTH PORCH

HERBERT HOOVER SMILED ACROSS THE luncheon table at Henry Schricker. "You know, Mr. President, this view across the lawn was always my favorite. You see both the Jefferson Memorial and the Washington Monument. Thank you for inviting me for lunch."

Henry was delighted by the chance to consult with a man who'd been in this seat before. "My great pleasure, Mr. President. And I much appreciate your counsel. Especially your viewpoint on the assumptions of authority that a president's associates can make. I try to guard against unneeded confidences. In a more limited way, I discovered at Indianapolis that some most willing to help me often told others how influential they were with the governor. Some wanted praise. Some wanted remuneration for their influence. But, as my press relations man likes to say, I may be telling Noah about the flood."

Hoover chuckled. "President Schricker, you have a down-home way of putting things in context. Reminds me of the first Republican who lived in this White House. He issued his Emancipation Proclamation without his cabinet's concurrence."

The former and current presidents chuckled.

Then Hoover dropped his smile. "And as you may have already discovered, some of the decisions a president must make do not please everyone. I understand why my signing the Hoot-Smalley tariff still draws criticism. But I've never understood the hatred. I think the worst came from Texas. Those who claimed the depression caused them to eat jackrabbits were joking, but that did not keep some haters from calling them Hoover chickens."

WHITE HOUSE, CABINET ROOM

"LADY, GENTLEMEN, THANK YOU AGAIN, for your service to President Roosevelt. He relied greatly on his cabinet officers to work independent of any close oversight, and so will this president. And thank you for your sustained support since his death."

Henry swept his eyes around the table. Most of the cabinet members leaned over their yellow legal pad and a manila envelope with supporting data. They had sat in Congress when he delivered his "we will carry on" speech. Today was their first working meeting with the new president.

Henry wondered if they thought about how much loyalty they were expected to transfer from one president to the next. "I expect you all, especially Secretary Stimson, will hear from those who wonder how could I approve of the new recruit combat rule. You can assure them that I am well aware of the criticism that comes from those who have lost their youths to military service. You might also tell them I was once a captain in the Indiana State Guard where the young men were strong and learned quickly. I have no doubt that six months of training before sending an eighteen year old to a battle station will improve the odds that he will survive."

Henry waited for comment. He took the nod from Secretary of War Stimson as all the affirmation he needed.

"I decided to sign the bill Congress sends me. On future decisions, you may expect that I will call on you to help me respond. But you can also expect that I will follow an example I found in my previous Abraham Lincoln readings."

Stimson sat closest to Henry. He couldn't miss that the secretary of war throwing back his head and raising his eyebrows.

"Oh, yes, Secretary Stimson, I know that Lincoln was a Republican before you were."

A few chuckles told him others saw Stimson's reaction as well.

"But you can expect me to share some of my 'Lincoln Lore' that I started receiving in the mail over a decade ago.

Stimson gave a feeble salute. Some Cabinet members laughed.

Henry continued "I'm referring to the Lincoln story about his decision to issue the Emancipation Proclamation. When Lincoln canvassed his Cabinet on whether to issue the proclamation, all members voted no. Lincoln announced he voted yes. He would issue the proclamation freeing the slaves. But he urged his Cabinet members, in all deliberations, to continue to speak their opinions. I ask the same from all of you."

BLAIR HOUSE

HENRY SHUT OFF THE BEDSIDE lamp, but continued to talk. "Maude, as expected, my evening in the Map Room helped me learn more about troops, planes, ships, and war zones. I won't wake her, but I have a report for Margaret about her USS *Indiana*. When the lieutenant reported the *Indiana* was steaming from Okinawa to Ulithi for replenishment, I showed my new-on-the-job ignorance and asked where exactly Ulithi was. What do our people do there? Rigdon said we know the Japanese know about Ulithi, but the atoll is still classified, a military secret. He saw no reason for me not to tell you and Margaret.

"Ulithi is a Pacific atoll with coral reef, palm trees, and white sand. Last year, the US Navy landed. Found four hundred natives and three enemy soldiers residing there. The natives were relocated, and the Navy set up shops to maintain and repair over a hundred of those landing craft vehicles that ferry troops and tanks ashore.

"On one of the four atolls the Seabees built an airstrip. Douglas DC-3s each week deliver sacks of mail, supplies, and people from Guam. They have a radio station. And, sad to say, a cemetery. It's a crowded place, I was told. Have about six thousand repair people there. Ship fitters, carpenters, electricians, and welders. Even have a floating dry dock. And a ship that distills water but also bakes pies and bread.

"Without the Ulithi base, I was told, we would have had a difficult time supplying the troops who landed at Okinawa. Because our ships this past October defeated the Japanese fleet in the Leyte Gulf, we can set up supply and repair depots closer to the Japanese homeland.

"But, for now, the USS *Indiana* will refuel when the battleship gets to Ulithi.

"You know, Maude, I'm beginning to understand what Churchill must feel. They say the sun never sets on the British Empire. Well, with all of our fighting men and women in the Pacific, the reports keep coming to my desk all times of the day."

CHAPTER 9

"HITLER IS DEAD. YES, MAUDE, Hitler is dead. I'm telephoning from the Map Room. I will be over to Blair House for supper, but I just had to tell you the news. Map Room staff picked up a report from a Nazi radio station in Hamburg. Announced Hitler died fighting the Bolshevists in Berlin. But also report from Berlin underground radio says Hitler committed suicide in his Berlin bunker.

"I've alerted Mike Quinn we need to make a special press announcement. I also plan to comment on the *New York Times* bulletin that our troops have liberated thirty-two thousand inmates the Nazis tortured in their Dachau prison.

"Also the bad news: thirty-nine boxcars full of mostly Polish bodies. Nine thousand died of hunger. And fourteen thousand died this past winter. Newspaper called what the Nazis did a holocaust."

Maude agreed, "Oh, Henry, do comment. So horrible. The *Times* used the correct term."

"Well, tonight, you will not have to wait for Gabriel Heater to broadcast the good news. You just heard the good news about Hitler. You and Margaret cook something special so we can celebrate."

WEDNESDAY, MAY 2, OVAL OFFICE

HENRY READ IN THE MAP Room. *"Berlin surrenders to Russians after 12 days of street fighting. German Army surrenders in Italy."*

Henry thought, *Gabriel Heater will have some more "Good News Tonight."*

THURSDAY, MAY 3, OVAL OFFICE

THE LANKY PRESS SECRETARY SAT close to the desk. Mike Quinn opened his manila folder and passed a paper to Henry. "Mr. President, this is a draft copy of the press statement. We will release at noon that you have appointed Associate Justice Robert H. Jackson of the Supreme Court as the Chief counsel of United States preparing charges against war criminals. And you promise 'no delay' which is consistent with our traditional insistence upon a fair trial for any accused."

Henry nodded. "And, Mike, let's add 'Those who face the court will be the men primarily responsible for the atrocities.'"

Quinn flipped open his reporter's notepad and penciled the quote. "Mr. President, I have written—for your approval—some press release words for you to celebrate the 1942 naval Battle of the Coral Sea."

Henry smiled. "By all means, let's read what you said I said."

Quinn passed the paper and waited while Henry read.

> *Today, we commemorate the Naval Battle of the Coral Sea. From May 3 to May 8, 1942, our valiant Navy flyers fought it entirely by aircraft.*

> *The Japs planned to confront and destroy the American Pacific fleets by a raid on Midway Island. But Allied Intelligence discovered the Japanese plans and ordered Task Force 17 and a number of support craft to stop the enemy.*

On May 7, American planes found the Japanese light carrier Soho and sank it in 10 minutes. "Scratch one flattop!" was the signal received by Adm. Fitch on the Lexington.

On May 8, the final day of the battle, two large Japanese carriers were damaged so badly they could not take part in the Battle of Midway, a major American victory less than a month later. Because of their losses in the Coral Sea, the Japanese cancelled plans to invade Moresby. Thus their advance in the South Pacific was halted.

But Task Force 17 also was severely mauled in the Coral Sea. Both Yorktown and Lexington were heavily damaged by Japanese aircraft. Yorktown, known as "Waltzing Matilda," limped first to Pearl Harbor and then to the Battle of Midway, where she was finally lost.

The Lexington went down in the Coral Sea.

There were more words, but Henry thought, *This copy needs editing.* He reached into a top drawer and took out a pen with blue ink.

Henry said "Change 'Japs' to 'Japanese.' Don't give them another reason not to surrender. Better edit 'intelligence.' Don't want them to know but ..."

Henry frowned, dropping his editing pen on the desktop. "But, Mike, better we don't send out this press release at all."

Quinn laid his notebook in his lap.

Henry saw Quinn's slumped shoulders and hurried with an explanation. "It's not your copy that worries me, Mike. Couldn't help reverting to my old 'green-eye-shade' newspaper editor habits. What really worries me is I think this is no time to start memorializing. In our county, we had a farmer who also preached on Sunday. Church located on the farm road between Knox and North Judson. I remember because about five years ago, when I was looking for votes, I attended his little church. I even remember his sermon scripture. Looked it up in my pocket *New Testament* while he was preaching.

"Luke wrote at end of chapter nine, '*No one who sets his hand to the ploughing and then keeps looking back is fit for the kingdom of Heaven.*' Every farmer's kid there who had driven the tractor knew what that meant. Keep looking ahead. Look back and you may not keep the row straight.

"That's where we are now, Mike. No time to look back. We'll leave that to the historians. They can go all the way back to first airplane landing on a carrier and Billy Mitchell predicting the rise of air power."

Henry took a deep breath. "Also many Gold Mothers wouldn't understand why we would memorialize one battle and not name the one that took their son."

Mike took the copy Henry handed back to him, thanked his fellow Hoosier president, and left.

Henry bowed his head and thought, *The scripture I quoted also says "Leave the dead to bury the dead."* He thought a silent prayer, *Oh, Lord, help us end this war.*

⊰——⊱

FRIDAY, MAY 4, BLAIR HOUSE

MARGARET POURED HENRY THE SECOND cup of breakfast coffee.

Maude held up the folded newspaper. "Let me read you what else Eleanor wrote in her column."

> *"I always have a pride in the beauty of the rooms, their proportion, the woodwork and the historically interesting furnishings which remain the same no matter what individuals may live here. It was good to find Mrs. Schricker appreciative of the things I have loved."*

Maude grimaced. "Oh, my goodness, Henry. Bless her heart, but we were so disappointed with what she showed us."

Margaret nodded. "Pop, Mom's so right. Walls streaked with dust. Outlines of all the pictures that had been taken down. Shabby furniture in need of upholstering. Threadbare carpets that hadn't been cleaned in years. Draperies that were actually rotting."

Henry finished his coffee. "I guess Eleanor has been too busy to pay attention. I put my banker eye on the White House budget, and saw she has left untouched fifty thousand dollars that Congress allocated for upkeep and repair. You've got some funds for cleaning up the old house.

"Also, my banker's eye saw some other White House expenses we can eliminate. President Roosevelt needed the swimming pool in the basement. Polio hit him hard. But I never spent much time swimming after I learned how over at Bass Lake. Maybe we could turn the pool into a bowling alley. That would give the staff and the secret service guys a place to exercise."

Maude slapped the paper on the table. "Good idea, Mr. President, but how about fixing the upstairs before reworking the basement? We didn't see the presidential quarters. But while Mrs. Roosevelt told Margaret about the pianos, the White House butler Alonzo Fields told me that the upstairs was a mess."

Henry thought of an exit line. "Well, Indiana historian Boomhower wrote how President Benjamin Harrison's women fixed up the old house during the last century. I know another set of Hoosier gals that know just what's needed this century."

Henry blew kisses. At the front door, he grabbed his white fedora off the hook and crammed it on his head. *I need a less furious place, say like the Oval Office where I can learn about a war in Europe.*

WHITE HOUSE, OVAL OFFICE

Henry read the urgent message from the Map Room and smiled. "German forces in the Netherlands and Denmark agree to surrender."

SATURDAY MAY 5, OVAL OFFICE

Henry put the Map Room paper notes in his inner coat pocket for Maude and Margaret to read that evening:

USS Indiana shot down two Oscars.

American troops liberate Mauthausen death camp.

> *Also report Japanese have been launching bomb-carrying paper balloons with no property damage.*

Henry knew he would need to explain the paper balloon story that was yet to be told. Intelligence did not want the Japanese to know their balloons had crossed the Pacific. But the futility of their effort was just too good to keep hidden. Besides, the situation was no secret to many people who lived in Oregon.

⁂

SUNDAY, MAY 6, WASHINGTON, D.C., GENERAL MARSHALL'S OFFICE

COLONEL WATSON WISHED HE WAS going to church with his wife, but he explained to Katherine he was on call. He was glad he had great news for the general, because he would not like the *Post* story. He held the folded newspaper behind his back and waited until the general sat.

"Good Morning, General. Great message from Ike. Grand Admiral Karl Doenitz has ordered U-boats to return to bases, ordered armies to cease fighting."

Marshall grinned. "Great. A new Führer of the German Reich. What Intelligence reported as possible yesterday was true. What Donovan's OSS picked up in the Vatican was close, probably too early for their identification."

The colonel laid the newspaper on the general's desk. "I don't know if you saw the *Washington Post* this—"

"Damn right, I did. Read the story at breakfast. What stupid Congressman leaked my testimony?"

"Well, sir, that was supposed to be an executive session, but the *Post* did call the Congressman 'irresponsible.'"

The general growled, though he doubted that any damage had been done.

"Hell, yes, I read their damn 'speedy and broad' crap." *Firing squads were a good idea,* the general thought.

Marshall unfolded the paper and read aloud. "Get this:

> *Our soldiers, their families and the rest of the civilian population will be greatly relieved to learn that*

demobilization is expected to get underway speedily and proceed on a fairly broad scale after Germany's surrender."

"Dammit, Colonel, that's the wrong message. Get me our information officer. We'll release the whole demobilization plan in detail. You can bet people who read this will get the wrong impression. Hell, we've still got men fighting and being killed in Germany."

OVAL OFFICE

THE PRESIDENT'S PRESS SECRETARY MADE a confession. "I don't think I could have resisted. I would have filed the bulletin. Third Reich surrenders. Enjoyed the consequences."

"Mike, what are the consequences?"

"He's ordered home. Bet the Associated Press won't fire him. I bet Edward Kennedy will become a historical footnote as the journalist who scooped the world. Mr. President, what do you want me to tell the press?"

Henry Schricker strained to keep what they call a poker face after being dealt four aces. He thought, *Back in my newspaper day, I would have had the same problem trying to resist breaking the end of World War I story. But my answer needs to sound presidential. Or maybe now's the time to buck the story to General Marshall.*

"Mike, think this is one of those 'we can neither confirm or deny' answer to your press buddies. Let's refer them to General Marshall's office." And, Henry thought, *Marshall will refer the reporters back to Ike's command, and then …*

Three knocks on the door interrupted. Chief of Staff Leahy entered. "Excuse me for interrupting, Mr. President, but Churchill just went on BBC and told England that Germany surrendered."

Messages kept pouring in to the president's desk. One of the first said the USS *Indiana* was underway for Okinawa. Henry would later pass that one from the Map Room to his daughter, now somewhere in the White House. He knew Maude and Margaret were moving their belongings from Blair House to this big house. Eleanor had needed military trucks to move the Roosevelt collections. The Schrickers only needed a van.

Henry reread Eisenhower's request for formal orders if he was to pull troops back, withdraw our troops south of the Elbe River to previously agreed occupation lines. Ike's request repeated what Henry had already heard. German troops wanted to surrender to Americans or British because they feared Russian troops would abuse them.

The cable from Churchill was most Churchillian. It said something along the lines of the tide of Russian domination swept forward 120 miles on a front of 300 to 400 miles. Churchill didn't stop there. He predicted Russia would now dominate other capitals besides Berlin. His cable warned Russia now would control Vienna, Budapest, Belgrade, and Sofia.

Henry addressed his men. "Secretary Stimson, Admiral Leahy, thank you for coming to my office on such short notice. You have also seen the message from General Eisenhower. The Russians don't appear to give him any choice. And I don't blame him for passing the decision on to us. Before your president answers Ike's formal request, what do you think?"

Leahy nodded toward Stimson. "I know I'm passing the buck, but Secretary Stimson brings more diplomatic and Army experience than this Navy Man."

Henry dropped his head. *I need counsel, not buck-passing.*

Stimson didn't smile. "Mr. President, apparently the Russians want a propaganda favor. I say, concede their request. And, if needed, remind Stalin of our cooperation when you meet."

"Thank you, gentlemen. Secretary Stimson, please have General Marshall authorize Ike to accede to the Russians' demands. Call it a request, and don't mention that the White House approved. Thank you both for coming at this hour."

Henry wondered what other rewards would the Soviets demand in order to get Stalin to declare war against Japan.

WHITE HOUSE, PRESIDENTIAL QUARTERS

HENRY NOTICED THE DISTRESSED LOOKS from his wife and daughter, and asked, "Why do my girls look so downcast?"

Margaret answered, "Pops, your girls have discovered how much tender loving care this old house needs. And we're going to give it."

Henry uttered an "Oh?"

Maude added, "But, Margaret, you need to tell him the good news."

Margaret nodded and took her father's hand. "Come with me, Pops. I want to give you the piano tour. Mom and I were briefed yesterday by Mrs. Roosevelt's house manager. She's such a stickler for formality, I didn't bother telling her you played the piano in the morning to wake up the boys and me. Now you've got a house full of them. Let's go to the East Room and see the famous Steinway they call the Eagle-Leg Piano. They told me in 1938 they designed American Eagles for the legs that hold it up. FDR helped with the design, but bet he couldn't play as well as my pop."

Henry grinned. "And I presume you think flattery will get me to play a rendition you request."

Maude winked. "Well your two boys in the service called. Said tell Pop to find a piano and play that old Democrat campaign song *Happy Days Are Here Again.*

Henry pointed toward the door. "Okay, girls. East Room. Here we go." But Henry thought, *Happy days yet to come, the war is only half-over.*

CHAPTER 10

TUESDAY, MAY 8, WHITE HOUSE, ADMINISTRATIVE OFFICE

THE CAPITOL PRESS CROWDED INTO the room, pads and pencil at the ready for him to announce the bulletin they already knew. Henry's wristwatch said 8:29 a.m. The time that he should have announced Germany's surrender was 2:12 a.m. the day before when Ike signed the surrender papers. But the Russians insisted on a joint announcement.

"Gentlemen and ladies, as Prime Minster Churchill explained on the radio yesterday, the delay in announcing the Nazi surrender was agreed upon by all parties. Time was needed to notify all troops in Europe to cease firing. In thirty minutes I will announce to the nation that Nazi Germany has surrendered. I will declare this great day 'Victory in Europe' day. I will also remind my listeners that much fighting and sacrifice remain before we defeat the Japanese warlords."

WHITE HOUSE, OVAL OFFICE

"MR. PRESIDENT, WE WILL JOIN all networks at exactly 9 a.m."

Henry nodded. "Thank you. I understand." He arranged his notes, adjusted the glasses on his nose and smoothed his script. Some of the words were dictated and a phrase here and there was edited into the last draft. But they were all his words.

Editor and Publisher Henry F. Schricker had sold the *Starke County Democrat* 25 years ago, but he still remembered how to meet a deadline.

When he'd announced the Nazi surrender to reporters gathered in his office, he saw their bored look. Of course, those reporters knew Germany had surrendered. Henry knew many "Extra" editions waited in type for his announcement. America's radio audience was also waiting on a celebration starting line.

"Fellow Americans" were the words Roosevelt used to open his fireside chats. Henry penned in the same opening. The director stood in front of his desk. The portrait of Franklin Delano Roosevelt looked over Henry's shoulder.

"Ready, Mr. President in five, four, three, two, one." He pointed to the microphone on Henry's desk.

The announcer said, "We take you to the White House in Washington, D.C. with the President of the United States of America, Henry F. Schricker."

Henry brought air up from his diaphragm, just as his attorney mentor taught him in 1910.

"Fellow Americans. Today we can thank our God for this Victory Day in Europe. Nazi Germany has surrendered. The world has survived Adolph Hitler. Peace in Europe is again possible. But only because of many sacrifices.

"Many have died. Many have suffered crippling pain, endured untold hardship on the world's battlefields, separated themselves from family and loved ones, traveled around the world to carry out their sworn duties.

"And our gratitude includes those many who have contributed creative skills—in shipyards, factories, munitions plants, laboratories—to insure freedom will prevail.

"Today, your president declares Victory in Europe. VE Day has arrived.

"I wish you were listening to President Franklin Delano Roosevelt deliver this great news. President Roosevelt deserves our deepest admiration for his leadership through these darkest hours.

"If he were alive, President Roosevelt would praise victory in Europe, but also remind us that a day in infamy has yet to be avenged. His call for unconditional surrender has yet to be met by the military rulers of Japan—and we will never rest until the Japanese warlords surrender."

WHITE HOUSE, PRESIDENTIAL QUARTERS

MARGARET LAUGHED AT HER PARENTS. "You would think we were back on South Main Street, gathered around the radio to hear Gabriel Heater."

The first lady turned up the volume.

"There's good news, tonight. Wild celebrations in New York, London, Paris, Moscow …"

Maude turned down the radio volume. "Henry, the boys called while you were in the Oval Office. They will call again around seven."

Margaret interrupted. "Before they start really celebrating."

"Shush, child."

Henry laughed. "Margaret's right, honey. I've been taking calls and telegrams before people started celebrating all day. The best phone call was from Senator Truman, who sounded like he had already had a little bourbon. Harry's celebrating both VE Day and his sixty-first birthday."

WEDNESDAY, MAY 9, WHITE HOUSE, PRESIDENTIAL QUARTERS

MAUDE POURED A SECOND CUP of coffee for Henry. Then she spoke to Henry and Margaret.

"I'm reading a *Washington Post* story that should sober up a bunch of yesterday's celebrators. Here's the headline, "Killing Japs Only Okinawa VE Observance.""

WHITE HOUSE, OVAL OFFICE

"Mr. War Secretary, you're here early to discuss moving troops to the Pacific. But before you brief me, let's talk about General Grove's report that Oppenheimer will soon test fire a nuclear bomb. I'm cognizant that if our scientists succeed, decision to employ this new weapon needs presidential approval. I don't intend to shift the burden to you or others. But from that day in April, when you and Grove told me about the Manhattan Project, I go to sleep worrying how to decide.

"Secretary Stimson, I'm asking you to help me justify—if the test succeeds—employing such a weapon.

Stimson nodded. "Of course, I'll give you my most honest opinion."

"Thank you. Now before you convene the committee to identify targets, help me organize a decision presentation."

Henry reached into a desk drawer and pulled out a small book. "This collects the writings of French philosopher, Blaise Pascal. His nineteenth century approach to decision-making shapes my thinking. I reread his essay last night, and made notes."

Henry read from his notes. "Pascal wagers whether there is, or there isn't a God. No maybe. Just is there a God? Either yes or no.

"If you bet no God and there is no God, then you lose nothing, but gain nothing. But if there is a God, and you wager no God, probably every preacher you and I have known can tell you about the fire and brimstone that waits for you.

"On the other hand, if you bet there is a God, follow his commandments, and there isn't a God, you still gain. Your neighbors will commend you for living a good life, praise your honesty, applaud your generosity for others.

"If you wager there is a God, we have heard all our lives of the heavenly blessings we will earn. Therefore, Pascal advises us to wager God exists and enjoy an infinity of blessings. I think Pascal furnishes us with a decision model that's hard to refute."

Henry Stimson, twice Secretary of War, nodded his agreement.

Henry Schricker put his note into a coat pocket. "My use of Pascal's reasoning, of course, presumes our scientists can build a nuclear bomb. Thank heaven, Hitler's scientists never succeeded."

⁓ — ⁔

THURSDAY, MAY 10, WHITE HOUSE, OVAL OFFICE

"THANK YOU, MR. STEVENSON, FOR coming to see me early on a one-day notice, especially with celebrating still going on."

Adlai almost laughed aloud.

President Schricker didn't wait for a reply. "Your dad and I knew each other as editors and publishers, even before you cubbed on his newspaper. We've served in state governments at the same time, not to mention some rip-roaring Democrat conventions when Illinois and Indiana delegations were seated next to each other."

"When you talk to the family back in Illinois, give your dad my regards. He won't be surprised what I've asked you to do. I talked to Navy Secretary Forrestal. We think we can share your talents, just as he has shared your quick wit with Eleanor Roosevelt."

Adlai said, "I'd happily assist however I can with your speeches."

Henry smiled. "Before we start composing, I must confess to you, another staunch Democrat, that I've often looked to our first Republican president as a model for presidential speechmaking. For years, I've been receiving a Fort Wayne insurance company publication, the *Lincoln Lore*. Here's a copy. Notice the peacemaking Lincoln quote. I'm sure you can find other notable quotes that suggest we need to bind our wounds."

Adlai nodded.

The president frowned. "Several important people have advanced positions they want me to take. I'm sure you already have heard some of these contrary views. Here's my summation.

"Secretary Morgenthau and Churchill want Germany's military industry destroyed. Stalin wants to steal it. France wants the Germans to rebuild their country. Poland wants the Germans expelled. Tito expects to keep three different races in Yugoslavia under the same roof.

"Adlai, all those agendas could tear the United Nations apart. How about both of us think of words that would help cement adoption of the UN charter?"

Henry picked up the paper, placed his reading glasses on his nose, and read aloud. "We stand today at the threshold of a great event both in the life of the United Nations and in the life of mankind. This Universal Declaration of Human Rights may well become the international Magna Carta to lift people everywhere to a higher standard of life and to greater enjoyment of freedom.

"Adlai, if you don't mind me dispensing with formalities—I'm sure that Eleanor Roosevelt wasn't without words, but the man who helped her put together that speech knew his business. That speech worked so well at the General Assembly of the United Nations, that your new president wants you to help him write another speech that I will deliver to the U.N. Can do?"

"Yes, sir."

"Good. I envision a Lincoln parallel. Lincoln's vision for reconstructing the South after the Civil War and the job ahead reconstructing Europe. I will be at the Pentagon this afternoon, you may need to read some Lincoln before I see you here tomorrow afternoon at three o'clock."

⛇ —— ⛇

WASHINGTON, D.C., DRIVING TO PENTAGON

THE TWO MEN RIDING IN the back seat of the limousine paid little attention to the Virginia landscape. The chief of staff grinned as he handed the president the list of Interim Committee participants.

"Mr. President, think they all read your Pascal's Wager homework?"

"Jimmy Byrnes reported that John Jay McCloy, under-secretary to Stimson, made sure everyone had a copy.

President Schricker chuckled. "Bill, I think I've turned education upside-down. Here's a Hoosier with one-year business training at Valparaiso College, only eight years of public schooling, who assigns religious reading to presidents of universities, graduates of military academies, and nuclear scientists.

"I owe thanks to Congress and the framers of our Constitution for specifying citizenship and age requirement for political candidates, but not requiring a college degree."

Leahy smiled. "Abraham Lincoln did well without a college education."

"Yes, he did. But he read the law and qualified as a lawyer."

"Mr. President, so did you. Plus edited a weekly newspaper. And, apparently, you read religious philosophy."

"Thanks, Bill."

"You're welcome. But if I may be so bold, I do believe there's a God. And my parents forbid me to gamble, so I'm not sure about couching the question of belief as a 'you bet your life' wager."

"I'll use that observation to open my presentation to the committee. I'll chalk my diagram on the blackboard, then we can erase. I presume there'll be chalk and eraser in the room?"

"Yes, sir. McCloy said everything is ready."

❧ — ☙

WHITE HOUSE, PENTAGON

"THANK YOU, MR. BYRNES, FOR representing me yesterday at your initial meeting."

Henry thought, *Not the time to announce James Byrnes would soon become his secretary of state.*

Henry swept his eyes across the assembled committee members. He thought, *I'm just a country lawyer, and I'm going to tell some of America's greatest scholars and military authorities how to make the world's most momentous decision.*

He kept short his welcome to government representatives, but enlarged on his praise for the three university presidents.

"We express our gratitude to Harvard, President Conant, to Massachusetts Institute of Technology, President Compton, to University of California, President Lawrence.

The educators only nodded at their recognition. *Probably not thrilled,* Henry thought, *to serve on a committee that decides whether to drop the first atomic bomb.*

"Gentlemen, as we have agreed, it is best that your president keep minutes today. Not only to ensure secrecy but to keep a historical record."

Henry looked around the large table and saw all nodded in acceptance. "Admiral Leahy told me he flinched when he read

Blaise Pascal's term deciding whether God is called a 'wager.' But placing a bet is a decision-making exercise. Let me add, long before I read what Pascal wrote in his French monastery cell, I had fully accepted a provident God exists, and I am sure you have all made your judgment."

Henry didn't wait for any confessionals. "I will repeat what you may already know. Pascal was a brilliant mathematician who as a young man developed betting probabilities and invented a calculating machine to help his father collect taxes for the state. All accomplishments before he repented and went to live out his life in a monastery.

Henry received smiles, but no chuckles. "We meet to decide upon a future decision that depends on a weapon yet to be tested. We're here because we're, if you will allow, betting our nuclear scientists will succeed.

"In the same way that Pascal states his wager of either yes there's a God or no there isn't a God, let me couch our decision. Do we drop a nuclear bomb like the explosive our scientists will soon test? Or not?

"I've asked for a blackboard to draw what you will recognize as a management device, a decision tree. When we finish, we will erase the chalk, but history—and the fiscal watchdogs in our Senate—will not let us erase an expenditure that General Grove tells us now exceeds $2 billion."

Henry heard several intakes of breath. "And, of course, that's one of the 'Why not?' questions, if we say no to dropping the bomb."

He wrote at the top of the blackboard. *Bomb?*

"Let's start with what may happen if we decide yes."

Schricker drew a diagonal line downward and wrote *yes*. Below that he drew and wrote lines to *Japan surrenders?* and then another line to *Japan doesn't surrender?*

"And, gentlemen, if Japan doesn't surrender, I think we have our first question repeated."

Henry drew two lines from *Japan doesn't surrender* downward to *bomb Japan again* and *don't bomb again*.

Secretary Stimson broke the silence. "Mr. President, I'm sure I'm not the only one here who isn't amazed that all of the fire bombs we've so recently dropped on their homeland hasn't caused them to surrender."

General Marshall answered, "Iwo Jima and Okinawa tell us they intend to fight to the death."

Conant added his voice. "But, general, the world has never seen anything as destructive as a nuclear explosion. Or the probable radioactive after-effects. Our scientists hypothesize destruction of a whole Japanese city."

No others interrupted, so Henry continued to print on the blackboard. "Let's look at alternatives if we choose no to dropping an atomic bomb."

Schricker drew a diagonal line down from *no*. Then wrote *starvation, casualties*.

Henry decided not to add another option for not dropping an atomic bomb. The Russians could develop their own. Some nuclear scientists in New Mexico were known communist sympathizers and could return to their European homelands. Some of those scientists might give Russia a balance of power. If only Russia had that ability, how would Stalin use that threat?

Henry laid down his chalk. "I'm confident that many who come after us may compare a nuclear device to poison gas and germ warfare that nations have long deplored. But a prolonged war and blockade leads to mass starvation—not only in Japan, but in those countries they've conquered. It also delays what relief we have pledged to give those countries freed from the Nazis."

At the bottom of his second diagonal downward line, Henry wrote *Invade Japan* "How many millions of lives—ours and theirs—will be lost if we invade? When will a kamikaze populace and their ritualistic fight-to-the death military surrender? I think our question of whether to bomb may have been largely decided by my predecessor and the British prime minister. We see few indications of any Japanese willingness to surrender.

"Now, gentlemen, I need to hear from you. If you are of the same mind that your president should order the first bomb that's operational dropped on Japan, then we will pick targets we should consider bombing."

❧ — ☙

AFTER THE BREAK, HENRY STARTED up the discussion again. "I think we all agree that remaining new targets should have been previously spared, the better to assess damage. And, as Secretary Stimson has well stated, that we should spare Japan's ancestral home. Do you want to add to that statement?"

Stimson responded, "Thank you, Mr. President. I would hope we all agree not to give the Japanese any warning. We don't want to concentrate on a civilian area, but at the same time, we want to make a profound psychological impression on as many Japanese as possible."

President Schricker nodded to Stimson. Then read from his notes. "Here's the summary that I will include in my historical notes of this meeting. We agree to drop the bomb."

Henry nodded toward Stimson. "I note $2 billion spent on the project." He saw some blink, some drop their heads. "President Lawrence, our notes will show you favored a prior demonstration, but that you reported a contrary opinion from Robert Oppenheimer, your colleague now directing completion of the project from his laboratories in Los Alamos, New Mexico.

"Professor Oppenheimer told you to tell the Interim Committee that he could not conceive of a technical demonstration that would be spectacular enough to actually induce the Japanese to surrender."

Lawrence nodded yes.

"Doctor Compton submits—and the Secretary of War agrees—that the most desirable target would be a vital war plant employing a large number of workers even though closely surrounded by worker's houses."

Compton nodded agreement. Stimson returned the nod.

Henry continued, "My notes include that our military planners project that a proposed invasion of Kyushu could cost 500,000 American lives and many more injuries. *Some other military planners estimate an invasion could cost a million lives.*"

Henry paused to look around the room. "It's agreed that we keep an element of surprise. We note that fire bombing of cities hasn't caused the Japanese to surrender. May have caused more determination to resist to the death."

He took a deep breath. "We agree a second bomb can be dropped if Japan resists surrender. We will issue warnings by leaflets and radio broadcasts. We will warn if Japan does not surrender, we will drop a second atomic bomb, with enough force that many nearby civilians may also die."

Secretary of War Stimson waited until Henry finished. "Mr. President, I can add a somber report I have received. Casualties for both Army and Navy are nearing the million mark."

Henry clenched his teeth and thought, *We may all die if we have begun the destruction of our planet.*

CHAPTER 11

FRIDAY, MAY 11, WHITE HOUSE, MAP ROOM

Okinawa. Japanese suicide plane crashes into USS Bunker Hill. First report, nearly 400 American sailors killed.

SATURDAY, MAY 12, OVAL OFFICE

HENRY READ THE UPDATE SENT from the Map Room.

USS Indiana on station at Okinawa. Task Group 58.1 Shot down 16th enemy warplane.

MONDAY, MAY 14, WHITE HOUSE, OVAL OFFICE

UNDER SECRETARY OF STATE JOSEPH Clark Grew stood close to the president's desk so he could point out the multiple places needing signatures. "Mr. President, your signatures will let us complete negotiations with the Russians. Unfortunately, they think the old Lend-Lease agreement that President Roosevelt signed should continue after the Germans have surrendered."

"Secretary Grew, I understand you want me to immediately sign off on this agreement. But I don't intend to sign anything I haven't read twice." Henry thought, *I'm not going to forego a good banker habit.* Besides, he wasn't in a forgiving mood. "Mr. Grew, forgive my tone. Before you arrived, I had just read the bad news that Leahy's office delivered from the Map Room. We lost over seven hundred men when the Japanese dive-bombed the USS *Franklin.* The carrier was still afloat and was being brought back for repairs."

⊰——⊱

TUESDAY, MAY 15 , WHITE HOUSE, MAP ROOM

HENRY EXPECTED MAUDE OR MARGARET upstairs in the presidential suite to put his evening meal in the refrigerator. He needed to finish his self-imposed geography lesson so would miss dinner. The map of Japan was spread across the Map Room table.

The lieutenant had brought him the map and now waited at his desk. Rigdon knew Henry studied maps he'd seen projected earlier today. Henry started at the top. His eyes followed the Sea of Japan down and left to the Korea Strait. Then right across to the lowest island, Kyushu. Henry remembered the briefing, The sixth army would come ashore on the south and west coast.

This first invasion of Japan was code named *Olympic.* Three Marine divisions and six Army divisions were assigned.

The Marines would establish a southern beachhead, after frogmen swam ashore the night before to reconnoiter. *Damn risky business*, Henry thought. To the Marine's right, three Army divisions would land. To that group's right, another three Army divisions would land.

Henry ran his finger up the map to the next island, Shikoku. There was no landing planned, but three Army divisions would arrive offshore. They called it a feint.

Above Shikoku, Henry traced the island of Honshu, Japan's mainland. He ran his finger from Hiroshima on the Korea Strait, northwest up to a northern city named Hirosaki. *Wonder if that's where their whiskey is made.* Henry chuckled to himself.

He consulted a miles chart and used his fingers to calculate that Honshu island was over a thousand miles long. And Tokyo was on the Pacific coastline.

Henry recalled the gist of the briefing that afternoon. *Coronet*, the invasion of the mainland at Tokyo, would follow after *Olympic*, the invasion of Kyushu. Joint Chief planners had code-named both invasions *Downfall*. Henry thought, *Someone in our military has a gallows sense of humor.*

‍‍‍

SUNDAY, MAY 20, WHITE HOUSE, PRESIDENTIAL SUITE

HENRY REMOVED HIS GLASSES AND folded the newspaper. "Maude, I'm reading a sensible opinion piece from Andy May, a savvy Kentucky Congressman. He wants Congress to pass a universal service bill. I would sign that bill quickly."

Maude laid her *Saturday Evening Post* in her lap and gave the president the attention he occasionally demanded from his "kitchen cabinet."

"Couple of things I like about the Kaintuck's proposal. First, he wants all those finishing high school, both young men and young women 'cause they aren't children any more. And many are already working part-time during the war to serve their country for a year."

Maude questioned, "Compulsory military training for both sexes?"

"Depends on whether the graduate wants to enlist. And whether the military wants them. But we do need to keep up our military preparedness. A reserve of trained military men we didn't have when Japan and Germany declared war on us. As for young women, they could teach immigrants better English language or help clean up brush in the national forests to reduce chances of forest fires, like the CCC young men did before the war. One of the best programs in our New Deal legislation. I'll wait and see what Congress sends for me to sign, but I hope some planning for peace included. Though I would expect some legislative log-rolling. The congressman could remind his colleagues they could keep spending money on local military bases if barracks that we've built across the nation become dormitories."

Henry thought, but didn't say, *And if some of my Democrat friends in the South vote to integrate those barracks.*

MONDAY, MAY 21, WHITE HOUSE, OVAL OFFICE

YESTERDAY, HENRY SAW THE SECRETARY of Labor was scheduled for today's appointment. He asked Leahy to furnish biographical information before she arrived. He noted she turned seventy-five last month and had joined Roosevelt's cabinet in 1933 as secretary of labor.

When she told him she was resigning, Henry came from behind his desk and took Secretary Francis Perkin's hand and asked her to sit with him on the couch. He asked, "Why?"

She explained, "I offered to resign in 1936. In 1933, I'd only agreed to serve if Franklin agreed to several changes."

Henry raised his eyebrows.

Secretary Perkins smiled. "You know, the policies that helped us get out of the economic depression. I wanted a forty-hour work week, a minimum wage. Also unemployment compensation, a child labor abolition, direct federal aid to the states for unemployment relief, social security. Franklin said he wanted the same policies. So I joined his cabinet. My husband, Paul Wilson, had been a great supporter. Our daughter, Susanna, now grown, appreciates her mother broke some ground as a female cabinet member."

Henry nodded. "And I appreciate what a fine choice Franklin made."

Perkins smiled. "Just let me say, Henry Schricker, he made a good choice when he chose you for his successor. I'm sure someone told him what a fine first lady you would bring. I'm impressed she once taught at the country school near where she made her homestead. Somehow, Franklin always recognized depth in those he chose."

⚜ — ⚜

WEDNESDAY, MAY 23, WHITE HOUSE, OVAL OFFICE

HENRY READ THE STATE DEPARTMENT update that a sad-faced Admiral Leahy handed him.

Prime Minister Churchill resigns.

Will force first general election in ten years.

Election set for July 5.

Henry asked his chief-of-staff to get the secretary of state on the telephone. Henry wasn't sure how the president was expected to comment or what would be the appropriate note to send Winston.

＊—＊

THURSDAY, MAY 24, WHITE HOUSE, MAP ROOM

LIEUTENANT RIGDON SMILED.

"Mr. President your state was well represented. Both the USS *Indiana* and the USS *Indianapolis* have joined Task Force 59. We've got ships controlling Japanese waters, now. Intercepting their food supply from China and Korea.

"And what's really great, we've got ships that can rescue pilots who have to ditch after they bomb the Japanese homeland."

＊—＊

FRIDAY, MAY 25, WHITE HOUSE, MAP ROOM

"MR. PRESIDENT, TWO NIGHTS AGO, LeMay's headquarters reported 520 Superfortress B-29s dropped 3,646 tons of incendiaries on mixed targets, industrial and residential area west of Tokyo's harbor and south of the Imperial Palace"

"Pardon me, Lieutenant, you say industrial and residential targets?"

"Yes, sir. The Japanese have placed their factories in the middle of residential areas. We think their intention was to house workers close by. But, yes, sir, Tokyo Rose highlights our bombing residences. She tells our boys listening that they should be ashamed of our, to quote her, "atrocities.""

❦——❦

SATURDAY, MAY 26, MAP ROOM

"THANK YOU, MR. PRESIDENT, FOR coming to the Map Room. I could have sent you the usual daily update that our bombers have laid waste to Tokyo. But this information should be most confidential."

"Thank you, Lieutenant Rigdon. I came to my office a little later than usual or I would have been here sooner."

Henry didn't say, *Saturday morning for a president not like family time, second cup of coffee, back home in Indiana.*

"Give me the 'for my ears' report, Lieutenant?"

"Yes, sir. We know definitely that the Emperor's Imperial Palace was not targeted and was not bombed."

Good, Henry thought, *the Japanese would make great propaganda out of a bombing of what they consider a sacred place.*

"My colonel thought you should know so you can refute any Japanese claims. Also, he thinks you need to know that the emperor was in a nearby, fortified bomb shelter. What's most confidential is the report that came from our code-named *Vessel 24b.* And that the report was relayed directly from within the Emperor's Palace."

Rigdon couldn't miss seeing the president's jaw drop.

"Our agent in their palace has a special Navy radio circuit. Our submarines operating in Japanese waters received and verified the sender's code. Source also reported Emperor still assured by military that Japan can fight until the Americans sue for peace."

Henry thanked Rigdon, but Henry thought, It *takes any fun out of my next day off to take my girls to the annual congressional dinner.*

❦——❦

SUNDAY, MAY 27, WHITE HOUSE, PRESIDENTIAL QUARTERS

MAUDE SETTLED INTO AN EASY chair, kicking off her heels.

Margaret slipped off her heels, before she leaned back on the couch. "Wow, Pop, that Burning Tree is one fancy club. Thanks for taking us. You and Senator Truman were stars on their piano."

Henry smiled at his daughter. "I was just part of the introduction for Harry's piano solo. Senator Truman was the star. Paderewski's *Minuet from Mozart's IX Sonata* is not easy to play. But Harry was winning piano contests when he was a teenager.

Playing his part of *The Old Missouri Waltz* and *Back Home in Indiana* was easy. But he was glad he met early to practice the short duet—glad his staff furnished the sheet music for him.

"Harry didn't need sheet music. As he said, he probably could get a job playing piano in …" Henry paused and searched for another word. "A bar room."

Henry sat on the piano bench, his back to the keyboard. "Don't worry, girls, I'm not going to play the piano any more tonight. Just afraid that if I sat in my recliner, I would go to sleep before I got this monkey suit off."

Margaret beamed at her father. "Pop, you look great in a tux. 'Sides, when you men wear the same uniform, we gals can show off our difference in finery. 'Course, we had to listen to those tributes to gone members of Congress. Thanks for keeping your few words to a few words."

Maude nodded. "I'll second that. Plenty of words tonight. Maude Byrnes and I even got a chance to gossip a bit about the people we have met at Perle Mesta's parties. Maude is the nicest lady I've met in our half a year living in Washington."

And her husband is truly a Southern gentleman, Henry thought, *who I will need to do some negotiating with when I meet with both British and Russian staffs.*

"Hey, Mom, you were seated next to Bob Hope. I noticed he was doing all the talking. Bet he wasn't selling you War Bonds. What will the ladies back in Knox have to say when I tell them about you spending the evening sitting next to Bob Hope?"

"Honey, Hope wise-cracked the whole time. Ever hear about the man who brought a bear to the movie theater?"

"No, Mom. What's Hope's punch line?"

"Because the bear read the book."

Margaret laughed. "I understand why the troops enjoy his appearances so much. I asked him about those shows, and he said he saved the really good jokes for when he visited the boys in the military hospital. They are our real heroes."

Henry interrupted. "And Hope slipped me a compliment about you. 'Good-looking first lady,' he said."

Maude laughed. "Before or after they served more wine? Henry, that's a clever thing your staff does to make sure you and I get grape juice."

"Hah!" Margaret rose off the couch. "At our table, they didn't serve juice. Gotta head to my bedroom before I go to sleep on this couch. Think I best wait and call my husband tomorrow. Night, Mom. Night, Pop."

Maude told her to sleep tight.

Henry turned half around on the piano bench and with his right hand tapped out *Lullaby and Goodnight*.

TUESDAY, MAY 29, WHITE HOUSE, OVAL OFFICE

GENERAL MARSHALL HANDED THE FOLDER to the president with the words Henry was beginning to see daily: *For Your Eyes Only*. Henry had seen the words so often that he had begun the habit of running his fingers across his desk and tapping out the tune and lyrics for *I Only Have Eyes for You*.

"Mr. President, this draft from General MacArthur's staff planners arrived yesterday. My staff immediately prepared a summary for you. This draft provides more details than the *Downfall* invasion plan presentation you received two weeks ago. You will note that the proposed November attacks rely on replacement troops moved from our mainland, plus Marine divisions now staging in Hawaii. We do not expect to deploy troops from Europe until the early part of 1946."

Henry translated. "You're telling me we'll need reinforcements in spring, maybe early summer of next year. In other words, we'll still be fighting a year from now."

General Marshall nodded his agreement, before continuing, "Mr. President, you will note that the assault on their main island, Honshu, begins after we establish control of the southern half of Kyushu and build airfields there."

Henry felt glad he had spent time in the Map Room researching the geography of Japan.

Secretary Simpson had named Nagasaki as a possible target for an atomic bomb. Henry remembered Nagasaki was located in the northern part of Kyushu.

Henry thought, *I wonder who I should ask. If we bomb western Nagasaki with a nuclear device, how far south would the damage spread? Would the explosion help our troops if they had to establish a beachhead in the south of Kyushu Island?*

⁂ —— ⁂

WEDNESDAY, MAY 30, WHITE HOUSE, MAP ROOM

THE STAFF NOW KNEW HIS routine. When Henry came to the Map Room on or before ten o'clock in the morning, he welcomed their cup of coffee. Henry sipped while Lieutenant Rigdon read from his notes. "Mr. President, report from General LeMay's headquarters. I will summarize for you. Yesterday our B-29s bombed Yokahama. Report says 2,600 tons of bombs wiped out nine square miles of the city's commercial and industrial district. Some of the Japanese shipyard facilities again escaped bombing. The Japanese have quartered many of our American prisoners of war in camps there."

Thank Heavens, Henry thought.

"Mr. President, LeMay's headquarters have issued more details than usual. Different from when the Japanese didn't send up night-time fighters to contest incendiary bombings from seven thousand feet."

Henry clinched his teeth and thought, *I was told they had to fumigate some planes because of the odor of burned flesh*

Rigdon noted the president's frown and hastened an explanation. "Maybe because this was a daylight raid. P-51 Mustangs flew escort, as usual. The Japanese engaged our fighter planes. Reported 150 Mitsubishi A6M Zekes scrambled to defend."

The lieutenant continued, "I will see you get our casualty report as soon as received."

Henry hoped the report Harry Hopkins sent from Moscow brought news he wanted to read. He opened the *FYE Only* envelope and extracted the pages, laid them on his desk, tapped a few notes of the Volga boat song across the stack, and concentrated on the summary:

1. American policy vis-a-vis Russia—assured Stalin no abrupt changes.

2. Polish Government policy.

3. United Nations Security Council voting.

4. Yalta summit promise renewed.

Henry chuckled as he leafed through the pages. *Harry knew I would skip to his number four first.* His grin widened when he read Hopkin's on page four.

> *Stalin renews his promise given to Roosevelt and Churchill. Russia will go to war against Japan in three months now that Germany has surrendered. Will deal with Chinese Nationalists, instead of Chinese Communists.*

He sure should, Henry thought, *because England and America have prepaid Russia with D-Day invasion and gave Uncle Joe, as Churchill liked to call the dictator, the second front against the Nazis.*

CHAPTER 12

BILL DROVE OVER THE RAILROAD tracks, turned left, and parked in front of the white house. The back car doors flew open and the two sisters and their brother yelled as they ran toward the house. "Grandma! Grandpa! We're here."

Grandma Nelice came out the front door, followed by Grandpa John. She knelt, spread her arms, and hugged the girls. Young Bill waited his turn. When the girls went to grab their grandfather's outstretched hands, Young Bill snuggled into Nelice's arms.

John Elam put one hand on Bill's shoulder, as he shook his son's hand.

Maudie waited inside, but her children Rhon and Colleen didn't. They rushed outside to see their cousins. Mary's teenager Alton went outside to see his cousins.

Grandma Nelice puckered up. "Thank the Lord. And we'll have more family here than we did last year. Ben and his family are coming from the farm south of Knox. Bill, honey, your sister Maggie wrote from Michigan that they couldn't take time off from their Willow Run job. Albert, his Louisville wife and Dickie, aren't here, but, Lord willing, may come from Texas this summer. Albert called long distance and said to tell you he's too busy in the oilfield right now. Don't know exactly where the Army has stationed your brother Edward, but, thank heavens, he's still in the United States."

Grandmother Nelice couldn't hold the tears back. "It's a great day. As the hymn says, *Will the Circle Be Unbroken*? Bless y'all."

When Thelma went inside, his brother-in-law went with Bill to unload the suitcases.

Ollie unleashed his sarcastic grin. "Bill, now that you're here from Tennessee, looks like we've got a grand Memorial Day weekend. Got a Kentucky hillbilly reunion going right here in northern Indiana. You're still deferred from the draft, right? Understand you're doing some sort of plumbing job at Oak Ridge. How's that job going?"

WHITE HOUSE, OVAL OFFICE

"THANK YOU, ADLAI," HENRY SAID. "I appreciate you listening to my reading. Appreciate your coaching how to best deliver our words Monday. Your president appreciates that a Memorial Day speech should praise defense work, extoll our military victories, and promise to always honor those who gave their lives for our country. My Maude has been attending Mothers of Servicemen meetings. And she confided the other night that she prays often that we don't have to bury one of our sons in the Arlington National Cemetery. Of those who hear our speech tomorrow, many will say the same prayer."

Henry ran his fingers across his desk and tapped out *We Did it Before and We Can Do it Again.*

"Adlai, to tell you my innermost thought, at the end of each and every paragraph I'm tempted to add 'but there's still a war yet to be won.' That's the president's job. To keep everyone focused on the present, not the past. Let's end this war and bring the boys home."

CHAPTER 13

H ENRY READ THE MAP ROOM memo.

USS Indiana Okinawa Support, 0950, bracing for severe weather, possible typhoon building from the east.

He ran his fingers across the desk and picked out *Stormy Weather*.

Before he sat in front of the president's desk, Stevenson laid one copy of the United Nation's speech on it. Adlai held his copy, ready to make revisions.

Henry scanned through the three pages. "Adlai, your draft reads well. I think your Lincoln quote is appropriate. You think, maybe, we should add another FDR quote?"

Stevenson wrote the suggestion on his draft.

"Also, I want to run a couple of paragraphs past Harry Hopkins when he returns from Moscow. Make sure the Russians understand that the veto compromise they demanded is intended only for large policy decisions, not administrative adjustments the UN hired help can make.

"I think we now have framework for a UN charter to which our senate can consent. And, Adlai, I hope you don't mind that, tonight, I'll read aloud what you've written and get my first lady's reaction. Maude was a big help preparing my speech to Congress in April."

Stevenson nodded understanding. "By all means, Mr. President, share our words with your first lady. Good that you have her for a sounding board."

Henry leaned back in his chair and put his fingers together. "Yes, indeed. Maude listened and made many suggestions in Indianapolis. But I can't get her help here. A governor isn't burdened with the intense secrecy required of a president."

President Henry Schricker looked to the ceiling before he fixed his gaze on his speechwriter. "I'm not going to burden you, or Maude, with a decision only I must make. Only a few, here and abroad, know the details. It's secret now, but I'm sure whatever course I choose, the world will long remember."

Henry dropped his frown and smiled. "Even the *New York Times* is sitting on this story." He pulled a plug of Red Dog chewing tobacco from his inner coat pocket. "Want to join me?"

"No, thank you, Mr. President. But, by your leave, I might smoke one my cigars?"

"By all means. I have a few also. Maybe I'll join you another day when I'm not masticating—and spitting."

Henry reached under his desk and pulled out the spittoon. "Leahy's aides had a little trouble finding a cuspidor in the White House storeroom. Found this old one that they think may have gone back to before Lincoln's residency."

Both men smiled

"Adlai, after we have helped restore some peace in this world, the Lord willing, I can envision mounting the podium and putting your name in nomination for this presidency. And the nation will ask, will Adlai Stevenson handle his military crisis the same way Henry Schricker did?"

Stevenson drew on his cigar.

Henry spit into the vessel. "You know I'm a God-fearing man. But, never, never, did I ever think I would be asked to make a decision that belongs only to God."

Both turned when they heard the knock on the Oval Room door. Schricker spit out his "chaw" and shoved the cuspidor under the desk. Stevenson crushed his cigar in the ashtray, then stood.

"Come in," Henry said.

The door opened and Admiral Leahy announced, "The gentlemen from Congress await, sir."

Henry nodded a thank you to Stevenson and stood. Adlai nodded in return.

"By all means, please show the two distinguished gentlemen in," Henry said.

Speaker Sam Rayburn and Minority Leader Joe Williams shared handshakes with Adlai Stevenson, who excused himself and left the office.

When the men were seated, Henry gave them his cultivated county-fair smile.

"Sam, Joe, don't expect you want to talk about how high the corn will be on July Fourth? That's how the Hoosier farmers in Indiana often begin their conversations. Got a pretty good idea you're here to tell me what your congressmen think about our administration's fiscal year budget proposals. What's their reaction?

Minority Leader Williams answered first. "Mr. President, you pleasantly surprised many of my Republicans. But you didn't surprise those Republicans from your state. They told us you were a Democrat governor whose Indianapolis budgets kept the state of Indiana in the black."

Henry turned to Speaker Rayburn. "You think our Democrat brethren will, as you like to say, go along with our budget proposal?" Henry didn't wait for an answer. "I hope so. We are getting deeper in debt. And when we defeat the Japanese, we'll be even deeper. In addition to rebuilding Europe, we have promised to give our returning military money for college, business loans, home mortgage support, job placement. Plus we owe those women wartime workers who'll file for unemployment compensation. And, gentlemen, don't forget lots of people will cash in their war bonds."

Rayburn smiled. "And buy cars and refrigerators and a bunch of other goods we quit making during this war. Manufacturers will go back to paying taxes."

"Joe, you Republicans will need to go along when we increase the tax on those manufacturers."

Williams puckered his lips and frowned.

Rayburn's smile widened into a grin.

"Mr. President, I think we can pass your skinny budget. But I must tell you, Henry, that some New Deal Democrats wonder why Franklin picked a nitpicking banker."

TUESDAY, JUNE 5, WHITE HOUSE, MAP ROOM

L<small>IEUTENANT</small> R<small>IGDON</small> <small>TYPED THE REPORT</small> to the president.

> *USS Indiana reports typhoon reducing cruising speed from sixteen knots to ten knots. Eighty knot wind tears port side floatplane off davit. One plane crashed onto deck.*

WEDNESDAY, JUNE 6, WHITE HOUSE, PRESIDENTIAL QUARTERS

M<small>AUDE</small> <small>LOOKED OVER THE NEWSPAPER</small> at Henry. "Honey, I'm reading your story. Where did you get all these numbers?"

"Quinn's staff collected the numbers. Mike wrote a first draft. I edited his copy, and I added a couple of my own sentences about how we made Hitler's divisions fight two armies. Told Mike to use all his outlets to make sure my words got noticed in Moscow. Then Mike's people polished and released the copy. Sorta like the gals loading shells near Knox. I guess you could say we've got a wartime production line loading words. To tell the truth, I liked it better when I stuck a thumb in my mouth and tried to figure what word to type next."

OVAL OFFICE

> *USS Indiana*
>
> *0704 eye of storm*
>
> *0711 lost steering until 0746, regain, steering motors dried out.*
>
> *Heavy cruiser Pittsburg lost 50 feet of bow*

Henry tried to envision what the battleship crew endured. His main frame of reference was an Indiana tornado. That kind of big wind sent people in North Judson, his birthplace, to their storm cellars.

OVAL OFFICE

ADMIRAL LEAHY GAVE HENRY THE invasion plan that needed his final approval. Henry scanned the outline for *Olympic*. The Kyushu landing was set for November. He needed to approve before sending to the British.

Henry thought, *I hope the Brits appreciate we're deploying 1.5 million Americans and half a million soldiers and airmen from Europe to the East Asian and Southeast Asian theater of war. Need to ask our brass how many Brits plan to make the trip.*

GUAM, ARMED FORCES RADIO STATION

MAJOR WESLEY WALLACE READ WHAT he had just written to Caroline. He didn't want his words blacked out, because some nincompoop in mail operations thought he violated military security. Surely, back in the states newspapers had reported a typhoon hit Guam. His letter didn't reveal any Navy or Army whereabouts. But he knew the corporal in the mailroom needed to mark out some words to show he was on the job. Maybe he would spare these words.

Dear Caroline,

I've told you before that the movie actor Lew Ayres was assigned to my command. Like I wrote before, Lew received all sorts of bad press because he said he was a 'conscientious objector.'

On our island a typhoon—meaner than any hurricane we ever had on the Carolina coast—blew out all the bulbs on our radio tower. Made our unlighted tower a hazard for the planes landing here. With the wind still blowing and dark approaching, Lew hung a bag of light bulbs over his shoulder, climbed the tower and replaced the broken bulbs.

Lew Ayres may be a conscientious objector, but he is no coward.

Thank you for the well wishes you sent from the folks back in Chapel Hill.

Love, Wes

SUNDAY, JUNE 10, WHITE HOUSE, MAP ROOM

A NOTE TYPED FOR PRESIDENT Schricker read:

USS Indiana, 220 miles east of Okinawa at Minaui Daito Jima.

WEDNESDAY, JUNE 13, WHITE HOUSE, MAP ROOM

Leyte, San Pedro Bay, USS Indiana joins USS Philadelphia for two weeks replenishment.

CHAPTER 14

PRESIDENT HENRY SCHRICKER SURVEYED THE military advisers that General Marshall had assembled. They wore their full dress uniforms adorned with service ribbons. "Thank you for coming early today. I understand that some of you will now go to hear Ike speak to Congress. I will read his prepared speech after we adjourn. I appreciate your varied views on our prospects for invading Japan. I have the report presented to me by General MacArthur's staff. I plan to ask General Eisenhower for his observations."

Henry thought, *Not just about invading Japan, but Ike's opinion about using a nuclear bomb.*

"Before I adjourn our meeting, I also want to hear from you, Mr. McCloy. We have heard from all others, and no one leaves this meeting without standing up and being counted."

John McCloy glanced at Stimson before responding. McCloy was more than Henry Stimson's assistant. He was a former artillery officer, a banker like the president had been. And McCloy knew about the atomic bomb project from the outset. FDR told McCloy what he never told his elected vice president. Henry wanted to hear his innermost thoughts.

McCloy frowned. "We ought to have our heads examined if we do not seek a political end to the war before an invasion. First, we could assure the Japanese they could retain their emperor. Second, we could warn them of an atomic bomb—something I know shouldn't be said aloud even in this restricted company."

McCloy swept his eyes around the table as several heads lowered, then he sat down.

Henry responded. "Mr. McCloy, a warning, by all means. But I don't know how much we should tell. I am sympathetic to your point about the emperor. If you read press clippings when I campaigned as President Roosevelt's vice president, I was once a country lawyer. One thing I learned from another country lawyer named Alexander Eastus. He often reminded me regardless of what the Law said, if the Judge sent the case to a jury, you needed information about the members of the jury panel. With the help of our intelligence services, we need to identify the emperor's advisors we want on our jury. Who would vote to surrender? I think you're telling me to scratch Susuki. choose Emperor Hirohito who will most likely be the foreman of their jury, which is a good point."

Henry stood. "Gentlemen, thank you for your counsel this morning."

WHITE HOUSE, OVAL OFFICE

HENRY PUT HIS READING GLASSES back in his coat pocket and thought about General Eisenhower's return to Washington. He'd commanded three million men in Europe and deserved a hero's welcome.

Chief-of-Staff Leahy entered with documents to sign.

Henry talked as he signed. "You know, Bill, I think Ike is a man I could support, as a Republican or preferably as a Democrat."

Admiral Leahy smiled. "You sound like you're ruling out a re-election campaign in three years."

"Well, in Indiana you can't run again at the end of your first term as governor. And nobody, yet, has run after they were out of office four years. Besides, I appreciate Ike saw first hand those atrocities when they liberated concentration and forced labor camps. He knows the Holocaust was no myth. If he ran for president as a Republican, he might get a lot of the Jewish vote that usually goes for the Democrat. Also when I speak to the United Nation delegates in San Francisco, let's arrange for me to spend a few days in my hometown of Knox. I'll get some good advice from my old friend Israel Mishkovsky."

—⟡—

FIFTEEN MINUTES LATER, ADMIRAL LEAHY came back to the Oval Office "Mr. President, terrible news. I was just informed that Japanese snipers on Okinawa killed Lieutenant General Simon Bolivar Buckner, our commander of all forces on Okinawa. I've taken the liberty of having my staff contact Mike Quinn to come and help you prepare a news release."

—⟡—

HENRY MARKED THE PAPER THEN handed back the news release draft to his press secretary. "Well, Mike, another one of those tough press releases. You gave me some good words to go with the body count. But after my words applauding our troops for bringing an end to the battle of Okinawa, I think you should move 'General Stilwell placed in command of Tenth Army, which conquered Okinawa' ahead of 'Americans lost 6,900 men, killed or missing, and nearly 30,000 wounded.'"

Henry considered any other changes. "Very thoughtful to include 'Japanese casualties were about 95,000.' Hope the Japanese newspapers repeat that information. Most of all, hope the emperor hears the casualty numbers."

—⟡—

SATURDAY, JUNE 23, WHITE HOUSE

"MAUDE, IF YOU CAN PUT off packing for a few minutes, I want you to read and tell me what else I need in my San Francisco speech."

"Henry, couldn't I do that on the airplane tomorrow before we land at the Indiana airbase?"

"Maude, I told staff I would call them tonight if I needed any changes."

"Well, in that case, let me read. Presume we can hear you on the radio in Knox when you broadcast from Frisco."

Maude critiqued. "Like your phrasing of 'to keep the world at peace and free from the fear of war.' Bet more than one of your editorial friends will ask how you intend to end the war with Japan. Will want an answer they can print."

Henry thought, *As usual Maude's on target. Wish I could tell her what could be our most horrendous solution. But I won't ask her to help me shoulder that burden.*

CHAPTER 15

Two Secret Service guards were already aboard. Two more waited for Henry, Maude, Margaret, and Adlai to walk up the ladder. When Maude spotted the female pilot in her WASP flying clothes waiting to greet them, she grinned and nudged Henry.

Henry got her 'see women also fly planes' message. But thought *maybe we should rename this airplane. Not* Sacred Cow *but* Holy Cow, *what the good old Hoosier boys might say when they discovered a woman was driving.*

"Welcome aboard, Mr. President, Mrs. Schricker, Mrs. Rollins, Mr. Stevenson. I'm Lieutenant Jimmie Glasser, Women's Ferry Command. I'm one of your co-pilots."

Lieutenant Glasser pointed toward the closed door. "Captain Tom Young and Lieutenant Bill Wright are going through takeoff procedures. They look forward to meeting you later during the flight."

Glasser introduced the WAVE standing next to her. "Mr. President, per your staff's request, Seaman Margaret Abel will show you and Mr. Stevenson to the president's quarters. The ladies and I will sit in the main compartment. Make sure you are all strapped in before we take off. Again, welcome aboard."

After passengers buckled their seat belts, a welcome was repeated over the intercom.

"This is Captain Tom Young. Mr. President, our crew is honored to have you aboard. We are pleased to have First Lady Schricker and your daughter aboard for our flight to Indiana. We look forward to ferrying you and Mr. Stevenson on to San Francisco. This plane is a converted four-motored Douglas VC-54. A lift was designed so President Roosevelt could be boarded.

I also noticed the underneath portal that was engineered so they could raise Franklin in his wheelchair, Henry thought.

Captain Young continued his intercom introduction. "The window glass is bullet proof. If you want to take a nap in the president's sleeping quarters, be sure to strap yourself into bed. If Lieutenant Glasser and Seaman Abel will secure themselves in the reception area, we will be ready for takeoff. Again, welcome aboard, Mr. President."

MAUDE THANKED THE WAVE FOR the coffee.

Seaman Abel nodded, went to her kitchen, and returned with coffee for Margaret and Captain Young. Then took a rear seat and adjusted her safety belt.

Captain Young nodded to the Schricker women.

"It's a pleasure having you ladies aboard. Feel free to inspect the president's quarters if you choose."

Maude replied, "Thank you, Captain. But I'm glad we aren't in the presidential quarters. Margaret and I don't need to listen to Henry and Adlai practice his United Nations speech."

Margaret chimed in, "Right, Mom. Also Adlai may be overdoing the hand gestures." She added chops to dialogue with both hands. "Free. Fear. War."

Maude shrugged her shoulders. "Think not. Big auditorium, different languages. Hand movements will signal when to applaud. Also news reel cameramen like animation."

"Maybe so, Mom. I guess some of those cheerleading hand signals that Adlai is coaching work best with a male audience. That's mainly who he's addressing in San Francisco."

Maude saw Young's raised eyebrows and hurried to explain. "Captain, my daughter and I are fond of the men in our lives, but we would like to see more women in government roles. Mrs. Perkins was the only woman on President Roosevelt's cabinet. I hope my husband can add a few more. Maybe Oveta Culp Hobby, who has done such a good job with the WACs. And I'm pleased to see two women were assigned for our flight."

Young chuckled. "Not just for this flight, Mrs. Schricker. They're regular members of our crew."

"Then, Captain Young, I presume Lieutenant Glasser is the co-pilot now."

"No, Ma'am. She's now the command pilot. Knows this plane well. She was one of the pilots who ferried the plane from the California factory to Maryland. Jimmie was a co-pilot when we flew President Roosevelt to Yalta. Like other women pilots with whom I have flown, she has a smooth, gentle touch. When her turn comes to make a landing, I think she handles the craft better than most men."

"Oh?"

"Not surprising, Mrs. Schricker, considering Jimmie started flying her dad's single-engine plane when she was in high school. She got her pilot's license before she was old enough to get a Texas driving permit."

Young looked back. "And, Margaret, you went up in an airplane early in life, didn't you?"

Seaman Abel smiled. "Captain's correct. My Dad, Harry Abel, owned a bi-plane when I was in grade school. He let me fly with him one day when he flew from Pueblo to a nearby Colorado town."

Margaret Schricker joined the conversation. "Margaret, I like that name."

Abel replied, "So do I, but now I'm most often called Seaman Abel. Or a few wise acres, like our co-pilot now in the cockpit, likes to call me Able Seaman Abel."

"Well, you will hear Margaret from this Schricker, Margaret. When did a Colorado gal join the WAVES?"

"Not when the war began. I was in Mills College, Oakland, when the Japanese attacked Pearl Harbor. Sorry to say, my mother worried about the enemy landing in California and ordered me home.

"When I graduated from University of Colorado, I joined. And, then—"

The intercom voice interrupted. "Lieutenant Glasser, here. In twelve minutes we land at Naval Air Station Peru. Crew and passengers need to prepare for landing. Fasten seat belts."

Captain Young rose and turned toward the pilot's cockpit. "Excuse me, ladies. I'll send Lieutenant Wright to sit with you.

And you'll be pleased to know a woman will make our landing. It's Lieutenant Glasser's turn."

The president's daughter talked to the other Margaret. "I understand you'll be in Frisco several days. Are you going to visit your alma mater Mills College in Oakland?"

"No. I left there in 1942. Then graduated from University of Colorado. And tonight I've got a date with a graduate from there. He's in Frisco waiting to be shipped to the Pacific."

"What service?"

"Intelligence. He's a Chinese language interpreter. They studied Chinese language at Boulder. Great guys. Even came and serenaded our sorority one night."

"Oh? What sorority? I belonged to Pi Beta Phi at Indiana University."

"Wow! I was a Pi Phi at Boulder."

The sorority sisters leaned against their seat belts and embraced.

PERU NAVAL AIR STATION, INDIANA

BILL SHAW WAS THE FIRST to greet the Schricker party when the three came down the rolled-in stairs. Henry shook his hand then pointed to his two women.

"Bill, I want you to take good care of my girls until I get back to Knox Thursday night."

"Yes, sir, Mr. President."

"Hey, old timer, it's still Henry. And you and I will talk about those old times when they fly me back from San Francisco."

ROCKY MOUNTAINS, AIRBORNE

HENRY SAT BEHIND CAPTAIN YOUNG, who had his hands on the wheel, earphones on. He listened to Lieutenant Glasser who sat in the right hand co-pilot seat.

"Glad you joined us up front, Mr. President. You will get a better view as we pass between some of the peaks. Since the plane is not pressurized, we'll fly below ten thousand feet. Pick our way around some Rocky Mountain peaks that lay ahead. When we get to San Francisco, you won't see much. Our landing in Oakland will be dark. By the time you get to your hotel and get to bed, bet you'll appreciate the west coast wakes up two hours later than Indiana."

⊰——⊱

TUESDAY, JUNE 26, CALIFORNIA, OAKLAND NAVAL HOSPITAL

HENRY WAITED OUTSIDE THE DOOR until the attendant removed Lieutenant Keith Wells's breakfast tray. Then he and the hospital commandant walked inside.

The commandant announced them. "Lieutenant Wells, the president is here to see you."

Keith swung his feet over the side of the bed and pulled himself up with the help of his crutches.

Before Keith could manage a salute, Henry extended his hands and placed them atop the Marine's hands. "At ease, Lieutenant Wells. It's your president who should be saluting you. Please ease yourself back on your bed."

Wells sat back on the bed and dangled his bandaged legs over the side.

Henry smiled. "I think you know the platoon you commanded has made a lasting impression. When President Roosevelt first showed me through the White House, he identified many paintings and pictures he had asked to be hung on the walls. He took the greatest pride in the Rosenthal picture of your platoon raising the flag on Mount Surabachi."

Wells smiled. "I wasn't there Mr. President. A nurse on the hospital ship moved my bed so I could see my platoon members raise the second flag. That's the one Rosenthal photographed. We got word on the hospital ship to watch."

Henry nodded. He had seen both photographs. "I also know that you were struck by a grenade at the base of Surabachi, couldn't move, but continued to give orders to your platoon. You definitely deserve the Navy Cross that was awarded you."

Keith clinched his jaw. "Thank you, sir, but I wouldn't be here if it wasn't for Private First Class Donald Ruhl. He fell on the grenade thrown at us. I appreciate he has been posthumously awarded the Congressional Medal of Honor. Two of us owe our lives to him."

Henry took a deep breath. "If you don't already know, your president has been told that twenty-seven Medals of Honor have been awarded to men who fought at Iwo Jima. I understand three were Navy medical corpsmen and one a Navy gunner. The rest, Marines. Impressive. Want to tell me why you volunteered to join the Marines?"

"Yes, sir. I was in school at Texas A&M, housed with two sons of Army officers. When we went to war, I asked what's the toughest fighting unit? One said toughest is the German Panzer Corps. Next toughest is the United States Marines. Soon as I could, I joined the Marines."

Keith paused. "Mr. President, I'm honored to have been platoon leader of third platoon, Easy Company, 28th Marines. I think, now, the Panzer Corps is no longer the world's best."

Henry chuckled. "Lieutenant Wells, we need to get you repaired and out there recruiting more Marines."

MARE'S ISLAND, OAKLAND

WORKERS ON THE DOCK STOPPED loading. Ship's crew watched from at the rail. Three secretaries huddled, watching through the office window.

President Henry Schricker was well aware of the eyes on him while his security scanned the dock. They probably all wondered why their president spoke with a junior grade officer.

Lieutenant Bob Shaw had known Henry long before he had a security detail. "Mr. Schricker, err, Mr. President, I wish I were going back to Knox with you today."

"So do I, Bob. Wish we could send everyone on this wharf home. Sooner, the better."

"Yes, sir. Those are the wishing words here."

Henry looked over Bob's shoulder, saw the secretaries at the window, and waved to them. They waved back.

"Bob, I saw your Uncle Bill when we landed at Peru Naval Air Station. He had a cavalcade waiting to take my Maude and Margaret on to Knox. I promised Bill I'd find time to see his nephew. Explain to your buddies here that your uncle got me elected in Indiana. Why you got a presidential visit. It's been good to see you. I got accustomed to you bumming a weekend ride from Indianapolis to Knox. You gave me different views about what people were saying in Indiana that some of my capitol staff hadn't heard."

Lieutenant Shaw beamed. "Thank you, sir. You coming here reminds me of one special weekend when I caught a ride to Knox from Indianapolis. That Saturday you let Howard, Trooper Bashore, drive me on to the barber shop. Boys there found I wasn't making things up. I really had been riding in the governor's car."

Henry grinned. "I'll pass the word to your uncle this weekend. I've got a bone to pick with him already. Talked long distance with Maude after I got here. Soon as Bill got her back to Knox, he had a crowd waiting at our home to greet her. Had Maude speak, while standing on the front porch, to our neighbors. Speech making is supposed to be my job.

"Bob, now that I don't have anything left to run for, your Uncle Bill will probably put my Maude up for office. And she would win. "

DOWNTOWN SAN FRANCISCO

PRESIDENT HENRY SCHRICKER STOOD AND waved from the open car. The motorcade drove through the streets headed for the meeting of the United Nations. Cars were in front of him; cars lined up back of him as far as he could see.

Two things working here, Henry thought. *My first public appearance since Franklin died, and they're cheering the office not the man.*

Henry waved his white fedora toward people cheering from the street. He looked up and waved at those heads cheering from office windows. Some threw paper or ticker tape. Some threw pieces of cardboard. Henry wondered if the cardboard was all they had to throw or whether the throwers were Republicans.

When he saw a baby crying in a mother's arms, Henry thought, *I know just how you feel, but you keep objecting and I'll keep smiling and wave my hat.*

⋆⋆ ⸺ ⋆⋆

ASSEMBLED UNITED NATION DELEGATES, CONFERENCE ON INTERNATIONAL ORGANIZATION

MEN AND WOMEN OF THE U.S. Armed Forces stood in the background. President Schricker watched Adlai Stevenson move into a seat to the right of the podium. When they made eye contact, Henry winked. He listened to his introduction and thought, *The speech that Adlai and I wrote is shorter than this build-up. We respond in kind. Diplomacy requires we praise the delegates from fifty nations, and Adlai has included several praise sentences.*

I've witnessed a bunch of real estate and loan signings. This United Nations Charter signing reminds me of when our forefathers signed the Declaration of Independence. *Wonder which one of the fifty delegates here thinks he's John Hancock and signs with the largest signature.*

More to wonder if the United States deliberates and ratifies this charter before October 24 when the charter is supposed to take effect.

Even more to question, will we defeat the Japanese by that time?

Henry paused his ruminations and looked down at the words Adlai had wrote. He noticed Adlai's check mark. So he raised both hands, outstretched toward his audience.

"You have created a great instrument for peace and security and human progress in the world. The world must now use it. If we fail to use it, we shall betray all those who have died in order that we might meet here in freedom and safety to create it.

"Our pledge. Keep the world at peace. And free from the fear of war."

The delegates stood and applauded. Henry caught Adlai's eye again and winked.

CHAPTER 16

WEDNESDAY, JUNE 27, AIRBORNE, DESTINATION INDIANA

"THIS IS CAPTAIN YOUNG SPEAKING. Clear skies ahead. We will be cruising at nine thousand feet. Estimated time of arrival at Peru Naval Air Station is 2200 hours. You can unbuckle seat belts and move as you please."

Henry hung his jacket over the back of the swivel chair. He loosened his tie before he opened the file folder handed to him when he boarded the *Sacred Cow*.

The report from MacArthur's headquarters brought a smile. *Island of Luzon conquered.*

Good news in the first report. *The usual staff tactic*, Henry thought.

The report from General Groves read, *"New detonators arrived at Los Alamos from DuPont Co. Reduce risk of misfire from 1 in 300 to 1 in 30,000. Ninety percent success expected by scientists."*

The success percentage made Henry clench his teeth. Spending $2 billion with a 10 percent chance of failure would make a banker think twice before he made another loan.

Bad, really bad news. One report said that 373 were killed on carrier *Bunker Hill* when a Japanese suicide plane and bomber scored a hit off Okinawa.

How much is one child's life worth to a mother? More than we have spent, Henry thought.

At the bottom of the file he found some good news to tell Maude and Margaret when he landed. *Suggested White House repairs and replacements underway.*

❊——❊

KNOX, INDIANA

The caravan of three black limousines—driven from D.C to Indiana to ensure presidential security—turned south off Highway 30, crossed over the railroad, and passed between the cornfields.

Henry rode in the middle limousine, alone in the back seat. Beside him rested the briefcase he had closed after he scanned files handed him at the Peru Naval Air Station.

Moonlight helped him see the cornfields. It looked like corn could be knee-high by July Fourth. That was always a good predictor of bumper harvest in September. Out the left window, Henry saw the new, one-story building. Lights from the small shop shone on cars parked in front. *Second shift working*, Henry thought.

Henry remembered when he'd cut the ribbon on the tool and dye shop. He'd made a gubernatorial speech about Knox's 1942 contribution to the Arsenal of Democracy.

As they approached the Yellow River Bridge, a siren blared. Probably, the Sheriff had his patrol car waiting to lead the president's cavalcade into town.

When she'd agreed he should accept the vice-president nomination, Maude had worried there wouldn't be as much time in Knox as they had when he was governor. Tonight was the first time he had been home since he became president. Once again, Maude had been right.

Their headlights illuminated the Yellow River sign. Henry had a wry thought, *I hope Wild Bill Donovan's demolition agents don't get confused and blow up this bridge instead of their target in China.*

After they crossed the Yellow River Bridge, Henry leaned forward so he could see out both side windows as well as the front window.

People lined up on each side of highway 35. Shoulder-to-shoulder, his Knox neighbors waved as they drove by. Some children waved small American flags. *Bless their hearts, they ought to be in bed.*

Henry leaned forward, put his hand on the back of the front seat, and asked Tom Gohr if he had directions to 501 South Main Street.

"Just follow the sheriff, we were told, Mr. President. He directed us to drive really slow when we turned onto Main Street at the Courthouse. There it is. That's an impressive three stories of stone. Pretty big clock on the top. How old?"

"Built at the end of last century, and I rode over from North Judson with my family for the dedication. We made the trip in a wagon."

Henry wished he rode in an open convertible so he could wave to the citizens standing in the lights beaming from Main Street stores.

At the railroad crossing Henry saw the sheriff's deputies had closed off South Main Street. But the people who lived between the railroad and his home waved from their lawn.

Maude and Margaret waited on the front porch. Henry thanked Tom then waved a thumbs up to the other drivers and secret service men standing by their autos.

At the top of the stairs, he hugged Margaret. Then he hugged and kissed Maude.

Maude whispered into his ear, "Welcome to the Indiana red-brick White House, Mr. President. Welcome home, honey."

෯ — ෯

THURSDAY, JUNE 28, KNOX, INDIANA, 401 MAIN STREET

THE FREIGHT-TRAIN WHISTLE WOKE HENRY up. He looked at the bedside clock that read 5:31. The train rumbled through the Main Street crossing, only four blocks north. He'd forgotten how loud the thing could be.

Henry slipped out of bed without wakening Maude. He took his clothes to the bathroom and started his morning rituals. When he was dressed, he went downstairs to the kitchen, where he pumped and drank a glass of well water.

Henry stopped at the piano near the front door, but he decided dawn was a bit early to play piano wake-up music. Though it was not too early for him to walk to the Mishovsky house.

He took his coat off the rack, put it on, and straightened his tie. If the governor was expected to appear with coat and tie, for sure the president should. He donned the white fedora that identified him, going back to his 1910 lawyer days.

When Henry stepped on the porch, secret service agent Doyle Guthrie sprang from the church swing.

"Good morning, Mr. President. My goodness, sir, you're up early."

Henry chuckled. "Mr. Guthrie, no earlier than usual. In Washington, you only see me after Maude and I have eaten our breakfast. This morning, I'm letting her sleep in. Hope you're ready for my customary morning walk."

"Yes, sir. And I see Rex just opened the door of our communications van parked across the street. Chris is on station in the garden behind your house. I'll call him on my walkie-talkie. Men in the other shift are still at the motel. Chris will call them."

Henry sighed. "Doyle, I had state patrolmen Howard Bashore drive me when I was governor. He usually waited in the car. I still haven't gotten accustomed to the way you secret service gentlemen hang so close."

"That's what we volunteered to do, Mr. President. Pardon me for asking, but to where are we walking? We like to have someone ahead of you."

Guthrie fell two steps behind as Henry walked toward the railroad track where uptown Knox began.

"Well, Doyle, we'll walk another twelve houses north. I used to walk three more blocks to the bank. But this morning when we get to the railroad track, we'll turn west and walk on this side of the tracks. We're going four blocks to Israel's house."

Guthrie almost stuttered. "To-to where?

"To the Mishovsky home. Israel is a junk dealer. And a corn farmer. Expect he's already put on his long-sleeve work shirt and overalls and made coffee. He lets his wife sleep in. Says she's the smart member of the family who buys and sell stocks. Doyle, off-the-record, when I was their banker, the Mishovskys were our biggest depositor. And Israel and I were the early birds who met for a second cup of coffee at the restaurant nearest the railroad track."

The agent dropped back a step, spoke softly into his walkie-talkie, then walked briskly to keep up.

When they reached the railroad, Henry turned left and led Guthrie west on a red brick sidewalk. Four blocks later, they walked south to the back door of a two-story house. Henry knocked on the back door. A minute later, it opened. The squared-off man in overalls dropped his jaw then smiled.

"Goodness gracious, hello, Henry, or I should say Mr. President. How about a cup of coffee?"

"Good to see you, Israel. Coffee, you betcha. And how about a cup for this fellow who controls my apron strings? Meet Doyle Guthrie. He's one of eight men the Secret Service sends with me wherever I go."

"Pleased to meet you Mr. Guthrie. Please, come in. And, yes, coffee's made. Sit. I'll pour one for both of you. But first, I think I need to let Elizabeth know who's here."

He went to the kitchen door and shouted up the stairwell. "Wake up, Elizabeth! Lee. Norman, get dressed. Come down! The president's here!"

❧ — ☙

A FLUSH-FACED DOYLE GUTHRIE STUTTERED, "You-you are going… Mr. President, you are going to a corn farm?"

"Yes, Doyle. And Israel is driving me there in his 1937 red Studebaker. And his daughter Lee and his son Norman are going with us. It's only a mile or two east of here. Want to go with us? Ride in the back seat with the kids?"

"Yes indeed, President Schricker, that's my duty. But please, sir, can you wait just a few minutes. Your escort cars are headed this way. I called while you were drinking coffee." Guthrie pointed at the approaching vehicles.

Two black limousines followed by the communications van drove up behind the old red Studebaker.

Guthrie signaled them to follow west. Doyle worried that one limo wasn't in front before he squeezed into the back seat beside seven-year-old Norman and teenager Lee. Henry sat opposite of Israel who looked into his rearview mirror at the cavalcade assembling.

"Henry, this parade reminds me of an old Russian and Lithuanian saying that I heard as a boy. 'All the dogs bark when the caravan passes through the village.'"

The president pointed at the steel bridge over the river.

"Mr. Guthrie, Israel and I are going to walk to that bridge over our Yellow River. That's the north boundary of his farm. More information than you may want to know, but that old bridge is where Israel and I used to sit, dangle our feet over the stream, and pretend to fish. We dropped our bait in the river, but hoped no fish took our bait and interrupted our serious discussions about the world and how our county was going to survive the depression.

Henry asked, "You think, Doyle, you and my other nursemaids could just watch from a distance? Maybe guard my coat and tie I left in the Studebaker?"

The Secret Service agent grinned.

"Yes, sir. Will do. But I hope you understand, we will send one car over the bridge and up that country road to check for any oncoming cars."

"I understand, Doyle. I'm getting used to living in a fish bowl."

Guthrie chuckled. "Make sure they don't run over your friend and our president."

⸙ —— ⸙

THE PRESIDENT AND ONE OF the richest men in Starke County sat and dangled their feet above the river.

Henry reached in his shirt pocket and took out his chewing tobacco.

Israel shook his head. "I'm guessing you don't use that filthy habit much in the White House."

"You're right. But I do have a cuspidor, left over from when Lincoln was there, hid under my desk. But I will just send this load down the river."

Israel chuckled.

Henry chewed for a minute. Then addressed Israel like the old friend he was. "Sometimes, when I was soliciting votes from a Hoosier farmer I knew well, I offered him a chew. Always asked how his crop was doing? Israel, you don't have any nicotine habits, and I saw your corn looks pretty good."

"Yes. Good so far. This July Fourth the corn will be a little higher than your knee, as we say. Though right now, we could use a little rain."

"How's the rest of your family doing, Israel?"

"Thanks for asking. Our older daughters, Celia and Bertha are working Chicago defense jobs while their husbands are away. Lee is in high school, but works our farm vegetable garden. You probably noticed, she started helping with weeding soon as we got here. Norman is only seven, but as you can see he's big for his age. He helps me load scrap metal into the railroad cars."

Henry spit tobacco into the river before he spoke. "Israel, last time we visited, you told me your son Leo was serving in the Army Air Corps. How's he doing?"

"Pretty good. He got promoted to First Lieutenant. Said he couldn't give me any details, but he's a training officer for navigators on the biggest bomber, the Superfortress. But you know more about that than I do, Mr. President."

Henry thought, *I know we've spent a ridiculous amount of money on the B-29. And the crews are firebombing Japan. But the Japanese won't surrender.*

"How's Elizabeth doing with her stocks? Hope she's made some money to put in our Knox bank."

"Mr. President, she's putting her money in your newest bank. My smart wife buys U.S. War Bonds."

Henry nodded approval. "Smart. Some of my worried advisers think that when we defeat the Japanese we will need to continue federal controls. Invent government jobs for those who have worked in war production or served in the military. But when we lick the Japanese, I predict we will have a boom manufacturing civilian products. After the last world war, that was our history."

Israel sighed. Picked up a rock on the bridge road and tossed it into the water below. "Ah, yes, history. We all say we are supposed to learn from history. I think of that word 'history' when I sit by this Yellow River. A word invented by an ancient Greek named Herodotus. Before I immigrated to America, I was studying to become a medical doctor. Learned to read Greek. And learned Heraclitus's famous statement. The one where he says we stand in the same riverbed, but new waters flow past us. Same place, different events. Different choices."

Henry nodded understanding.

"Mr. President, tough job for you. But I know, from our years together, that you study how the waters flow around you. And you're not afraid to make a decision. I don't think you know how to part the Red Sea—my people often use that as a real test—but we're counting on you to end this calamity."

Henry rested his hand on his old friend's shoulder. "Thanks, Israel. I'll work some of your wisdom into the speech Bill Shaw has scheduled tomorrow in North Judson."

KNOX, INDIANA, 401 SOUTH MAIN STREET

HENRY ENJOYED A NEW VENUE for this press conference. To sit at the top of your front steps and answer questions from two-dozen reporters felt more natural than facing 300 reporters crowded into an Administrative Office.

Studying the attendees, he noticed the *Capitol Press* pool reporter didn't look too awake. He couldn't miss that *The New York Times* and *Washington Post* byline reporters had decided to skip a trip to farmland. He expected they would use wire service coverage to back up what their young reporters phoned to the copy desk.

Henry waved a hand. "I see some new faces I haven't seen at previous White House press briefings. Welcome to the 'Red-brick White House' on the red-brick Main Street."

Henry almost laughed at the look on the faces of the big city and wire service reporters. He deliberately took questions first from the three weekly newspaper editors in Starke County. Hadn't their journalism professor taught them all news was local?

"Members of the press, let me introduce you to Leonard Fenwick, the editor of our *Starke County Republican* and M.E. Cannon who edits the *Starke County Democrat*. You may know the *Democrat* was once published by a young lawyer named Henry Schricker. What you may not know, I was once an elected officer in the Indiana Press Association. But that was after World War I. I want to call first on Mildred Kren, the editor and publisher of the *North Judson News,* to tell you—and add some details I haven't been told—about arrangements for me to speak in North Judson tomorrow."

Henry thought, *I made points with Maude and Margaret sitting nearby in the porch swing when I called first on the woman who published fifteen miles west of 401 South Main Street.*

❧——❧

FRIDAY, JUNE 29, KNOX, INDIANA, SCHRICKER HOUSE

MAUDE LOOKED OVER THE BREAKFAST table and caught Henry's eye. "Well there's some good news in this morning's newspaper. Associated Press reports the United States will make 12 percent more butter available for civilians. Henry, if there's anyway you can take credit for that news, you might improve your favorability percentage in the Gallup Poll. Maybe you can work some good news into your speech at North Judson. And, honey, do you really want Margaret and me to go with you?"

Henry grinned. "Yes. You don't have any choice. Political boss Bill Shaw has already written your recognition into the mayor's introductory speech. Shaw is feeling his oats. He used to boss a governor, and now he's telling a president how to operate."

❧——❧

NORTH JUDSON, INDIANA, CORNER LANE AND SYCAMORE

FROM THE PLATFORM, RINGED ON two sides by high school band members, Henry waved his white hat at the people. Then Henry put his hat back on, because the day was hotter than usual in Northern Indiana. Temperature had climbed to ninety degrees. His girls seated beside him waved fans, gifted from the good ladies of the Lutheran Church. The Hoosiers who filled Lane Street and overflowed onto Sycamore Street cheered and applauded.

Henry asked the women to forgive him for departing from a proper presidential dress code. He took off his coat, rolled up his sleeves, and told the Hoosier men to do the same. The citizens laughed.

"And men, women, you boys and girls working part-time, keep those sleeves rolled up because America still has more work to do, a war in the Pacific yet to win."

The crowd applauded louder than before. Henry heard a few loud "Amens!"

He placed both hands on the side of the lectern and leaned forward to orate. "As a native son of North Judson, I esteem it an honor and a privilege to serve as the first, and I hope not the last, president from Starke County."

Henry waited for the chuckles to subside. "You have already honored me as your governor by placing a plaque on that small two room cottage over there on South Lane Street, where I was born in 1883. I remember four young men in the North Judson high school Blue Jay barbershop quartet sang for that plaque dedication. They're all now in the military. I later learned that our Superintendent of Schools, Mr. Lucas, told his son and the other three not to harmonize on *How Dry I Am* because this governor was a teetotaler."

Henry didn't wait for laughter. "Folks, this old self-taught musician gets intoxicated when I hear those barbershop-singing overtones and undertones. Let's give our current Blue Jays a round of applause."

Henry faced the four boys, applauded, and turned to the applauding crowd that filled streets and sidewalks. When the applause subsided, Henry looked around the temporary stage, nodding to dignitaries. He winked at Maude and Margaret. Then he turned to the crowd with a serious face, as he surveyed his audience.

"Where else, except in America, could the son of a poor emigrant who came from Bavaria in 1867, whose mother came three years later, become the chief executive of this great land? What a great honor. And such a tremendous responsibility. Many emigrants have come to our county from European countries. Irish, Germans, Bohemians, Austrians, Poles, and a few from Scandinavian countries and Africa. But now, we are privileged to call ourselves, unhyphenated Americans. I am unhappy with some big-city newspapers. They thought they had to call Private First Class Frank Ono an Asian-American when they reported he received the Distinguished Service Cross. That's our Frank Ono. A soldier from North Judson. A Hoosier. An American."

Henry held up the report. "I quote from a portion of the medal citation:

Private First Class Frank H. Ono distinguished himself by extraordinary heroism in action on 4 July 1944, near

Castellina, Italy. In attacking a heavily defended hill, Private First Class Ono's squad was caught in a hail of formidable fire from the well-entrenched enemy."

Henry paused. "I'm sure many of you have read how Private First Class Ono opened fire with his automatic rifle and silenced one machine gun 300 hundred yards away. How he advanced through enemy fire and killed a sniper with another burst of fire. Hurling hand grenades, Private First Class Ono held back the enemy while the rest of the platoon moved forward. Then, you have read, Private First Class Ono boldly ran through small arms and mortar fire to render first aid to his platoon leader and a seriously wounded rifleman. Volunteering to cover the platoon, Private First Class Ono occupied virtually unprotected positions near the crest of the hill, engaging an enemy machine gun emplaced on an adjoining ridge and exchanging fire with snipers. Completely disregarding his own safety, he made himself the constant target of concentrated enemy fire until the platoon reached the comparative safety of a draw. He then descended the hill in stages, firing his rifle, until he rejoined the platoon. And I read that Private First Class Ono's extraordinary heroism and devotion to duty are in keeping with the highest traditions of military service."

Henry laid the citation on the podium. "Your president looks forward to when I will meet Frank Ono, and we can compare our younger days in North Judson. That day will also be a sad day because there are eleven men from North Judson who will not be coming home. I have asked our North Judson editor and publisher Mildred Kren to read our present roll of honor, and the year of their sacrifice."

Mildred prefaced her reading with "I know there are relatives here who still mourn, as we do, the loss of their loved one. Know that North Judson, Starke County, will not forget their sacrifice."

She read the names of eleven killed in action from 1943 through May of 1945 and three missing in action dated 1942, 1943, and 1944. The one prisoner of war was Marine Pfc George Ciboch. He was captured by the enemy in May 1942 and was in a Manchukuo prison camp.

Henry returned to the podium. "Thank you, Mildred. When I return to Washington, D.C. Monday, I will be there only a few days before I fly to the country from which my mother and father emigrated. Outside Berlin, we will meet with both British and Russian delegations and discuss the fate of those countries from which many of our North Judson and Starke County families came. I am scheduled to review our American troops there. I will not forget those who made our VE Day celebration possible. Especially our sons from North Judson. But today, we still have a war thrust upon us by the warlords of Japan that we must win. If I were playing the organ at the church nearby, you would hear the old hymn *Onward, Christian Soldiers*. We still have a cross we will bear."

Henry paused. "God bless you. And God bless America."

The North Judson High band played *Hail to the Chief*, the song they had practiced for a week. Henry waved his white hat. North Judson folks cheered. Henry turned again toward his girls and winked.

⚜ —— ⚜

SATURDAY, JUNE 30, KNOX, INDIANA, 401 SOUTH MAIN STREET

THE SUN HAD JUST CLIMBED above the Drew house across the street when the Army car parked in front and the officer got out. Colonel Britt Watson saluted when he reached the top of the stairs.

"At ease, colonel," Henry said. "We're on a three-day vacation. Come sit beside me on the swing."

"Thank you, sir."

Henry smiled. "For what reason do I deserve your early-morning visit?"

Watson handed the president a paper. "Admiral Leahy telephoned for me to pass on today's Map Room information."

Henry unfolded the paper and read, *Chinese troops invade Indo-China.*

"Well, Britt, Gabriel Heater will have some good news to tell us tonight. The Philippines are now ours. Some mopping up still needed. Now, the Chinese are helping us drive the Japanese back to their four-island homeland. Good news to start our day visiting the homefolks before lunch with the Schillings."

⊰——⊱

KNOX, INDIANA, SCHRICKER HOUSE

HENRY GREETED RUSSELL SCHILLING WITH a double handshake. Then gave thirteen-year-old Jim a three-fingered Boy Scout salute. Young Jim smiled, now glad he wore his Scout uniform to meet the president. He stood upright and returned the salute.

Maude hugged Edna then led the Schilling family into the dining room, where Margaret waited with coffee and a glass of milk for Jim.

Henry started the conversation at his end of the table. "Russ, how's the crop going on that sandy island you call a farm?"

"Gonna be a bumper crop, Henry. This year we planted half of our fields in soybeans."

"Also your other hat. How's the bank doing, Mr. Director, over at Culver?"

"Deposits are high, Henry. Seed's about all the farmers need to finance. No new equipment for sale. Everybody's got a job and not much to buy. You're pretty kind to ask about my business. But now that you're president, some folks wonder if you will move back into this house. Or should we honor you by making 401 South Main Street a presidential museum?"

Henry smiled. "Well we'll see. You're kind to think that far ahead." Henry turned toward the Schilling's son. "And I see, Jim, by your badge you've made Second Class. How's our old Troop 13 doing?"

"Gathering lots of scrap paper to help the war effort, Mr. President, and by the next Court of Honor I expect to make First Class, sir."

And I hope that's all you need do, now. Don't want to send you overseas to fight, Henry thought.

At the other end of the table, Maude ended her description of the White House presidential quarters. "But we will be busy readying here until the president gets back, after he meets with Churchill and Stalin in Germany starting week next."

Edna held up three fingers. "South Main Street, once governor's Knox Mansion, now the red brick White House. Maude, you've got lots of experience fixing up homes. And a lot of help from Margaret, I'm sure."

Margaret chimed in, "The governor's mansion in Indianapolis you visited, Mrs. Schilling, was in better shape than what Mrs. Roosevelt left us to clean up."

Maude nodded. "But, Edna, we've had lots of help from the staff." Then Maude spoke from behind her hand so the men at the other end of the table couldn't hear. "We've got pianos all over the place. But we have to beg Henry to take time and play one. Used to be Henry didn't bring the office home with him. Now, our home is also his office."

From his front porch swing, the president visited the invited townsfolk.

First to visit was Howard Bashore the state trooper who lived in Knox and drove Governor Schricker wherever he went. "Mr. President, I still remember that banquet when you were governor and invited me to sit at the head table with you. The persons in charge of the event did not think that was appropriate, but you said, 'He is not only my driver, he is my friend!' I'll never forget that. Who's driving you now?"

Henry answered, "Tom Gohr. And you two would get along fine. 'Course the driving gets complicated when the Secret Service boys demand that one limousine go ahead and another follow. They even drove three limos from Washington to the Peru Naval Air Station just to meet my plane from California and drive me here. Tomorrow, Tom drives me back to the plane. Bunch of the Secret Service guys get aboard and fly with me back to D.C. Being president makes getting to places complicated. But I know you could handle the driving job."

The morning political audiences had not been much different from the appointments his chief of staff scheduled for the Oval Office. In Knox Political Boss Bill Shaw replaced Bill Leahy as the gatekeeper. And politicians and diplomats had been replaced with locals that Shaw said he could arrange for the president to meet. The big difference from the Oval Office was that Henry enjoyed all the visits on his Knox front porch. But wished he had time to talk with more people than those Shaw had recruited.

Henry asked his Knox chief of staff, "Bill, now you've got no one here right now, Maude asks if you want to come in for lunch?"

"Thanks, but tell Maude I've got some more politicking to do. She'll understand."

"Well, thank you for inviting folks. Ted Haye's recording for the radio station was a lot of fun. He interviewed Maude and Margaret earlier this week. But things got pretty serious with the Collins family. Their son wrote them he's being rotated to the Pacific. His letter joked he was going to join General MacArthur. I couldn't tell them what's in store for him. Told them I would share their prayers for his safety. The Rubbis reminded that I had signed their lot purchase deed when they bought at Bass Lake. Their teenage daughter Louise is a knockout. She would make Mickey Rooney forget about Judy Garland. The Rubbis told me about their two sons in the infantry who fought at Guadalcanal. Eddie is recovered from a boat accident, but his brother Nick is still in the hospital at Greenbrier, West Virginia. Japanese sniper ruined his shoulder. I think I might arrange to visit the hospital, like I did in Oakland, to thank the wounded and especially Nick."

Shaw beamed. "Hope you can. Nick's father is a native Italian. But he's been an American from teenage on. Your speech yesterday reminded us we are all just Americans. Period. I liked that, Henry."

⚜ — ⚜

MAUDE CAME OUT TO THE porch carrying Henry's white fedora. She wiggled onto the swing, bumped Henry's hip, pushed her feet against the porch floor, and made the swing move.

"Henry, you're supposed to act surprised, but I know that you already have figured out there's a parade coming this way. That's why you've been sitting out here in the porch swing, right?"

Henry grinned. "You don't say? Maybe that's why all of my secret service detail started pacing nearby some thirty minutes ago."

They faintly heard the bass drums, then the snare drums, and then the city fire alarm sounded.

Margaret appeared at the front door and clapped her hands. "Stand up. Stand up. There's a president out here, somewhere. Here they come, Pop. Jump up and start looking."

Across the street, the Drew family emerged from their house. Grandson Jimmy and his sister Shirley waved small American flags.

The Knox High School band, wearing their Redskins red uniforms, marched in one long line. On the opposite side of the street from them, the North Judson High band marched in their Blue Jay blue uniforms. In the middle column, old men in white shirts marched who had served in Captain Schricker's state militia and some as a Knox Volunteer Fireman. Siren blaring, the Knox Fire Department truck followed, with firemen waving from the sides of the truck.

The marchers stopped in front of the red brick house at 401 Main Street and turned to face the president on his porch.

The bands played *Hail to the Chief* as the men saluted.

When the refrain ended, Henry returned the salutes. He started to speak, but Maude raised one hand to hush him.

She whispered, "You're supposed to speak to the crowd waiting at the court house. They want you to do what you used to do, ride there on the fire truck. We'll follow."

Maude smiled but didn't say who would be waiting at the courthouse.

Henry grinned and put on his white hat. As he walked down the stairs, he waved to the bands and the men dressed in white shirts. After he'd climbed aboard the fire truck, he shook hands with the driver. He waved the entire four blocks to the court house.

My opening words, Henry thought, *will paraphrase the son. "Bless you, all. I'm back home in Indiana."*

CHAPTER 17

THREE BLACK LIMOUSINES WAITED AT the west curb of 401 South Main Street. Henry kissed his wife, donned his white fedora hat, and stepped down the front steps to where his driver and longtime campaign manager waited.

"Tom Gohr, meet Bill Shaw," Henry said. "He's riding with us back to my airplane."

Henry told his driver more after Shaw joined him in the back seat. "Tom, this fellow is the man who got me into banking and politics. Bill Shaw is our number one political man in this part of Indiana. I already told Bill about how you drove this fancy, bullet-proof limousine, along with two other limos, from D.C. out to Knox. After you get me loaded on the plane, I won't see you until you drive back to Washington."

Tom nodded. "Understand, Mr. President."

Henry continued, "To avoid any more complications, Mr. Shaw has a car following to take him back to Knox. I'm going to slide this glass panel so you won't have to hear us talk. Just want to keep you out of trouble with the Civil Service, because we're going to talk politics. Big-time Knox, Indiana politics."

Tom chuckled. "No problem, Mr. President."

Henry shut the window panel and turned to Shaw. "Bill, let me lay it on the line. Nobody likes to be beholden without a chance to repay. And I know patronage is the coin of the realm for the elected. I didn't miss what you said yesterday about getting me elected again in three years. I'm beholden to you for supporting my career changes. From lawyer to publisher. From bank clerk to lieutenant governor, then governor. Then you rallied the Indiana delegation to support me for vice president."

Henry paused. "But Neighbor Shaw, this time you've got to know, I have no intention of running for reelection."

Shaw frowned.

"Sorry. Bill. You've done much to advance my career. Both financial and political. But being a trustee of other people's money is much different than being a trustee of other people's lives. You need to know that I'm considering an executive order that will alienate most southerners at the next Democrat nominating convention. It will likely scuttle any reelection campaign."

Shaw's large eyebrows shot up.

Henry continued, "I'm thinking about using a presidential executive order—just as Roosevelt did in 1941—to establish fair employment practices. And issuing the order after I go to the Potsdam Conference. My order will end segregation in the military."

Shaw's eye opened wider. "Surely, Henry, not before the war's over."

"That's a good point. I'll consider waiting. But, Bill, last night I ran the flag up the flagpole on this executive order idea, confided with my best sounding board. Last night I told Maude what I had in mind."

"And?"

"Maude said if anyone reads Eleanor Roosevelt's columns like she does, they would know Eleanor would have written this 'end segregation in military' as an executive order when the war started."

Shaw inhaled deeply.

"Bill, you don't need to tell me about the political damage. But it's fairness long overdue. Race and color shouldn't divide us. You heard what I said in North Judson. We're not Asian-Americans, African-Americans, or Bavarian-Americans—if you want to classify your president. We're Americans."

Shaw crossed his arms but didn't comment.

"Did you know our Negro soldiers get more respect in England? Did you hear about the pub owner who banned white officers after they snubbed enlisted Negroes? And in Italy, the Tuskegee Airmen are welcomed like the heroes they are. As for my reelection, I know that integrating the military won't pass muster with southern Democrats. Three years from now, I don't think you could win a convention nomination floor fight. What's more, I predict Jimmy Byrnes still won't get enough northern Democrats to support him."

Henry watched Shaw swallow deeply.

"I'm not going to bring a problem without a solution. Think we need to nominate Dwight Eisenhower before the Republicans corner him. And when Adlai Stevenson gets elected Governor of Illinois, run him for vice president."

Shaw took a deep breath. "Henry Schricker, you have always been a straight shooter. But this time, I feel like you just dropped a big bomb on me."

Henry patted Bill's shoulder. *I may have to decide when to drop a bigger bomb, if I haven't approved a $2 billion dud. And that decision will end any thought of running for a second term.*

⋇ — ⋇

KNOX, INDIANA, ABOARD THE *SACRED COW*

ADLAI STEVENSON SHOOK HANDS WITH Bill Shaw then followed Henry up the steps into the four-engine plane.

Henry and Adlai followed orders when they heard, "This is Captain Young speaking. Welcome back aboard, Mr. President. Everyone buckle up. Tail wind today. Will be a shorter flight from Indiana back to Andrews."

Good, Henry thought, *this* Sacred Cow *needs some pasture time before she flies to Germany.*

Once airborne, Henry opened the folder on the small luncheon table that served as his desk. Adlai waited while Henry read dispatches. "Adlai, this dispatch will please the daughter I just left in Knox." He read aloud, "USS *Indiana* joins Task Force 38.7. Now in Japanese home waters, to remain there.*"*

Adlai waited until Henry quit reading his dispatches. "Well, Mr. President, how did your visit to Knox go?"

Henry smiled. "Best reception I ever had. Parade. Speech at the courthouse. Big surprise there. My sons got weekend leave. Surprised me. My Army and Navy boys escorted me from the fire truck to the podium that was erected. In the speech I repeated some of your United Nation phrases, thank you. Saw a bunch of my friends. Made some new ones. Don't want to take any praise away from our White House chefs, but it was a pleasure to eat Maude and Margaret's fine home cooking. How went your few days back in Illinois?"

Adlai beamed. "Better than I could ever hope. Some of my Democrat friends talked to me about the possibility of running for governor. I acted surprised, but sure didn't say no."

Henry nodded several times. "Adlai, I'm not surprised. You're well qualified. You will make a great campaigner. And I will support you. Want you to get that job." *Then I can nominate you for this job Roosevelt left for me,* Henry thought.

Henry paused. "And as much as I hate to lose your services, I think you should leave Washington soon and get back to Illinois. Do a little of your own speechmaking there."

"Thank you, sir. I will take you up on that idea. But I want to report on one assignment you gave me. I went to the library and searched for more information about Churchill. Read some of his writings. And I think I found one item that will help 'break the ice' when you meet him in Germany."

Henry smiled. "Tell me."

"Churchill wrote a short tribute to Baden-Powell, the founder of Scouting. In one paragraph, he speculates that the motto Be Prepared reflected Baden-Powell's 'B-P' initials And I know you started a Boy Scout troop in Knox before World War I. That information work for you?"

Henry lightly pounded his desk with both hands. "You bet your boots. Baden-Powell even visited Culver, near Knox, in 1908. I didn't get to meet him. But I read his book *Scouting*, and we started Troop 13 in year 1913. I've read many of Churchill's writings. He and I can also agree about universal military training. I remember when our Civilian Conservation Corps got young men off the streets. That New Deal program even helped build facilities on the Tippecanoe River between Knox and Winamac, over in the county south of Knox."

Henry leaned across his desk. "One thing I keep telling Republicans, who will listen, those boys helped save our forests. Fires grow in brush that needs clearing. And our boys did the clearing."

Henry smiled. "And you know what, Adlai. Bunch of those boys even sent some of their small pay back home to some parents who needed help. The Prime Minister and I will have something to chat about in addition to smoking his good cigars while figuring what to say to Uncle Joe Stalin. If Churchill doesn't know that in 1913, I organized a Boy Scout Troop back home in Knox, Indiana, we need to see that he gets that information before we meet in Germany. Bet you know how to get that done."

Adlai smiled.

Henry laid the paper on his desk. "When Churchill and I are alone, I will probably need to refuse a drink from him. I already had one Scouting idea in mind before you found these additions. Last year, at a Scouting banquet in Indianapolis, young Bud Hooks, the drug store owner's son, told us how gracious Baden-Powell could be. I remember, young Hooks said he had learned at Jamboree that the father of Scouting didn't smoke but always proffered a cigar if wanted. A teetotaler who always offered wine to those at his dining table.

Henry grinned. "I predict that Winston and Henry will find much common ground—journalists, scouters, and politicians."

Henry thought, *Also, I won't be surprised if Churchill suggests that the United States forgive some of England's wartime debt to our country.*

"Good work, Adlai. The prime minister and I will have something to chat about in addition to good cigars and what to say to Uncle Joe Stalin."

CHAPTER 18

H ENRY SMILED AS HE LISTENED to the telephone call. He winked at
Admiral Leahy who stood before his desk. "Good work, Senator
Barkley. Congratulations. You got the Senate to confirm Byrnes.
Let's swear in our new Secretary of State in my office tomorrow."

Henry nodded. "Okay, yes, Byrnes needs to get packing today.
I will send him ahead on the Navy cruiser that takes our delegation
to the Potsdam Conference."

Henry listened before he replied, "Get with Byrnes and then
call Admiral Leahy's office and work out a time. Then Mike Quinn
will get the press people here to witness the ceremony. Again,
thanks Alvin. Good work on speeding the confirmation. As for my
appearance before the senate this afternoon, my speech will be short
and to the point and all about ratifying the United Nations Charter.
We live in a world where we must get along. I'll repeat a few of the
challenges that Mrs. Roosevelt offered when the delegates first met
in San Francisco."

Henry had an afterthought. *Two speeches for the price of one,
because Adlai wrote both challenges.*

"Okay, Leahy, let's see if I understand what's organized? If I
heard the number correctly"—Henry raised his eyebrows—"this
afternoon you and a trainload of advisors and negotiators, plus a few
military, secretaries, communication specialists, are going to make a
secret trip to Norfolk to board a Navy cruiser. Then you'll sail, steam
that is, to Antwerp in Belgium."

Leahy nodded in acknowledgement of Henry's information.

Henry continued, "While crossing the Atlantic, advisors and experts will discuss diplomatic problems and solutions we might accept. Good plan. But your president could wait for a briefing after we get to Germany. There you could supply me, I hope, with clever words to say to Stalin in the presence of Churchill, a man with many words. When we reach Antwerp, I understand you people plan to have the *Sacred Cow* there to fly me and a few others to Berlin.

"In Potsdam we move into a movie suburb, talk with the Brits about the general election they're calling. Attend daily conferences in Stalin's fancier mansion. And we, when our turn comes, host a big dinner party for all. Eventually, I talk with Joseph Stalin—a man who will not bother to listen to as many advisors as your president is scheduled to hear—and convince Uncle Joe our objective is to divide control of Europe sanely and urge Russia to start war with Japan.

Bill, I don't want to sound too sarcastic, but I don't think you need me cruising for eight days, since I'll just be waiting to be coached, say, the last three days."

Henry thought, *The admiral can either laugh or cry.*

Leahy chuckled. "Mr. President, I'll arrange to meet you halfway there. You could fly to, say, the Azores Islands. A good port where we can pick you up. Take you from shore in the USS *Augusta's* captain's fancy motorboat. Welcome you aboard."

Henry smiled. "That sounds better. As for today, I see by your daily schedule that the *New York Times* has sent an artist—S. J. Woolf, says here—to do a sketch of the president at work. Send him in. I'll pose. Might be a good time for me to put on my reading glasses like the ones Franklin used on his nose. Won't tell him I'm reading a biography of Joseph Stalin."

WHITE HOUSE, PRESIDENTIAL QUARTERS

Henry wrote his promised daily letter.

Dearest Maude,

Your man is feeling down about going to the conference in Germany. Wish it was just you and me going there looking for my Bavarian roots.

Henry stopped writing and wondered how much of his concerns he should unload

I didn't invite Stimson because I'm concerned about his health, so Stimson invited himself. He'll go by plane and arrive in Berlin ahead of me.

Morgenthau is not invited. He was eager to go and upset at my decision. He wants to close their manufacturing and reduce Germany to farming.

Stimson opposed including Morgenthau. He wants an economically strong and productive Germany. He say it's the only hope for the survival of Europe.

Henry rubbed his left arm over his eyes and resumed writing.

But, honey, your great concern about Germany's concentration camps will not be overlooked. Our delegation already agrees we should punish Germany's war criminals in full measure: take her weapons, guard governmental action until the Nazi-educated generation has passed from the stage, but not deprive her the means to build a better Germany.

Sorry, you won't be in Potsdam to hear me unload the day's worries. I've arranged to get my letters, secure overnight delivery, back to you. Will try to write you each evening before I go to sleep. But wish you were going with me.

Love and Kisses, Henry

⊰⊱ ── ⊰⊱

TUESDAY, JULY 3, WHITE HOUSE, OVAL OFFICE

Henry thanked his press secretary for coming in early. "Mike, I'm going to keep this meeting short. Put some extra burden on you."

Quinn nodded. "Understood, Mr. President. You leave after the Fourth. I also understand your travel arrangements are under wraps for security reasons. Just tell me what you want me to do."

Henry looked at the "to do" list on his desk.

"Mike, you need to write my Independence Day statement. Commend our national heritage. Need a tribute to armed forces. Follow with our promise to carry spirit of independence to the world. After the Fourth, you need to report that I'm not making appearances, because I'm meeting with cabinet members on the budget that Congress has sent over. That's no spin. I'll be spending time with some cabinet members on the ship going to Europe."

Henry looked at his list. "And Mike, put some words in about how I managed to keep Indiana finances in the black when governor. You were in Indianapolis part of that time. See if you can dig up something nice a Hoosier Republican said about my, ahem, fiscal responsibility."

Mike grinned. "Can do. Think I remember a few grudging admissions we printed."

As Quinn left the room, Henry thought, *But what will Republicans say when they find out we have spent over $2 billion on a bomb that has yet to explode? Dare I hope Admiral Leahy is wrong when he says the "fool thing" won't work.*

Colonel Watson entered and turned on two lamps in the Oval Office. "Getting late, Mr. President. Adlai Stevenson is still waiting for when you need him. And Congress is still meeting. But Speaker Rayburn asked if his delegation could come later. Speaker knows you are leaving after the Fourth. Wants to make sure you know his, err, Congress's concerns. I said yes for you."

Henry winked. "That's admiral for a colonel. Do ask Adlai to come in while I wait for Sam."

Stevenson sat in front of Henry's desk and took the legal pad from his briefcase.

"Relax, Adlai. Don't need to compose any lofty words. For the next weeks, I'll be listening to declamation by the greatest, Prime Minister Churchill. And who-knows-what from Commissar Joe Stalin."

Adlai put his legal pad back in the briefcase.

Henry leaned back in his chair and loosened his tie. "When we asked the Secretary of the Navy to reassign you to writing speeches for the president, pretty sure he thought that was because Eleanor had already identified your talent. Don't know if he knew older Schrickers and Stevensons farmed nearby on the Indiana and Illinois border. Probably only knows our families are connected politically. Adlai, I'm sure if you were an Illinois farm boy, or know a few, you understand there's a time when you need a chew."

Henry pulled his chewing tobacco from his inner coat pocket. "Adlai, you get an extra burden today. Need you to take Maude's place and give me some frank reactions. Tell me, man-to-man, how does a small town banker and a farm-state governor meet for the first time and confide with, the Prime Minister of the United Kingdom? A man who has spent more hours than I ever did confiding with President Roosevelt. What can I say that's new to Churchill, a man of many talents? He's been a journalist, an author, an artist, and a statesman."

Stevenson chuckled. "Mr. President, it occurs to me you've got two of those titles already. Don't think you want to be an artist but bet you could if you wanted. I'll research the prime minister a little further. Right now, bet he doesn't play the piano or the organ. He does know a little bit about farming, I've read. Never heard of any man drinking more spirits than Winston Churchill. But I know you don't drink anything. Hope he knows not to offer you alcohol."

Henry smiled. "As to bad habits, my once-in-a-while cigar won't compete with his constant companions, either. Doubt the prime minister would understand if I offered him a chew."

Adlai chuckled. "I'll work up some notes for you to read as you travel."

Henry leaned forward. "Adlai, my Maude is back home in Knox. I sometimes ask her to hear my concerns. Ask her how she would react. Not often, because it's the president's job to make decisions. I'm not going to burden you with a decision only I must make. Won't tell you the particulars. But a few, here and abroad, know the details."

Henry paused. "You are a trained newsman who will appreciate it's a big story. So big, the *New York Times* is sitting on it. Adlai, I can envision some day mounting the podium and putting your name in nomination for this presidency. And the nation will ask, what would you have done in my situation? I'm afraid that long after Mom and I are gone, even after you are gone, another president could face this same, bitter question."

Henry spit into the vessel. Adlai waited.

"Adlai, you know I'm a God-fearing man. But, never, never did I ever think I would be asked to make a decision that belongs only to God. I'm sure whatever course I choose, the world will long remember."

Both men turned when they heard the knock on the Oval Room door. Henry spit out his chew, shoved the cuspidor under the desk, and tightened his tie.

Adlai crushed his cigar in an ashtray and tightened his tie, then stood.

"Yes. Come in," Henry said.

The door opened and the colonel announced, "The delegation from Congress, Mr. President."

Henry nodded a thank you to Adlai, as he stood. "By all means, please show the distinguished gentlemen in."

CHAPTER 19

MARINE COLONEL BRITT WATSON, DRESSED in his summer khaki uniform, held the door open. "Good morning, Mr. President. I received a message from Admiral Leahy. He's enjoying seeing the sea on the USS *Augusta*. And I've good news from the Map Room. MacArthur's headquarters announces liberation of all the Philippine Islands."

"Yes indeed Britt, good news."

The colonel continued, "MacArthur's message asks when we should give the press details?"

Henry chuckled. "I'm sure General MacArthur prefers to announce this triumph to the press." Then thought he should probably act like he was the Commander and Chief. "Send a message from President Schricker that the president wants the general to announce the good news. Send it now, because the sun is already setting in Manila. I'll read the correspondence you put on my desk while you send the message."

Colonel Watson saluted then went to Leahy's office.

Henry took off his sport coat and hung the jacket across the back of his chair. He had read through official business and had started on personal correspondence when the colonel returned.

"Message to MacArthur sent, sir. I will notify you when Manila replies. I'm sure, Mr. President, that your stack of personal correspondence is much higher this Fourth of July. Many happy birthday greetings for our country. Before you leave for the National

Press Club, I have several copies of the sing-along words for you. Copies for the service people were sent yesterday. We have collected a portfolio of the music, although I'm told you can play all of these tunes from memory."

Henry laughed. "I think my wife or daughter must have spread that word. But I'm glad I've got the sheet music in case my fingers forget. I used to wake my family up playing those tunes downstairs at our home."

❧ — ❦

WASHINGTON, D.C., NATIONAL PRESS CLUB

SERVICE MEN AND ENLISTED WOMEN filed into the National Press Club auditorium.

Lauren Bacall waved to arrivals, tossed her blonde hair, blew a kiss to the incoming crowd. She turned to the president who sat at the piano. "Mr. President, I did a similar appearance with Senator Harry Truman right here during the winter. He's a very good piano player."

Lauren grinned. "The senator thought my agent had a good idea. He let me sit atop the piano while Senator Truman played."

Henry thought, *I saw the photograph. The National Press Club is proud of that photo. But not a similar picture this president wants the folks back in Knox to see. Yep Lauren, you are a pretty picture of a nineteen-year-old blonde. And the wolves back in Starke County—not only Humphrey Bogart—would whistle.*

"Yes, Miss Bacall. Senator Truman is an accomplished musician. When he was younger, he won national recognition in concert competitions. I can't compare my piano playing to his. But it's not the first time I've played music for a sing-along. The National Press Club people are passing out the words for our songs as the service men and women come in. I can play *Pack Up Your Troubles*, *Over There*, *Yankee Doodle Dandy*, *It's a Grand Old Flag*, and many more from memory.

"Also, the smart people working at the White House found us some sheet music so I could find the right keys, and let you sing the words. You stand out front and lead the singing. Bet the boys will appreciate you being here more than the piano player."

⊰——⊱

KNOX, INDIANA, 401 SOUTH MAIN STREET

MARGARET SANG A VERSE AS soon as Henry answered the telephone. "Back home in Indiana."

Henry laughed.

"Hey, Pop, you're the big news on radio tonight. Lauren Bacall got second billing. NBC says you're a star pianist. Gabriel Heater sounded surprised you could play. Walter Winchell puffing you to all the boys and girls at sea. My dad, the piano virtuoso. Whoopee!"

Henry answered from the White House residential quarters. "Thanks, honey. How's Mom doing after all the hullabaloo I created in Knox?"

"Pop, she's handled all the well-wishers just like the first lady should. She's made time for all of them. I'm going to go downstairs and get on the other phone. About time you told us about you and Lauren Bacall today. Did you remember how to whistle? Here's Mom."

Maude was laughing when she came on line. "Okay, Henry Schricker, tell your story. Better be good."

Henry laughed. "Honey, not to worry. That Bacall girl is no better looking than my Maude."

Margaret chimed in from the other line. "But younger, Pop. Younger than your daughter."

Henry chuckled. "And Miss Bacall is no prettier than my daughter. Here's my story, and like a good lawyer, I've got a room full of GIs to confirm my testimony. The good staff at the White House helped when I told them what I planned for the National Press Club sing-along. Told them what songs I was going to play, and they had sheet music ready for me when I left the White House.

"When I got to the auditorium, Miss Bacall very graciously told me she had appeared there with Senator Harry Truman for another GI gathering. She told me Harry let her stretch atop the piano and show her legs—"

Maude interrupted. "I heard at one of Perle Mesta's parties that Bess Truman didn't like that photo."

"Maude, back when I presided over the Senate, I heard the same from Harry himself during one of Rayburn's recuperation sessions—."

Margaret interrupted. "Well, how were her legs, Pop?"

"Young lady, my little lamb, your father plays organ at the Knox Lutheran Church. The choir doesn't show their legs."

Maude chimed in, "Good thing. Most of their legs have seen better days."

Henry and Margaret laughed.

"Okay. Ladies, let me finish my testimony. Besides furnishing sheet music for me and Miss Bacall, my White House staff also mimeographed the words of the sing-along songs I had Miss Bacall pass out. Most of them I played from memory."

Maude asked, "How did Miss Bacall do on the high notes?"

"Just what you would expect from an alto. She strained on the top notes. We needed your Knox soprano. But the GIs had a great time. And they found out their president could play the piano—for whatever that was worth. On a more serious note, White House staff suggests I choose some music to play at the banquet when the United States entertains the Russians and the British. It's going to be one state dinner after another.

"Maude, Margaret, we have arranged for me to send you guarded, private letters each day. I can also phone you on a secure trans-Atlantic phone circuit. But I won't use that phone unless I need an immediate response."

Maude answered, "I understand, honey. And we will pray for you every day."

Henry paused. "Thanks, honey. We need God with us. The worst of times may be yet to come."

THURSDAY, JULY 5, WHITE HOUSE, OVAL OFFICE

HENRY THANKED THE LIEUTENANT FOR the early morning coffee and the written reports.

Heavy air attacks by American fliers leave 10 Japanese cities in ruins, destroy or damage 128 enemy ships and 92 planes.

Henry envisioned the B-29s taking off from the small Pacific islands that we had won a high price, especially in lives lost. Joined in the air with escort planes on islands closer to Japan, bought with more lives. Then Henry signed the appointment of General Spatz as commander of Strategic Air Forces in the Pacific.

The other report reminded him of the sacrifices made in Europe that made half-of-the-world's oceans safer. He would be aboard soon enough.

USS Augusta *reports all well in Atlantic.*

WHITE HOUSE, OVAL OFFICE

HENRY DECIDED TO BRING THE argument to an end. "Secretary Morgenthau, you have left me with little choice. You say that you must be included in our delegation to Potsdam. You have challenged me. Either invite you to fly with me to the Azores, and then continue with me on the cruiser, or you will resign. Your many years of service to the president and our country are monumental. Your position on the repatriation of Germany is well understood. My affection for you as a person is tremendous.

"But your presence at Potsdam is not essential."

After Morgenthau left the Oval Office, Henry wasted no time. "Colonel Watson, please reach Fred Vinson. Ask him to call me, soonest. Thank you."

Henry thought, *Vinson will make a fine, new Treasury Secretary.*

FRIDAY, JULY 6, WHITE HOUSE, OVAL OFFICE

Admiral Nimitz describes powerful attack by U.S. Third Fleet, joined by British forces, as pre-invasion stage of war against Japan. 1,500 bombers over Japan.

Henry read the report before he read and initialed the news release of his appointment of General Spatz as commander of Strategic Air Forces in the Pacific.

Then he filled his briefcase with biographical paragraphs about Stalin and notes about Churchill from Adlai Stevenson.

Before he left the presidential desk, Henry squeezed his paperweight of bundled newspaper type. Then ran his hands across the desk and fingered out *Abide With Me*.

WHITE HOUSE, PRESIDENTIAL QUARTERS

HENRY SHED HIS COAT AND tie, kicked off his shoes, leaned back in the overstuffed lounge chair before he placed the call to Maude.

"Honey, I know we have been talking a long time, and you think I need to get some sleep. But I'll rest plenty between here and that fancy filmmaking town on the outskirts of Berlin. Twelve hour flight tomorrow. Then several days of briefing by our experts after I go aboard the cruiser.

"Yeah, Maude, it sounds exhausting. But what's really going to exhaust me is sitting around a big table and listening to a bunch of speeches. Already warned that Churchill will make a bunch of orations. Stalin, they tell me, leaves most of the talking to Molotov.

"Going to miss you too. Already too many days since I left you in Knox. Loves you."

SATURDAY, JULY 7, WHITE HOUSE

AT SUNRISE, HENRY LOOKED AT his watch. Time to leave for Andrews airfield. He would breakfast on the plane. His baggage had already been picked up from the presidential suite. Limousine drivers and Secret Service bodyguards were waiting.

᜔———᜔

ANDREWS AIRFIELD, ABOARD *SACRED COW*

HENRY SAW THE INSIGNIA AND remarked, "I see, Tom, you've been promoted. Congratulations, Major Young."

Young smiled. "Thank you, sir. I think when they scheduled your flight to Europe I was promoted because I will command Captain Bill Wright and his two junior officers. Those three now aboard. They will spell my crew during the different flights. Taking some berths we usually fill with flight attendants. Lieutenant Glasser's still flying, now in cockpit. She knows this route well.

"Flight to the Azores will take about eight hours. The Navy should arrive to take you aboard the next day. Glad sir, you decided not to go the complete voyage on the Navy cruiser with all your advisers and staff."

Henry thought, *I'm glad, also. Maude and I like to travel. I've seen the sea, but never the Azores. Remembered his North Judson grammar school history lesson. Columbus sailed west from the Azores to discover our new world.*

Young continued, "We will land you at Lajes in the Azores. Refuel. After you go aboard the USS *Augusta*, we lay over before we fly on to Antwerp. Meet you there. Then fly you and the advisers you select on to Berlin. Mr. President, I've flown through Lajes many times. Just to provide a little detail: it's on the island of Terceira. The nearest town is Angra, where the restaurants have terrific grilled swordfish, served simply with boiled potatoes. The island's mainly hilly grazing land. The wind blows all the time. Never very hot, never very cold. During the flight into Lajes, you will see the rims of extinct, submerged volcanoes that formed the Azores."

Henry thought, *Sounds like a place Maude and I need to visit. A peacetime president could schedule such a vacation. Lord willing, I will make decisions that will give us peace in our time.*

᜔———᜔

AZORES ISLAND, PRESIDENTIAL QUARTERS

Henry thanked his attendants. "Nothing I need at the moment. I'll call for breakfast in my room tomorrow morning. Leave any unpacking to me. The apartment is very nice."

Henry saw messages waiting. Probably, as usual, from the Map Room, War Department.

Henry thought, *Maybe I should have asked them, just this once, to take the telephone, desk, and messages away.*

But there was good news.

> *Secretary of State Cordell Hull discharged from Bethesda Naval Hospital, Maryland.*

> *Department of War announces 42 divisions fought in Europe to return by end of the year.*

The GI newspaper *Stars and Stripes* was at the bottom of the to-read pile. Henry laughed at the "GI Joe" cartoon. Funny, but not as good as the one Mauldin did about shooting the dilapidated jeep, like shooting horses because they could run no longer.

The newspaper's songs story grabbed his attention.

> *Hey, GIs counting your points in anticipation of when you get to quit occupying Germany and go home, Company E 335th Infantry held a GI hit parade contest that the Associated Press reported.*

> *The music on their mind tells how much they want to go home. The hits include Show Me the Way to Go Home, Hurry Home, Home Sweet Home, My Old Kentucky Home, Home on the Range, and My Home in Indiana.*

Henry stopped reading and tapped out that one on his desk.

Henry thought, *Here I am, far away, wishing I was sitting in the swing on the porch at 401 South Main drinking Maude's tea with honey. G.I. Joe, I'm feeling your pain. We've got to end this war.*

The telephone rang. "Mr. President, the cruiser *Augusta* radioed. The captain's boat will pick you up tomorrow afternoon. ETA between two and four."

Henry thanked the officer. Thought of what he needed to write in tonight's letter to Maude.

> *Honey, we need a vacation trip to this beautiful island.*
> *Not seeing much of the place this time …*

❦——❦

SUNDAY, JULY 8, ATLANTIC OCEAN, ABOARD USS *AUGUSTA*

THROUGH THE PORTHOLE HENRY WATCHED the Atlantic waters heave. His shipboard boarding had been one of his rare moments. The crew, dressed in their whites, stood at attention while the president's flag was raised. The ship's band played *Hail to the Chief.* Then broke into a jazzed-up version of *Back Home in Indiana.* Some Broadway musician who volunteered for the Navy probably scored that version.

The captain told him the band wanted the president to sit in at the piano sometime during the rest of the voyage.

Henry thought he would include that request in the notes he jotted down. He would send his first letter from the ship to Maude.

❦——❦

MONDAY, JULY 9, ATLANTIC OCEAN, ABOARD USS *AUGUSTA*

HENRY AROSE AT HIS USUAL 6:15 and dressed. He left his stateroom and climbed the stairs. He thought to himself, *Stairs are called "ladders" if he was going to use the proper nautical term.* Henry took and returned salutes from the three officers who waited on the deck.

He began his turn around the deck, followed by the same officer who followed him yesterday. Henry stopped walking and turned to the two stripes on the officer's jacket.

The officer stopped and braced.

"Good morning to you, Lieutenant. Rather than follow, come walk alongside."

Henry thought he saw the officer blush as he moved forward. "Good morning, Mr. President. My pleasure to walk the deck with you this morning."

Henry looked closer. The officer looked older than most Navy airmen. "I see, lieutenant, that you wear wings insignia. Are you, like me, a ship's passenger headed for a new assignment?"

"No, sir. I'm a ship's pilot. I fly a floatplane that we catapult from the ship. I'm sure you've noticed our canvas-covered, high-winged planes, as you've walked our decks."

"Yes, I have, lieutenant. I've also noticed that you have been nearby when I've been on the deck. Presume you were assigned as my security."

They crossed in front of the large guns and turned toward the stern "My orders, Mr. President, are to continually know your location aboard, in case I need to quickly fly you off the ship."

Henry chuckled. "Sounds like our Be Prepared motto. Tell me your name. Where's home? Were you a Boy Scout, lieutenant?"

"Yes, sir. Lieutenant Robert Havins. Brownsville, Texas. As a Scout, I made Life but not Eagle."

"Now, tell me, what to expect if you need to fly me off the *Augusta*."

Havins smiled. "Not much difference between any other single-engine, high-wing airplane, except for the catapult launching. You'll need to press your head against the headrest before they fire the catapult. The plane will settle a bit before we start climbing. Helps to keep your eye above the horizon. I hope we don't need to launch in the dark before we can see the horizon."

They turned near the stern and started walking back up the port side.

"Lieutenant, sounds like you've been there?"

"Yes, sir. Two years ago, flying off the *Richmond* in the Aleutians campaign. But only one launch just at dawn, when you've got a little horizon.

"You were flying to observe shelling or …?"

"No, sir. I don't want to create any problem, but I'm not going to lie to the President of the United States. The admiral sent me off at dawn to fly to the nearest Alaskan town to bring him back some fresh seafood for his mess."

Henry shook his head. "Understood, Robert. Don't tell me the admiral's name. And I can wait until we get to Potsdam to order fancy food. Although, I think I would enjoy a catapult launching, preferably with a bunch of horizon."

CHAPTER 20

ELHAM, KENT, ENGLAND

MANICURED FLOWER BEDS. CULTURED LAWNS. The cathedral bells tolled the noon hour. The village from where the first Elam emigrated to the New World.

Corporal Thomas J. Elam slowed his Jeep and drove past the Tudor houses. The stone cathedral ahead rose above two-story white houses bolstered with black wooden frames. Elm trees lined the sidewalks. The beautiful village was more quaint than the postcards tried to portray.

He drove past two women with shawls over their hair and carrying shopping baskets. Tom nodded and smiled at them. Maybe they thought he had lost his way to Canterbury, the usual tourist stop that was 14 kilometers north of Elham.

Tom returned their smile. They weren't the first English women to show a Negro soldier the respect you could earn with good manners. Unlike some brash white GIs, Tom and his buddies didn't make fun of old fashioned British autos, outdated plumbing, or even some bad food.

Several British had told him they preferred American black soldiers to their "overpaid, overfed, oversexed and over here" white countrymen. British women noted that, in contrast to some white GIs, the black soldiers did not cat-call them—something that back home could have seen them lynched.

A George Orwell quote from the *London Tribune* was posted on their barracks bulletin board. It said, "The general consensus of opinion seems to be that the only American soldiers with decent manners are the Negroes."

Tom parked his jeep in front of the Rose and Crown building. Before entering, he looked at the outside menu board. Per usual, the plowman's lunch topped the offerings. After two years in England, he knew that the required bread, cheese, and onions could also include ham, maybe a boiled egg, and occasionally a green salad. Ingredients for the plowman's lunch would probably include something not sold yesterday. That meal would last until he got back to his Folkestone base.

Tom entered and realized he was early for most lunchtime patrons. Only two men sat at the table near the pub owner's bar. They quit talking when they saw the black Army soldier.

The pub owner spoke first. "Welcome, Yank. How about a half-pint on the house?"

The two patrons smiled as Tom walked by their table. The pub owner had already drawn the beer from the tap by the time Tom arrived at the bar. "Thank you, sir. Much appreciated. But you don't have to treat me…"

The pub owner interrupted. "Call me Henry. Special occasion for me, corporal. Been a while since this pub owner heard about that segregation fight up at Lancashire. Back Corporal, when some of your opinionated white officers suggested the local pub not serve Negroes.

And I decided, like the owner up there, that Henry Evans would serve a free beer to the first Negro soldier who walked into this Rose and Crown. Welcome. You're the first one in two years."

The two patrons chuckled. One waved for Tom to take a chair at their table.

"Good show, Henry. Glad you're showing a little charity that Malcom and I have never seen. And I'll buy the refill, Yank. I'm Patrick."

He proffered his hand that Tom took and shook.

The stocky man next offered his hand. "And I'm Malcolm. Welcome." He shook Tom's hand and asked, "Where you based?"

"At Folkestone. Sandgate to be specific."

"What's your billet, lad?"

"I was a reserve added late to the Lancashire barrage balloon outfit that Mr. Evans was talking about. I wasn't in the group at D-Day. But joined my division in France after Paris was liberated.

Most of my platoon had enough points to rotate back to the States. I'm waiting. Had time to visit Elham. Have wanted to see your village long before they sent us to England."

Patrick leaned across the table and lifted his mug. "We are glad to have you Yanks. Here's to you."

The three touched their mugs. Tom followed the others and took a sip. Patrick raised his left eyebrow, asked. "Why come to *Elum*? That's the way most of us say the name."

Tom grinned. "Yes, sir, I know. I owe you a confession. As my bunkmate told me this morning, I'm just another American in search of my roots. My last name is Elam."

Henry put down his towel and leaned over his bar toward the table to listen.

"As a boy, I was told that Robert of Elham came to the Colonies in 1638 and settled on the James River near Richmond. Robert of Elham became Robert Elam on the Virginia tax roles. And my enslaved ancestors were part of his farm's property. And you probably know that Colonial enslaved took the last name of their owner."

The men nodded understanding.

Tom warmed to his presentation. "Robert didn't own as many enslaved Negroes as they had on the rich Byrd plantation across the river. But Robert kept enslaved Negroes that he freed or were later emancipated. Their children moved across the United States, some as far west as California. The last time my mother heard from Dad's relatives, she was told there are about one thousand United State Elam families that are white and another thousand families are black."

Malcolm asked, "Where's your home, corporal? You don't have a southern accent."

"That's correct, sir. That's because I'm from Colorado. My grandparents grew up in Kentucky, but they moved west before the war started. My dad got a job at the steel mill. I lost most of my grandfather's southern accent in Pueblo's high school."

The Englishmen paused to take a sip of their half-pint. Tom sipped his mug.

The pub owner waited for the three to drink, before he asked, "What's your full name, Corporal Elam?"

"Thomas J. Elam, sir."

"What's the 'J' stand for, corporal?"

Tom hesitated. He expected his middle name would get a rise—usually did.

"Jefferson, sir."

Henry grinned. "Thomas Jefferson Elam. That's a moniker that must have gotten you a rise or two. I'm guessing your dad decided on that name."

"Yes, sir. He did."

Henry chuckled. "And I'm betting those Colorado school friends had some fun with your name."

"Not much, sir. That's because I just went by my initials T.J. whenever anyone asked for my name. Or just Tom if they wanted more information."

Patrick chimed in. "I've got a pen-pal ancestor in America. Dabbles in genealogy. Some of her family left Ireland during the potato famine and her grandfather ended up working in Kentucky coalmines. She thinks some of her Kentucky neighbor families may have been run out of Virginia because they were Tories during the American Revolution. Apparently, her forefathers didn't think much of Thomas Jefferson's prose. Guess your dad did."

"Yes, sir. He read the Declaration of Independence to me before I could read. When I went to high school, he gave me a copy. Insisted I memorize the preamble, and recite it."

Tom blushed. "Pardon me if I have offended my gracious Elham hosts."

The pub owner answered, "Not at all, Yank. We're mighty thankful you Colonials came over to help us protect Elham. Here. Have another half-pint. But you best know, we didn't celebrate your July the Fourth."

CHAPTER 21

Henry frowned at the update he read. The Japanese military were still dominating decisions.

"Secretary Byrnes, not very encouraging this intelligence that you and Admiral Leahy bring. But I'm not surprised. Think the Japanese warlords who control their emperor want to prolong the suffering. Wait for us to tire? Agree?"

Leahy answered, "Agree. They expect to get a negotiated peace. No intention of accepting an unconditional surrender."

Byrnes raised a finger. "But if we let them keep their emperor, their God on Earth, I think they will accept surrender."

Henry a deep breath. "Jimmy, you were my personal representative to the Interim Committee. Remember, we heard that idea from under secretary of war John McCloy. Back in June. When we were trying to figure out where to drop—if we get one—a nuclear bomb. Are we back to square one?"

Henry kept his bedtime letter to Maude short.

> *Lunched with warrant officers. Excellent band of 30 pieces. Make cheerful music at all meals but breakfast.*

> *Good picture show—your favorite Bob Hope in*
> *Technicolor as a pirate's victim in West Indies. Good that*
> *Hollywood sends new films to troops early on.*

> *Love you, Henry*

TUESDAY, JULY 10, ABOARD USS *AUGUSTA*, PRESIDENT'S CABIN

HENRY READ THE CODED MESSAGE that Graham handed him.

> *Chinese troops capture port of Futing, 450 miles west*
> *of Okinawa.*

> *Australian troops invade Borneo, seize control of Brunei*
> *Bay on northwest coast.*

Henry complimented the commanding officer of the White House Map Room. "Colonel Graham, glad you are aboard for our trip to Germany. You and your staff do an excellent job of keeping us informed."

WEDNESDAY, JULY 11, ABOARD USS *AUGUSTA*

HENRY READ THE MAP ROOM message.

> *US Secy of Navy: over 17,000 Japanese planes obliterated*
> *since Pearl Harbor.*

Henry thought, *What will it take to make the Japanese realize they can't win this war they started?*

FRIDAY, JULY 13, ABOARD USS *AUGUSTA*, PRESIDENT'S CABIN

HENRY ANSWERED THE KNOCK WITH "Please, come in."

Secretary of State Byrnes entered, followed by Colonel Graham. Both men were beaming.

Graham spoke first. "Mr. President, we have intercepted another Japanese telegram sent to their embassy in Switzerland. Tokyo is again seeking Soviet mediation. An attempt to persuade Washington to moderate its demand for unconditional surrender."

Byrnes added, "And a second source thinks the emperor arranged for the message. We suspect Hirohito may be ready to go around Suzuki's military brass. When we see Stalin at Potsdam, we will ask him how Russia handles the requests."

⊰ —— ⊱

ABOARD USS *AUGUSTA*, OFF THE WHITE CLIFFS OF DOVER

A BLUE, CLOUDLESS SKY ROSE above the wall of chalk, occasionally lined with flint. Henry put his hands on the ship's rail, drew a deep breath of English Channel air, and let out a deep "yeah-h-h."

"Lieutenant Havins, this is one part of this voyage I didn't want to miss. But we are too faraway to see if bluebirds are flying there."

The ship's aviator looked confused.

"Bob, I'm joking about the *White Cliffs of Dover* song lyrics."

Henry used both hands to tap out the melody on the ship's rail.

Now the lieutenant understood. "Yes, Mr. President, you would think the birds are flying there now. No Nazi bombers or buzz-bombs flying overhead."

Henry almost said what he thought. *But the cliffs are a small portion of the British Empire. The Brits are still fighting in the Far East. The Aussies and the Kiwi troops will go ashore with Yanks when—maybe an if—we land on Japanese soil.*

"Well, Lieutenant, I hope we will not have to wait too much longer."

SUNDAY, JULY 15, ANTWERP

WHEN HENRY WALKED DOWN THE gangway, he found General Dwight Eisenhower waiting. Ike smiled and saluted.

Henry returned the salute and thought, *He's impressive. We need this fellow to run on the Democrat ticket three years from now.*

Byrnes would be in my C-54 plane's cabin for their three-and-a-half hour flight to Berlin, Henry reflected. *Maybe good time to put a bee in his bonnet that the Democrats could "Like Ike." Not too soon to let Jimmy realize he has yet to get my support for his presidential run.*

BERLIN, ABOARD THE *SACRED COW*

THE *SACRED COW* DESCENDED TO the Berlin airport. From his airplane window, Henry could see roofless, bombed-out buildings. The drive to the suburban movie colony district brought the destruction into closer focus. Entire blocks were flattened. Rubble that bulldozers had pushed into piles surrounded stumps of trees. Blackened dirt mixed with shattered concrete along Berlin streets.

When his limousine passed into the Potsdam suburb, Henry noted the mansions still stood, but were in need of repair. Yet the Russian mansion, where he was told they would hold their conference, looked pristine. The walls were freshly painted and blooming flowers were planted.

BERLIN, RUINED FRENCH CHATEAU

HENRY'S LETTER TO MAUDE THAT night told her about the differences in housing.

Honey,

All we Americans are staying in a ruined French chateau. Somebody suggested calling our housing The Berlin White House. More realistic to call it the Yellow White House. The building is painted a dirty yellow and red.

I'm told that the Russians stripped this place before we got here. Didn't even leave a teaspoon. An American commander caught the Russian looters, and recovered a bunch of the furniture. Nothing matches, like this birdseye maple wardrobe and an oak chest in my bedroom.

Big need for you and Margaret to fix up this place. Though it's probably better you continue to see our White House spruced up.

If anyone in Knox calls our brick house the Red White House, smack 'em.

Meanwhile, as they say on the radio cowboy serials, we will do what we came to do: get out of Potsdam as soon as we can.

Really missing you tonight.

Hugs and Kisses, Henry.

CHAPTER 22

MONDAY, JULY 16, BERLIN, PRESIDENT'S POTSDAM QUARTERS

THE BRITISH PRIME MINISTER KEPT his eleven o'clock in the morning appointment with the American president. They joined hands and smiled.

It's like we have known each other for years, Henry thought.

Henry commented that despite numerous trans-Atlantic phone calls, surprisingly, they had never met in person.

"Mr. President, my daughter is even more surprised. She told me she can't remember in the last four years when I met an appointment this early," Churchill said. "As for Stalin, Uncle Joe was supposed to be here today, but his people say he's on a train somewhere between here and Moscow. We could start conferring tonight. After you tour Berlin, would you do me the honor of dining at my Potsdam residence?"

BERLIN, PRESIDENTIAL MOTORCADE

HENRY SAT IN THE OPEN-AIR Lincoln convertible alongside Byrnes and Leahy. He reviewed the Second Armored Division that lined the Berlin street, deployed for his inspection. Behind the vehicles Henry saw rows of buildings ruined by British and American bombers.

He asked the motorcade to stop outside Number 2 Kaiserstrasse. An Army captain who commanded that area was assigned to accompany the president as he walked through the ruin.

"Mr. President, I know this area well. Big black market here. Lots of pretty ladies. I can send someone to share that big chateau with you."

Henry bristled. "I don't run around on my wife, and she doesn't run around on me. That will be all, captain."

Before Henry returned to his limousine, he confronted the officer-in-charge. "Don't want to know his name. But see he's shipped to, say, China-Burma Theater. Don't fly him; send him cross Asia the slow way. Make sure that captain is out of here by noon tomorrow."

❧——❧

POTSDAM, CHURCHILL RESIDENCE

"MR. PRESIDENT, MY PEOPLE IN Washington have forewarned me. I'm told you prefer fruit juice to drink, instead of alcohol, when toasts are in order."

Henry lowered his eyes and thought how to answer. "Prime Minster, I also secured some preliminary information about you. Found out we are both Scouters. I organized the first troop in my farmland town and am somewhat versed in the history and words of your countryman, Sir Baden-Powell."

Churchill interrupted, "Henry, I recall that as a young newsman, as I know you once were, I telegraphed back to London some of Baden-Powell's words when I was reporting the Boer War."

Schricker grinned. "And I recall, Winston, that Powell was a teetotaler who kept and offered a glass of spirits to his guests."

Churchill beamed. "That's true. And I might add, a non-smoker who always offered a cigar to his guests. I'm told you do enjoy a cigar."

"Yes indeed. When my Starke County company of state militia gathered for our smokers before the first war, Captain Schricker passed out the first cigars."

Churchill reached inside his coat and pulled out two cigars. "Then allow me to pass out fine Cuban cigars for the first, Potsdam smoker. And I did bring my clipper." Churchill produced the device and handed it to Schricker.

The two heads-of-state lighted their cigars. With a deep inhale and a generous puff, the two men blew cigar smoke into the room. Henry watched the clouds, thinking ahead. *When we meet, would Stalin be blowing smoke? Or did Roosevelt and Churchill strike a deal that Stalin will honor?*

Will Russia declare war on Japan, as Stalin has agreed?

⚜ — ⚜

TUESDAY, JULY 17, POTSDAM, PRESIDENT'S OFFICE

SECRETARY OF WAR STIMSON BRUSHED by greetings at the door of the president's aged mansion. Stimson beamed and laid the cable paper on the president's desk. "We did it. It's what we have been waiting for."

PRIORITY

WAR 33556

TOP SECRET

URGENT

FOR COLONEL KYLES EYES ONLY. FROM HARRISON.

FOR MR. STIMSON

OPERATED ON THIS MORNING. DIAGNOSIS NOT YET COMPLETE.

BUT RESULTS SEEM SATISFACTORY AND ALREADY EXCEED EXPECTATIONS.

LOCAL PRESS RELEASE NECESSARY AS INTEREST EXTENDS GREAT DISTANCE.

DR. GROVE PLEASED.

HE RETURNS TOMORROW. I WILL KEEP YOU POSTED.

Henry clapped his hands and grabbed Stimson by the shoulders.

Henry knew that George Harrison was the acting chairman of the Interim Committee while Stimson was in Germany. And "Dr. Grove" was General Grove, director of the Manhattan Project.

Great distance, Henry thought. *We'll find out how far when I get secret details later today.*

The Map Room officer brought another message.

> *Local press release: Explosion attracted enough attention. Public statement by the Army that an ammunition dump had accidentally exploded.*

Henry thought, *This time, Franklin, I'm not the last to know. Now comes the biggest decision.*

He read, a third time, the petition directed to the President of the United States.

Henry thought, *These nuclear scientists—well, not all of them, Oppenheimer didn't sign—want only a demonstration of an atomic bomb because people are not aware of what may affect welfare of nations in near future.*

Henry thought about their wording, *"fateful decision whether or not to sanction the use of such bombs." Fate, like the jury determines the fate.*

They're making the presidency some power that predetermines the chance of world destruction. They need to understand that the people are aware of war in the Pacific. Their boys are there.

Henry ran his hand across the desk and rested his fingers on the paperweight he brought in his briefcase, type wrapped in tape that would print *Abide with Me*.

⊰——⊱

A FEW MINUTES BEFORE NOON, Henry looked up from his desk, and there stood Stalin.

The Russian reached across the desk to shake hands.

Henry smiled, but he remembered what Harry Hopkins had told him: *Hands as hard as his mind.* Henry recalled the Stalin biographical facts he had read and committed to memory: height of 5 feet 5, crippled left arm from a childhood accident, gold star over left breast pocket, born in Georgia in 1879, mother wanted him to become a priest, studied a while for the ministry but chose a military career, Kremlin complexion with an indoor pallor, irregular and tobacco-stained teeth.

As Stalin accepted the invitation to sit, he lit a cigarette. Hopkins had told Henry that the Russian General gestured with his right hand only while usually holding a cigarette.

Charles "Chip" Bohlen had followed the Premier Stalin into the room. Chip translated, as he would for most of the conference meetings. "And Premier Stalin thinks you should be the presiding officer at the conference."

Henry was not surprised. *I'm the only elected head of a nation,* he thought. *Churchill is in the midst of an election. Stalin is named by the Politburo, even though he controls that group.*

Stalin left after he delivered another ham-fisted farmer's handshake. He had repeated his promise to join the war against the Japanese.

"Chip, what do you make of his promise to fight the Japanese?"

"Mr. President, I believe he means what he said. But he may intend to concentrate his forces in Manchuria, the Soviet east end of the Trans-Pacific Railway. Intelligence tells us Russian troops are already massing there. As for his mid-August entry prediction, I think we best not count on that. You can bet that Joe Stalin knows of our invasion plans. He's cunning. He will let us take the losses while he adds Manchuria and Korea to the Soviet Empire."

Henry nodded. *Afraid Bohlen's got that promise figured right.*

"Mr. President, you can be sure Stalin knows how to keep a secret. I've just found out he arrived by train the night before you arrived. It's a thousand miles to the Kremlin, and nobody reported seeing his railroad car go by."

AT 3:30 IN THE AFTERNOON Stimson brought the special courier report from General Groves to the president.

Henry had Byrnes and General Marshall Leahy summoned to his office. Then the doors were closed.

Stimson took nearly an hour to read to them.

Henry tried to keep the facts organized in his head. Stimson had suggested, firmly, that no notes be taken. Grove's report was extensive and celebratory. What you would expect from a story shared with few for three years?

> *No evidence Hitler learned how to make an atomic bomb. German scientists had failed with "heavy water" they developed in Norway.*

> *The blast had been terrific. An enormous column of flame and smoke shot up to the highest clouds. Devastation inside a mile wide circle was absolute.*

Henry wondered if this bomb could end the second world war. How many lives would it save on both sides compared to an all nations invasion? He had been briefed on the planned assault upon the homeland of Japan. It would involve intensive air bombing, shelling from the sea, and an invasion by very large armies. There was no reason to expect anything less than desperate resistance from the Japanese. Their highly trained and dedicated Samurai had a devotion to their death, like the battles pitched on Okinawa island.

Henry wondered, *How many thousands of Japanese, rather than surrender, would draw up in line and destroy themselves by hand-grenades after their leader had performed the rite of hara-kiri?*

To conquer the country yard by yard might well require the loss of a million American lives and half that number of British— even more losses from fanatic Japanese civilians.

Or could we end the whole war with one or two violent shocks. The courageous Japanese people might find in the apparition of this almost supernatural weapon an excuse which would save their honor and release them from their obligation to be killed to the last fighting man and woman. No need for the Russians to pour in their armies for the final and perhaps protracted slaughter. We had no need to ask favors of them.

If the United States didn't desire Russia to war against Japan, European problems could be faced on their merits and according to the broad principles of the United Nations. From some British,

Henry had already heard that to stop the butchery, and end the war, would be a miracle of deliverance. From the Americans in the room, the president heard a resounding agreement to employ the atomic bomb against a Japanese target already selected.

Secretary of War Stimson finished his presentation. "As General Grove concludes, 'the real goal is still before us'. He messages, 'the battle test is what counts.' He waits our approval to use this nuclear bomb."

Henry nodded. "Yes, and this accomplishment gives us new confidence. Henry Stimson, I thought this conference would be too much for your health. But I'm glad you decided to come on your own."

HENRY PENNED HIS NOTE TO Maude.

Honey,

I miss you even more now that I've got moved into my sleeping quarters. This note should reach you by your bedtime.

Big event today. Met Stalin. Spent two hours with him. Like his handshake. Think we can find areas of agreement.

Maude, wish you were here.

Love and Kisses, Henry

Henry leaned back from his desk. He wished he could tell Maude and the world, that he had accomplished one of his objectives for this meeting. Stalin would fight the Japanese. Instead he went to his office door, beckoned the waiting communications officer, and thanked him for sending his note on to Washington.

WEDNESDAY, JULY 18, POTSDAM, LITTLE WHITE HOUSE, PRESIDENTIAL OFFICE

HENRY DECIDED NOT TO WAIT until his bedtime. He had yet to read more dispatches on his desk.

Henry wrote,

> *Maude,*
>
> *We held our first plenary session today. I presided. Stalin suggested yesterday I chair the conference.*
>
> *We, the United States, made public our support for fair elections in Poland. We'll see if we can agree on other matters.*
>
> *Back in my office. It's been a busy day.*
>
> *Love you, always. Henry*

Henry handed the note to the sergeant. "Thank you, sergeant, for sending the message back to Washington. I understand this copy will probably reach my wife before she goes to bed."

HENRY READ THE NEWS DELIVERED from the Potsdam Map Room. The newspaper summary didn't surprise Henry.

> *Hero's reception for General Eisenhower in Washington. He commanded three million men in Europe. Addresses joint session of Congress.*

Henry hoped Bill Shaw, Harry Hopkins, Sam Rayburn, and some of the other bosses in the Democratic mule-like party got the message. *Let's run Ike, not against him.* Ike was born in Abilene, Kansas, so at least the Kansas Dems should like him, Henry figured.

CHAPTER 23

THE LETTER TO MAUDE WAS longer than usual. But today had been busy.

> Saw Omar Bradley who is going to take over the veteran's bureau. We got the flag raised over the U.S. sector of Berlin. Then we held our official Potsdam dinner. Know you will want to know how that went.

> Pretty well, I think. Staff served a wine Stalin praised. Told it was a well-known claret. Spelled it for me: Mouton d'Armailhacq. Also Pommery champagne, 1934. This old editor can spell celery, lettuce, tomatoes, and ice cream…all flown in from the USS Augusta, still berthed at Antwerp.

> Got some spelling for the local pate de foie gras, but can handle rest: caviar on toast, vodka, and cream of tomato soup. Perch with saute meuniere, filet mignon with mushroom gravy, shoestring potatoes, lettuce and tomato salad, French dressing, Roca cheese, vanilla ice cream, chocolate sauce, and demi-tasse.

*Maude, made me think of that old World War I song
that talks about keeping the boys in the country when
they've seen and eaten in these big European cities.*

*And, oh yes, we put on a floor show with the dinner.
Three nurses came from our base in Frankfurt and
performed their imitation of the Andrews Sisters.
Brought their own band and piano player. I could have
played some tunes, but didn't.*

*Russians laughed and also clapped their hands when the
ladies sang repeat verses of Deep in the Heart of Texas.*

*So you can relive some of my "doings" at Potsdam, I am
keeping a journal to bring home to you. Some notes that
can wait and not clutter our trans-Atlantic messages.*

*Churchill will leave us, go home to get the results of
the British election. It looks like we will not finish here
before August.*

Love you, always, Henry

After he finished the note to Maude, Henry made notes to the printed menu and used a paper clip to insert in his journal. Henry thought, *Mom will want to second-guess our printed menu.*

SATURDAY, JULY 21, POTSDAM, YELLOW WHITE HOUSE

HENRY MET WITH HIS MILITARY chiefs to hear the good news: they won the battle for Okinawa. Sadly, there was still bad news: America reported 6,900 men killed or missing and nearly 30,000 wounded. And the commanding general was shot and killed. The Japanese casualties were about 95,000. General Stilwell was placed in command of the Tenth Army, which conquered Okinawa.

Henry met with his diplomatic advisers. They were confident Stalin wanted to recognize the former German satellite nations of Romania, Bulgaria, and Finland. But not confident that it was wise to recognize those governments until they were satisfactorily set up.

As for Poland, Moscow-directed Poles had no right to seize German territory. They had to decide if they were going to maintain occupied zones or give them away to Germany piecemeal?

Later that day, Henry dined with Stalin. He ate little and drank only juice. But they did make more progress. Stalin reiterated Russian's promise of support against Japan.

Henry read the transcript. The United States direct appeal by radio told Japanese listeners to quit war or face total destruction. Though Franklin's unconditional surrender resonated in Europe more than it did in Japan, Henry still had hope it might work.

Dear Maude,

Today was our first three-hour meeting with Churchill and Stalin. Pretty tiring.

Relaxed with a little piano playing for Leahy and Byrnes. We harmonized on "Old Mill Stream" pretty good.

First I attended our protestant services then went to the Catholic mass 11:30 am. We need all help the Holy Father can give.

MONDAY, JULY 23, POTSDAM, PRESIDENT'S OFFICE

MAP ROOM LIEUTENANT WISCH DELIVERED the report.

One thousand carrier-based planes drop fire bombs on Nagoya and Osaka. Over 600 B-29's blast Japanese naval base at Kure.

Henry thought, *If this destruction doesn't convince the Japanese to surrender, will one or two more powerful bombs make them surrender?*

⅜ — ⅝

Dear Maude,

Well, honey, the battle of the banquets goes on. Tonight was Churchill's banquet, and his people brought the string orchestra of the Royal Air Force to entertain us.

Best number was Freire's "Mexican Serenade" Ay-ay-ay.

We had a choice of cold clear soup or hot turtle soup, along with a 1937 Hallgartener Riesling. (Yes, reading off the printed menu that I will clip into my Diary and bring home.)

Next course was fried sole. What Churchill called "good plain fare. Told me that was his personal choice.

Then roast chicken, oiled new potatoes, new peas.

Apologized for wines. Said 1940 Saint-Julian vines suffered wartime neglect, two stars according to some wine expert—and that wasn't the Lord of the Manor at 401 South Main Street, Knox, Indiana.

Dinner ended with sappers (what the British called these enlisted men) serving as waiters, who brought in Scotch woodcock served hot. The custom in Victorian age, we were told

Scrambled eggs, cayenne pepper, and Gentleman's Relish on buttered toast, with anchovies crossed over the top.

Accompanied by Stokes port, Prunier Brandy.

And, yes, something in which this teetotaler could debauch, cigars from Havana.

If you get the idea that one country tries to outdo the other, you're right on.

Love, kisses, and a footnote.

There are a bunch of gamebirds flying around nearby Bass Lake that taste just as good as woodcock, maybe better.

Henry

TUESDAY, JULY 24, POTSDAM, YELLOW WHITE HOUSE

CHURCHILL WAS SILENT, HENRY NOTICED, and looked a little sleepy. Of course, 11:30 in the morning was early for a prime minister who usually started business after lunch.

Maybe he isn't confident about the election in England. We did have to put this conference on hold while Churchill flew to London for final mail-in returns. Or Winston is feeling slighted. Henry thought. *He and Franklin had already made the nuclear decision. Or he is listening, deferring to our chiefs of staff. Or, the decision is now mine.*

Henry repeated the conclusion. "Gentlemen, unless there is some unforeseen development, the bomb will be used within a few weeks. We have given our chiefs of staff authority to start preparations to use what General Groves calls 'the device' against targets already selected by our Interim Committee."

❦———❦

JOINT CONFERENCE, RUSSIAN MANSION

HENRY HAD WAITED FOR THIS recess moment. He walked casually to where Joe Stalin and his interpreter were standing away from the large conference table. He smiled at both. He turned, so his back shielded his conversation from others, but knew that Churchill and Byrnes were watching.

"Please tell Stalin that we have a new weapon of unusual destructive force."

Stalin listened to his interpreter, showed no emotion, and replied in Russian.

The interpreter turned to Henry. "Mr. President, we're glad to hear it. We hope you can make good use of it against the Japanese."

❦———❦

PRESIDENTIAL QUARTERS

HENRY REPORTED THE RUSSIAN INTERPRETER'S answer from Stalin.

Secretary of State Byrnes repeated his position. "I still think we should reveal to the Russians as little as possible. If Stalin were made fully aware of the power of the new weapon, he might order the Soviet Army to plunge forward at once."

Henry responded, "Don't you think we need protective cover when Stalin learns his wartime allies developed an epochal new weapon behind his back?"

"He wouldn't tell us. Probably pity us for our diplomatic weakness," Stimson said. "There's a high probability the Russians were informed about the Trinity test anyway, by liberal European scientists on the project. General Grove confided to me they might have to arrest some scientists who talked too much."

⚜——⚜

POTSDAM, MAP ROOM

THE LIEUTENANT READ THE INFORMATION from Washington. Sato telegraphed from Switzerland that Japan "was entirely alone and friendless." No option but to surrender on any terms available. Tokyo replied that unconditional surrender was out of the question, and that Japan must fight on.

Secretary of State Byrnes needed that information. Even at this late hour.

⚜——⚜

WEDNESDAY, JULY 25, FRANKFURT, PRESIDENTIAL QUARTERS

HENRY READ THE MAP ROOM report.

Tokyo radio broadcasts appeal for terms less severe than unconditional surrender.

Henry shook his head. Remembered conditions that Great Britain, China, and the U.S. had laid down in the Cairo Declaration in November of 1943.

Japan would be reduced to its home islands. War criminals were to be brought to justice. Japan was to be occupied. Henry wondered if they allowed Japan to keep their emperor if would surrender.

Henry had arranged for his letter to Maude to be delivered to Washington through Frankfurt Army communications.

Maude,

Writing you from Frankfurt. Have been seeing our troops here while the British go home to wind up their election.

Reminded of that Kipling Recessional poem "The captains and the kings depart." Well Churchill stayed just long enough to get his picture taken with Stalin and me. When you see it, that's me in the middle, crossed arms, holding hands with both of them.

⊰ —— ⊱

THURSDAY, JULY 26, POTSDAM

WAR DEPARTMENT REPORT.:

Cruiser Indianapolis delivered new explosives to Tinian Islan.

A smiling communications officer brought more news. "Mr. President, we've received a remarkable message from one of our submarines operating in the Sea of Japan. Maybe our first landing of U.S. military on Japanese soil."

Henry raised his eyebrows and gave a hand signal to continue.

"Here's the report in full." Lieutenant Wisch handed the typed paper to Henry.

DAILY SCUTTLEBUTT X BARB REPORTS SINKING ONE FRIGATE AND BLOWING UP ONE CHOO CHOO TRAIN WITH LANDING PARTY AND OWN DEMOLITION TEAM PUT ASHORE X

Henry laughed. "Lieutenant, has Admiral Leahy seen this dispatch?"

"Not yet, sir."

"Then, I presume I may pass along to the admiral when I see him later today."

"Of course, sir."

"And, perhaps, you could bring me a map showing the location and additional information. Your President may have to invent a new citation for a submarine crew that sinks a train."

"Mr. President, there was more on their radio report. The crew sang a short song *Down in the Valley.*

Henry smiled. Atop his desk he fingered out the tune.

◆——◆

POTSDAM, PRESIDENTIAL QUARTERS

HENRY REREAD THE POTSDAM DECLARATION that would be released to the press later today.

Following are our terms. We will not deviate from them. There are no alternatives. We shall make no delay.

- *Japan to be reduced to home islands.*

- *War criminals to be brought to justice.*

- *Japan to be occupied.*

There must be eliminated for all times the authority and the influence of those who have deceived and misled the people of Japan into embarking on world conquest.

Conditions to give Japan an opportunity to end this war:

- *Limit Japanese sovereignty to four mainland islands.*

- *Disarm Japanese military forces, allow members opportunity to return to their homes with opportunity to lead peaceful and productive lives.*

- *No intention to enslave or destroy the nation, but we will mete out stern justice to all war criminals.*

- *Japan would maintain such industries as will sustain her economy.*

Occupying Allied forces will withdraw from Japan as soon as these objectives have been accomplished, and a peacefully inclined and responsible government has been established.

We call upon the government of Japan to proclaim now the unconditional surrender of all Japanese forces. The alternative for Japan is prompt and utter destruction.

CHAPTER 24

FRIDAY, JULY 27, TOKYO, JAPAN

J APANESE RADIO HAD PICKED UP the Potsdam Declaration. A cabinet member asked Prime Minister Kautora Suzuki how Japan should respond.

He answered, "Ignore it. Nothing but a rehash of old proposals. Kill it with silence."

POTSDAM, PRESIDENTIAL QUARTERS

COLONEL GRAHAM HAD DECIDED THAT he, not one of his junior Map Room officers, should inform the president.

"Mr. President, the cruiser named for your Indiana capitol was sunk by a Japanese submarine in the Philippine Sea.

Henry shook his head at the news. "Tell me more details."

"Yes, sir. After the *Indianapolis* delivered needed parts to Tinian for the *Manhattan Project,* she was steaming for the Philippines when a Japanese submarine torpedoed and sunk her. Crew members were discovered gathered in the water. Many were attacked and killed by sharks. We are asking Manila for more information."

Henry bowed his head. "Thank you, Colonel Graham. Please keep me informed about developments."

⁜ —— ⁜

SUNDAY, JULY 29, POTSDAM, PRESIDENTIAL QUARTERS

SECRETARY OF STATE BYRNES REPORTED to the president. "The good news. We have made a deal on Poland. Russians—who said they were supporting the Poles—get only a portion of Germany they conquered."

Henry liked that news. *My Schricker homeland will remain in Germany.*

"But, bad news. Japan has formally rejected our surrender ultimatum."

Lieutenant Ridgeon's frown lengthened as he handed Henry the first report.

Japan formally rejects surrender ultimatum.

Henry nodded. But the second news bulletin was unexpected.

Empire State Building struck at 78-79 floors by B-25 bomb.

Henry shook his head in disbelief. *One of our pilot's error. Struck him that this kind of an attack on a New York skyscraper that could have happened if the Nazis had defeated Britain, early on, and sent their warships to blockade our Eastern seaboard. Or landed saboteurs to steal and fly one of our warplanes.*

⁜ —— ⁜

MONDAY, JULY 30, POTSDAM, OUTSIDE PRESIDENT SCHRICKER'S QUARTERS

HENRY TOOK A DEEP BREATH. *Early morning air,* he thought. *Best time to walk whether in Bavaria, Potsdam, or Knox.* He searched for his customary Army walking partner. *Wait a minute. That's a Navy officer holding a briefcase and waiting for me?*

"Good morning, Mr. President," the Navy man said. "I'm Lieutenant David Winton. May I join you in your morning walk?"

Henry took a look. The naval officer was a handsome chap with high cheekbones that lengthened his smile. He looked a lot like Robert Walker from the movies, but looks older than the ensigns that he met on the USS *Augusta.*

"Of course, lieutenant. But I'm surprised the Army assigned the Navy to convoy me."

Lieutenant Winton's smile broadened even wider. "They didn't, sir. But General Donovan of the OSS suggested I might complete his promise to tell you about our successful newspaper operation in Germany. I confess. I used General Donovan's pull to get the honor of accompanying you on your constitutional."

Whoa, Henry thought. *Wild Bill said he wanted to tell me about his newspaper with large circulation. That was over two months ago. Now his man follows up. A secret agent? Not what I would expect in a Navy uniform.*

Henry started walking. Winton's longer legs, easily matched the president's stride.

"Mr. President, I don't know how many people bought your *Starke County Democrat* back in the 1910s. We started dropping our daily newspaper behind the German army lines in 1944. By spring of 1945 our circulation was over two million. The RAF dropped one edition at night. The American 8th dropped an edition in the daytime."

Ensign Winton pulled four copies of the newspaper and handed them to Henry.

Henry stopped walking and looked at the newspapers. Then handed them back before he turned to walk back to his quarters.

"Mr. President, we made no secret that the Allies produced this newspaper. This paper was not a black undertaking. Its Allied origin was no secret to it recipients. On the other hand, it was not strictly speaking official Allied propaganda. Nowhere on any of its pages does anything indicate that it was not published in Germany. British Political Intelligence organized much of the output, and—"

Henry interrupted. "Explain something. You said two million daily circulation. But how many readers? And how would you know?"

"Good question, Mr. President. We used prisoner interrogations to measure the success of our project. They were dejected. Hopeless. And they said daily receipt of this newspaper convinced them they were losing. Also, one general on the western front admitted he looked at our daily maps—he complained the newspapers fell on his headquarters before breakfast—to see where the Russians had advanced on the eastern front."

Henry thought, *Lieutenant Winton doesn't need to tell me that the Nazi general desperately wanted to surrender to Allies, not Russian troops. Stopping our troops from crossing the Elbe may have been good for Russian relations, but not for the Germans. Reluctantly approved by a concerned Churchill.*

Henry would never feel comfortable about turning Germans, of which he was a descendant, over to the Communists.

Winton noted another reader. "A German western front general officer said he knew only of the Russian successes and the great pincers around Germany from the daily situation map appearing in *Nachrichten*, which means—"

"News," Henry translated.

Winton stopped. Turned to face the smiling son of German emigrants. "Of course, you know the word. Forgive me for forgetting my own research on your career, Mr. President. I was happy to discover that you were involved in the insurance business. I was an insurance broker on Wall Street when we entered the war. General Donovan knew my boss. He recruited me for his OSS and sent me to England to work with the British in counter-intelligence. I was given a direct commission."

Henry grinned. *Atlee, and I bet Wild Bill recruited you to sell me on his civilian, counter-intelligence agency proposal.*

"And like you, Mr. President, I'm the father of a daughter. Two, actually, identical twins named Priscilla and Diana. And someday, they'll be proud of their old man when I tell them President Schricker took me on his walk."

Henry offered his hand. "Mr. Winton, I will commend you to General Donovan when he and I next meet. Also I will tell him that you discovered a shared previous business interest, selling insurance. You made a fine sales pitch, that is, to keep a civilian counter-intelligence agency as insurance counterweight to military intelligence and the FBI. Not that your pitch was too blunt. But I caught the comparison. Convey my best to your wife and daughters. Enjoyed the walk, David."

⊰ — ⊱

POTSDAM, PRESIDENTIAL QUARTERS.

SECRETARY OF THE NAVY JAMES Forrestal came to breakfast. Henry enjoyed their discussion of universal military training and Forrestal made a strong case for the Navy's preparatory academies.

Henry thought, *Don't think we need to sell preparedness insurance to this secretary.*

General Eisenhower introduced Henry to his son. Henry was impressed.

Hope he doesn't grow up thinking the military should be served, rather than serving, Henry thought.

Ike understood how to defer to others, Henry reflected, and knew-first hand the needs of Europe. He knew the principal leaders of the free world, knew how to organize, and had a mind trained to mobilize.

We need him on our ticket, Henry thought, *not campaigning against us.*

His secretary of state didn't bother to knock on the half-opened door. James Byrnes entered, looking a bit shell-shocked.

"Not sure, I can believe this, Henry. Churchill lost the election!"

Henry thought, *I'm surprised also. Now it's Atlee, Stalin, and me.*

"What's even more unexpected is that apparently, Winston lost when the soldiers mail-in ballots were delivered for the final counting. He thought he was cheered as a warrior, a bulldog. Looks like the bulldog bit him."

TUESDAY, JULY 31, POTSDAM, PRESIDENTIAL QUARTERS

HENRY WAITED FOR SECRETARY OF State Byrnes, and Secretary of War Stimson to take sips from their coffee.

"Thank you for meeting this early," Henry said. "Of course, like you, I want the Japanese to surrender. The alternatives, an invasion or a starvation blockade, will kill many more people. Secretary Stimson, as your man McLeod suggested over a month ago, I think we all agree that we will let the Japanese keep their emperor, but only as a figurehead. You saw the petition from the scientists who have suggested we drop a demonstration bomb. And you heard General Grove's concerns that some European nuclear scientists at Los Alamos have already shared our nuclear research with a foreign power. Also the Air Corps general who will send our planes urges the drop of a demonstration bomb on Tokyo Bay.

"You will recall that at our Interim Committee meeting over a month ago, I asked for opinions from the scientists on our committee about alternative targets. I asked, what if we drop a bomb on a Japanese volcano? Or into the water. That could happen if the B-29 had to ditch into the Pacific. If I get a response, I'm afraid it will come too late to be of any consideration. We should also note two other generals with contrary opinions. Both Eisenhower and MacArthur oppose using a nuclear device that they say is a too-powerful addition to warfare. They argue that if the incendiaries already dropped on Tokyo and other targets haven't moved the Japanese to surrender, a larger bomb won't bring surrender either."

Henry turned to his Secretary of War. "Well, Secretary Stimson, I haven't forgotten when you and General Grove first informed me of the Manhattan Project. The recent explosion in New Mexico settled one fear. We don't have to explain to Congress and the American people why we invested all of that money in a bomb that didn't work. But I have heard arguments that we should not contemplate using an atomic device except in retaliation."

Henry thought, *The only two countries left that could match our production capacity are Japan and Russia. Our B-29s are destroying Japanese manufacturing. And we have to send additional arms to Russia. Will defer to Hopkins for an appraisal of the Russian's ability to build a nuclear bomb.*

He scanned the two faces before he spoke. "If the Japanese will not accept our proclamation for surrender, our departed president and the deposed prime minister have left this president with a nuclear alternative. The moment for our historical decision has arrived.

Henry read aloud his copy of the top-secret cable from Washington. "The time schedule on Grove's project is progressing so rapidly that it is now essential that a statement for release by you be available no later than Wednesday, August 1.

"I have answered Grove's request. With a lead pencil I wrote a large and clear answer on the back of that pink paper: "Request approved. Release when ready, but not sooner than August 2. Then I handed the pink paper to the Map Room Commander who has now transmitted my approval back to Washington."

The secretary of state asked, "Why August 2? That's Thursday. Two days away.

Henry didn't want a longer delay. "You need to mobilize your people to get the conference closed by Thursday. No staying for celebration. If Japan doesn't surrender, I will order we drop the second atomic bomb on the next selected target. Let's get your president back in Washington, or steaming that way before one of our B-29s turns the world upside down."

President Henry F. Schricker made a silent prayer. *And may God have mercy on our souls.*

⚜ — ⚜

POTSDAM, PRESIDENTIAL QUARTERS

HENRY KNOTTED HIS TIE, TURNED to the secretary of state. "Okay, Jimmy. Before we go over to the plenary session at the Russian mansion, school me. What did we give up? Where are you in agreement with Molotov? And what are our sticking points? And what do I say to Atlee? I see your Labour party sold the English on more government, not less? Don't think so."

Byrnes laughed. "I guess congratulations will suffice for Atlee.

Henry wrinkled his forehead. "Wish the Russians were that easy."

Secretary of State Byrnes leaned forward, put one hand on his knee, and raised fingers on the other hand as he counted off. "Henry, one, I think we had to give up the German territory in Poland that the Russians already command. Two, we agreed to give some limited recognition to their regimes in Romania, Hungary, and Bulgaria." Byrnes closed his fist. "But I got Molotov to give up on reparations. No money. No Russian involvement in the Ruhr."

Henry returned the smile.

⚜ — ⚜

WASHINGTON, D.C., WHITE HOUSE, PRESS ROOM

MIKE QUINN REREAD THE *NEW York Times* editorial. Sheryl Lee waited, notepad in hand.

"Sheryl, here's a sentence the president will enjoy. Let's add this quote to the press summary I will give HFS when I see him in Norfolk:

> *And the further fact that the United States not only played the decisive role in the victory, but that its president also presided over the conference to gather its fruits, has put a particularly large share of responsibility on America.*

Quinn handed the marked page to his assistant. "Wouldn't be surprised if the old editor doesn't say something about particularly. He's got a thing about adverbs. Says he wants to stamp out the Tom Swifties. And Sheryl, when you go back to your office, tell Dennis to see me about newsreel coverage next week."

CHAPTER 25

FRIDAY, AUGUST 3, KNOX, INDIANA, 401 SOUTH MAIN STREET

MAUDE AND MARGARET LISTENED.
A little dab of Beryl cream will do you.
Maude turned off the radio. "Well, my Princess Margaret, when your dad met King George's Princess Elizabeth, she wanted his autograph."

Margaret laughed. "When you see Pops next week tell him I also wanted his autograph when I was twelve years old: his signature on a check."

Maude grinned. "Come help me pack to fly back to Washington tomorrow."

USS *AUGUSTA*, PRESIDENTIAL QUARTERS

THE MEMBERS OF THE PRESS corps gathered about the small coffee table to hear the president.

"What I am going to tell you, soon all the world will know. But I'm alerting you, because you have been cleared for top secret information. That's why the military put you through so much questioning and background checking. It's likely that before the *Augusta* returns us to Norfolk, our B-29 planes may drop the first, ever, nuclear explosive on a military target in Japan. Here are the details ..."

SATURDAY, AUGUST 4, USS *AUGUSTA*

HENRY HAD HIS SEA LEGS back. His morning, and now sunset, walk around the ship with Lieutenant Havins was bracing. Henry was feeling positive.

This walk gets me ready to read all the messages delivered to my cabin. And I've got time to read. His time was usually spent dictating, answering the press, talking to congressmen, and making speeches. *It's getting difficult to squeeze in time for Maude and my family. Last time I played the organ was back in the spring at Luther Place.*

Merriman Smith joined Henry on his walk. "Mr. President, you know that what you told us yesterday has shaken up the other press members so much, we don't even talk about it amongst ourselves."

USS *AUGUSTA*, PRESIDENTIAL QUARTERS

HENRY WONDERED HOW MUCH INFORMATION he should enter in the diary that Maude and Margaret wanted him to keep. *And now that I have given the command to drop the first bomb, I'm just biding my time.*

Henry ran his fingers across his desk and tapped out a tune. *I recorded the radio speech, but hope there's a chance the Japanese heed our advance warning and come to the table. And what a blessing if the world never hears that recording I made before I left for Potsdam. It's a good speech. Tells the world about a nuclear weapon. Thanks to Laurence, the* New York Times *science editor, who wrote many of the technical words. General Grove hired him to handle the Manhattan Project. Bet that expenditure will get lost in the $2 billion story that's bound to come out.*

MONDAY, AUGUST 6, ABOARD USS *AUGUSTA*, MESS HALL

COLONEL GRAHAM CAME TO THE table where President Schricker and Secretary Byrnes were eating with six enlisted sailors. The Map Room Commander handed Henry a map and whispered in his ear. Henry whispered to Byrnes, jumped to his feet, his lungs expanded, and tapped his glass for attention.

"I have an announcement to make. We have just dropped a new bomb on Japan which has more power than twenty thousand tons of TNT. It has been an overwhelming success!"

The sailors cheered. Henry rushed to tell the others the news. The White House staff released the president's radio recording at 11 a.m. Washington time. Henry listened to his own voice over the ship's intercom.

The recording prompted thoughts that he wouldn't tell anyone, not even Maude. *Better I gave the go ahead to bomb one of eight Japanese cities than if I had to bomb my native Germany. Hope the tone of my recorded broadcast carries the remorse I'm feeling. The bomb worked. The nuclear age has dawned. A day I have no choice but to remember.*

Henry remembered a scientific story he once reprinted in his newspaper, a prediction now come true. At the end of World War I, the electrical genius Tesla predicted a new kind of "electrical" warfare was coming. *So prophetic. Would Tesla approve? Or did he predict an inevitable scientific development of destruction?*

The enlisted men sitting at his table had cheered. So did all aboard the ship. A few sailors yelled, "Remember Pearl Harbor!"

The daily log showed the ship's speed at 25 knots. The USS *Augusta* was returning to Norfolk at a calculated rate of 645 miles per 24 hours. Captain said the USS *Augusta* would dock tomorrow afternoon.

⇜——⇝

WASHINGTON, D.C., WHITE HOUSE PRESS OFFICE

MIKE QUINN PUT HIS STAFF to work gathering headlines to show the president. The headlines from the *New York Times* predominated.

BY GOD'S MERCY WE BEAT NAZIS TO BOMB

CHURCHILL SAYS: ROOSEVELT AID CITED

OUR RAIDERS WRECKED NORSE LABORATORY IN
RACE FOR KEY TO VICTORY

STEEL TOWER 'VAPORIZED' IN TRIAL OF
MIGHTY BOMB

SCIENTISTS AWESTRUCK AS BLINDING FLASH LIGHTED

GREAT CLOUD BORE 40,000 FEET INTO SKY

TRAINS CANCELED IN STRICKEN AREA

TRAFFIC AROUND HIROSHIMA IS DISRUPTED.

JAPANESE STILL SIFT HAVOC BY SPLIT ATOMS

ATOM BOMBS MADE IN 3 HIDDEN 'CITIES'

SECRECY ON WEAPON SO GREAT NOT EVEN
WORKERS KNEW OF THEIR PRODUCT

REICH EXILE EMERGES AS HEROINE IN DENIAL TO
NAZIS OF ATOM'S SECRET

BOMB DROPPED TINIAN TIME 0915.5

SEEN FROM ENOLA GAY: MUSHROOM CLOUD, FIRES,
FELT SHOCK WAVES.

⊰——⊱

USS *AUGUSTA*, PRESIDENTIAL CABIN

HENRY ALMOST PURRED OVER THEIR wireless connection. "Honey, I'll see you tomorrow afternoon. Colonel Watson will accompany you on the train from Washington. See you to the president's car. They say it's a three-hour ride from D.C. Boy, will I be glad to see you when the *Augusta* reaches Norfolk."

CHAPTER 26

TUESDAY, AUGUST 7, WHITE HOUSE, PRESIDENTIAL SUITE

M AUDE MOVED HER OVERNIGHT BAG near the door. She went to the dining table, reopened the *New York Times*, and finished her coffee while she read an article by Sidney Shalett.

Maude heard the knock on the door and folded the newspaper. That knock would be that redheaded Colonel Watson coming to take her to the Norfolk train.

ABOARD USS *AUGUSTA*, PRESIDENT'S CABIN

HARRY HAD JUST FINISHED FILLING his briefcase, when he answered the knock on his cabin door. "Please, come in."

Lieutenant Havins opened the door, stepped back, and waved in a tall civilian.

Henry grinned. "Mike Quinn, glad to see you. Did you bring the *Capitol Press* to Norfolk?"

Quinn nodded. "Some, Mr. President, but I'm mainly here to arrange for the newsreel people to film your return."

Henry's grin widened. He thought of the tune. "Mike, you think I ought to be in pictures?"

"Yes, sir. Cameras are set up on the dock to film you leaving the ship and walking down the gangway. Walk toward their cameras set up behind a tape barrier. Your wife is waiting in front of the tape. The Navy band is assembled to the left of the first lady. The band will play *Hail to the Chief*. Others in your Potsdam delegation will wait on board until you have stepped ashore and waved your white hat at the band and others."

Henry shook his head. "Mike, you sound like a Hollywood director. Where did the good old days go when you just passed out a typed press release?"

"Still do, Mr. President." Quinn read from the paper he carried. "You need to know that you are quoted, indirectly, as saying '...*our military is standing by long enough to allow the Japanese to recognize the power of our newest weapons. We hope and pray the Japanese will now surrender so we can begin rebuilding a world torn apart.*'"

"Mike, you put pretty good words in my mouth."

"Also, Mr. President, Admiral Leahy's staff collected quotes from other world leaders about the atomic bomb. They included letters they thought important for you to read. Colonel Watson brought those items. After you greet the first lady, Watson will escort you and Mrs. Schricker to the staff car that takes you to the railroad."

Henry smiled and gave a thumbs-up salute.

"Excuse me now, sir. I'll be ashore ahead of you. And I will be aboard one of the other railroad cars on our three-hour trip back to D.C. We have secure communications to the war office. If needed, I can also release other words to the press. Welcome home, Mr. President."

Henry conveyed his thanks to the ship's captain. He saluted the flag at the stern of the USS *Augusta*. Then he turned toward the band and saluted them, as they played *Hail to the Chief*.

His contingent of Potsdam advisers waited for Henry, with his chosen escort Lieutenant Havins, to reach the bottom of the gangway, as Quinn had suggested.

As they walked down the gangway, Henry thanked Havins. "Looking forward to flying with you next time aboard. That blast off the catapult ought to be more thrilling than any of the carnival rides at our Starke County fair."

At the bottom of the gangway, Maude waited. She stretched out her arms to Henry. He took both of her hands, pulled her close, and kissed the country doctor's daughter from Knox. *Time Marches On* cameras captured the moment.

Colonel Britt Watson kept a diplomatic pouch for Henry under his left arm. With his right arm he saluted. Henry didn't break his embrace of Maude. Instead, Lieutenant Havins returned the colonel's salute and grinned. Watson smiled back and waited until the couple was ready to walk past the newsreel camera to the staff car.

NORFOLK, VA, PRESIDENTIAL RAILROAD CAR

MAUDE LOOKED OVER HENRY'S SHOULDER. Through the train window, the Virginia farmland flashed by and faded into the dusk. The first lady watched her husband's frown deepen. *Don't ask. Henry will tell me if he wants me to know.*

Henry read the *New York Times* clipping a third time. Then he reread the English translation of the leaflet that was dropped on Japanese cities. *Wasn't there a better way than this leaflet?*

TO THE JAPANESE PEOPLE:

America asks that you take immediate heed of what we say on this leaflet. We are in possession of the most destructive explosion ever devised by man. A single one of our newly developed atomic bombs is the equivalent in explosive power to what 2000 of our giant B-29s can carry on a single mission. This awful fact is one for you to ponder and we solemnly assure you it is grimly accurate.

We have just begun to use this weapon against your homeland. If you still have any doubt, make inquiry as to what happened to Hiroshima when just one atomic bomb fell on that city.

Before using this bomb to destroy every resource of the military by which they are prolonging this useless war, we ask that you now petition the Emperor to end the war. Our president has outlined for you the thirteen consequences of an honorable surrender. We urge that you accept these consequences and begin the work of building a new, better, and peace- loving Japan.

You should take steps now to cease military resistance. Act now, otherwise, we shall resolutely employ this bomb and all our other superior weapons to promptly and forcefully end the war.

EVACUATE YOUR CITIES.
ATTENTION JAPANESE PEOPLE.
EVACUATE YOUR CITIES.

Because your military leaders have rejected the thirteen-part surrender declaration, two momentous events have occurred in the last few days.

The Soviet Union, because of this rejection on the part of the military, has notified your Ambassador Sato that it has declared war on your nation. Thus, all powerful countries of the world are now at war with you.

Also, due to your leaders' refusal to accept the surrender declaration that would enable Japan to honorably end this useless war, we have employed our atomic bomb. Radio Tokyo has told you that Hiroshima was virtually destroyed, with the first use of this weapon of total destruction.

The president pursed his lips, held back his tears. *Sodom and Gomorrah were warned, also. Oh, Lord, forgive us?*

Henry returned the papers to the diplomatic pouch. The letter from Berkeley he kept on his desk. Scolded himself for neglecting Maude.

The first lady sat nearby Henry's desk. Before he was a governor, her husband had said he didn't plan to bring his office home with him. When Henry was elected lieutenant governor, then governor, he sometimes broke his rule. The governor's mansion study became his office.

Now the office was a railroad car, and Henry had spent the last thirty minutes reading.

Maude was likely glad she had packed the latest edition of *Good Housekeeping* as well as *Colliers* and the *Saturday Evening*

Post. She had kept Henry appraised about the children while he was in Potsdam

Henry told her, "I looked forward to the letters you wrote. Most messages were waiting when I woke up. Good way to start the day."

But now Henry's long face suggested twilight was a bad time to end the day. "Maude, would you give me your reaction to something Leahy wanted me to read?"

"Sure, Henry."

Henry read from the newspaper clipping. "Here's what James Reston wrote in the *New York Times* about Hiroshima. *'Some of our scientists say that the area will be uninhabitable for many years because the bomb explosion made the ground radioactive and destructive of animal life.'* And he quotes from Leahy. Same information the admiral sent for me to read."

Henry thought, *This is the same admiral who told me he was an ordinance expert, and the bomb wouldn't work.*

"The lethal possibilities of such atomic action in the future is frightening, and while we are the first to have it in our possession, there is a certainty that it will in the future be developed by potential enemies and that it will probably be used against us."

Maude gasped, then covered her mouth with a hand.

Henry left the desk to put an arm around Maude's shoulder. "You don't need to tell me, honey. I share the same fear."

Henry went to his railroad car door. When he opened the door, he found Colonel Britt Watson and an Army sentry standing on the platform."Colonel Watson. Please follow me to my desk."

Henry took a pen from his inside jacket pocket, grabbed a piece of paper, and wrote rapidly. Finished, he capped his fountain pen and handed the paper to the colonel. "Colonel Watson, General Spaatz wants a written order. See that this presidential order gets sent immediately. Then notify Secretary Stimson, Undersecretary McCloy, General Marshall, Admiral Knox, Secretary Byrnes, and Admiral Leahy to meet with me in the White House Map Room an hour after our train reaches D.C. And add that you execute an order from Commander-in-Chief President Henry F Schricker.

"Britt, use whatever secured communications are available on this train. And as soon as we reach Washington, repeat these orders by telephone, and ask for confirmation. Request a secured confirmation from General Spaatz as well as from the members I have summoned for a war council before midnight.

"Now please read the command I have written. If not clear, tell me now."

Watson read Henry's written command and choked back a gasp. "Clear, sir. Most clear." The colonel took Henry's letter in his left hand, rose, and saluted.

Henry rose and returned the salute. When the colonel left the car, Henry smiled at the first lady. "Well, Maude, with that order we may be able to do something about limiting radioactivity."

Maude puckered him a kiss.

"But, Maude, it's a lousy homecoming when your husband goes back to work before bedtime."

❧ — ❧

WASHINGTON, D.C., WHITE HOUSE, MAP ROOM

"Thank you for coming at nearly midnight. Our Map Room hosts have served coffee. Join me." Henry raised his coffee cup to salute Secretary of War Stimson and his assistant, John McCloy, then he turned and raised his cup in a salute to Secretary of State Byrnes, General Marshall, Admiral Knox, and his Chief-of-Staff Admiral Leahy.

Henry thought, *When you're the boss, you don't have to apologize for calling a meeting. But I will.*

"Thank you for coming at this late hour. After the cruiser *Augusta* docked this afternoon, on my train ride from Norfolk, I read press reactions, and other information Admiral Leahy had gathered. He has prepared a synopsis for you, including a summary of the letter received from a nuclear scientist at Berkeley. While you drink your coffee, please read that synopsis. You who attended our target selection meetings will recall I asked our academic leaders to seek scientific opinion about possible nuclear targets."

Henry thought, *I wish this opinion had been forwarded to us in Germany before we decided to destroy Hiroshima.*

"I wanted us to meet in the Map Room, because I have asked Colonel Graham to brief us on the latest information received from inside the Emperor's Palace. And because we need maps displayed to show the second atomic bomb target I have designated."

Henry sat down his coffee cup and let his fingers tap *Onward Christian Soldiers* across the table. The wall clock said midnight.

CHAPTER 27

COLONEL GRAHAM WAITED UNTIL ALL had read the Berkeley scientist's letter, before he began his briefing. "Our intelligence source tells us the emperor is prepared to surrender. Intelligence also reports Russian troops are now massing and may already be moving into Manchuria."

Graham paused. "As you may know, not only have we broken the Japanese code, but we have a source in the Emperor's Palace whose radio signals are monitored by our submarine offshore. Our latest information from one close to Emperor Hirohito says the Russian invasion of Manchuria is now known at the palace in Tokyo. But when the emperor summoned his military men to meet, they did not respond on Monday. And when they did answer the summons— now is almost tomorrow in Japan because of their early position on the International Dateline—our intelligence reports the military still vowed to fight to their death.

"And the emperor has made no decision."

The colonel took a deep breath. "One of our interpreters thinks that the source's choice of words imply the military warlords threaten to kill the emperor should he choose to surrender. But that's conjecture, because the message our submarine received was very short."

Henry frowned. "I fear more devastation may be needed to end this war. And, frankly, reports of the amount of radioactive damage to Japanese citizens struck me as beyond appalling. And,

Admiral Leahy, to use your words to the press, exposing any person to radioactivity is beyond frightening. Gentlemen, I am well aware that modern warfare does not allow us the ability to spare civilians from collateral damage. But reports from the Hiroshima bombing tell us the civilians our atomic bomb did not kill will suffer from a radiation that will soon kill or disfigure."

Byrnes frowned. "But didn't we agree we needed to show we could invent more than one atomic bomb? One reason why we always planned to drop the second bomb?"

"Yes, Secretary Byrnes. But now we know, despite precision bombing, our nuclear device radiates over a larger area. And kills, and burns, civilians anywhere nearby. We planned bombings to destroy targets that were military, not mankind. That's why your commander-in-chief has chosen a different target."

Henry waited until all had exhaled. "Our three B-29s on Tinian Island will soon be in the air, one carrying our plutonium nuclear bomb. That plane will drop our second atomic bomb on a Japanese target recommended by General Carl Spaatz. Yesterday, your president made a command decision. We will attempt to avoid any more radioactive burning of Japanese people. But we will still drop a second nuclear bomb to encourage immediate surrender by their emperor. Which is why I have chosen a different target."

Henry noticed the military men took deep breaths. *By their oath to defend the Constitution, President Henry F. Schricker was their Commander-in-Chief. Hope they figured that out.*

Henry continued, "If the Japanese don't surrender soon, the Russians will conquer Japanese troops in Manchuria, invade Japan's northern island, and we will face the same problem we now have with a divided Germany."

Henry paused to wait for a different opinion. But he saw only nods of agreement.

"Gentlemen, you have read a copy of the letter from Berkeley physicist Dr. Paul Stewart. You saw his reference to the frequency of volcanic eruptions brought on by frequent earthquakes. Also, he notes that *tsunamis* often accompany earthquakes. You know the deep concern that not only I, but also Admiral Leahy, and I am sure others, feel for the added horror created by radioactivity.

Dr. Stewart's opinion suggests an alternative. Please, again read his opinion."

Henry waited until each man had finished reading. "Gentlemen, please note these sentences:

"*If a device is detonated in the harbor, in or over water, would not matter. Water itself does not become radioactive.*"

Henry shook his head. "I'm not sure I understand his second sentence. *The radioactive water in a reactor is from the dissolved nitrogen, which has a half- life of a few minutes, and dissolved cobalt from the stainless cladding, half- life of a dozen years (nasty stuff).*

"But his next paragraph explains why I have ordered General Spaatz to change targets.

"*The explosion radiation would be from the fission reaction products and the neutron activated dirt from the site. The shock wave would liquefy the mud and bottom sediment, and the resultant debris tsunami would wreak havoc on the shoreline.'*

"I also noted Dr. Stewart's closing sentence, which reads, *After the shock wave levels everything.*"

Henry made eye contact with each of the men before he spoke. "I shared Dr. Stewart's opinion in my order to General Spaatz. I reminded him of his original opinion that we should bomb Tokyo Bay as a demonstration of our nuclear power. I thought, but did not message, that a B-29 can navigate to Tokyo Bay with or without radar. We should not expect weather conditions to keep us from bombing such a large target."

Henry softened his voice. "If, as some scientists have said, 'God is the sum of all physical power,' then I pray we have his forbearance."

President Henry F. Schricker again looked at each man before he spoke. "If the Japanese don't understand the power of a nuclear bomb, you can be sure they will understand our power to start a tsunami—one of the greatest dangers to their seafood dependence—and give them added reason enough to surrender now. Your president will be in the White House until the Japanese respond."

＊ —— ＊

FRIDAY, AUGUST 10, ABILENE, TEXAS, NEWSROOM, *ABILENE REPORTER-NEWS*

BELLS CLANGED ON THE ASSOCIATED Press wire machine. Only the five people in the newsroom at that time of night heard the bells ring: two proofreaders, one sportswriter, the high school senior editing the sports page, one copyreader sitting at the horseshoe desk, and the night editor, Brooks Peden, sitting in the editing desk slot.

Peden opened the door of the wire room and tore the copy from the teletype. Moments later he announced to his late night editorial staff, "We dropped another A-bomb on Japan!"

The staff waited for him to read more of the bulletin.

Then Brooks yelled, "Tsunami flooding Tokyo! Atomic bomb started a tsunami! We're gonna drown 'em!"

Brooks sang as he pranced toward the back shop where printers were locking up the front and jump pages. The presses were scheduled to roll in thirty minutes.

The tune was *Suwanee* but not his words. "Soo Nommy, Soo Nommy, How I love you, Soo Nommy."

CHAPTER 28

> HIGH ALTITUDE B-29 RECONNAISSANCE. BREAKS IN
> CLOUD COVER. MAGNIFIED PHOTOS.
>
> DOCKS IN TOKYO BAY MISSING. FISHING BOATS
> ON SHORE. HOUSING SCATTERED, MUCH DEBRIS
> IDENTIFIED IN WATER.

WHITE HOUSE, OVAL OFFICE

HIS SECRETARY OF STATE DIDN'T wait for the president to welcome his visit. Byrnes shoved past Admiral Leahy and burst into the office.

"Hell, Henry, the Japs are stalling. The code message from Tokyo to their legation in Switzerland isn't ironic; it's moronic."

Henry held up open hands.

"Excuse the outburst," Byrnes said. "Here's the latest. Our cryptanalysis team say *Magic* deciphered a long message from Tokyo demanding we punish one of our submarine commanders. Get this." Byrnes read:

> *Demand exemplary punishment of the U.S. submarine commander responsible for sinking the Japanese hospital ship Awa Maru. Attached an itemized claim for damages*

*totaling 227,286,000 yen, together with a demand for
prompt payment by the United States.*

Byrnes took a deep breath then huffed. "A sarcastic note on the
Magic summary observed that no claim was made for the munitions
being carried by the hospital ship."

Henry shook his head. "Jimmy, this is not the answer we were
waiting for."

❦ — ❦

SUNDAY, AUGUST 12, WHITE HOUSE, PRESIDENTIAL QUARTERS

HENRY SAMPLED THE MEAL BUT pushed back his dessert. With little
appetite, Henry watched Maude finish her pie.

"You bet, I'm worried," Henry answered Maude's unasked
question. "So are our military."

Henry decided not to tell Maude about his concerns over
possible banzai suicide attacks by Japanese troops everywhere. Or
the probability of prisoners-of-war being killed. Or concerns the
Japanese warlords would kill their emperor.

When Maude finished eating, Henry went to the piano in the
other room and played *Abide with Me*.

❦ — ❦

MONDAY, AUGUST 13, WHITE HOUSE, OVAL OFFICE

HENRY WELCOMED ADLAI. "I'M TOLD this is the last time you'll help
me compose a speech."

"Yes, sir. My family and I will move back to Illinois before
Labor Day."

Henry winked. "Are you going to make any Labor Day speeches?"

Adlai grinned. "As a matter of fact, Mr. President, a labor leader
asked me to talk about what to expect when our boys—and girls—
leave the wartime workforce."

Henry nodded. "Same problem coming near my hometown, Knox. Quite a number of women, some men, who worked in the munitions factory will be out of work. I'm thinking of a World War I song parody that's not very presidential. Something about putting women back in the kitchen when they've worked outside the home for years now."

Henry tapped out the tune on the top of his desk.

Adlai smiled. "To tell the truth, I'm pretty sure invitation to speak came, because I've been working for 'Our President.'"

"That's fine, Adlai. I enjoyed some good labor support, especially the railroad union workers, when I was governor of Indiana."

Henry frowned. "Just a year ago. But as my Maude says, we've lived an eternity in less than a year." He took a handkerchief and wiped his reading glasses. "Adlai, some day I hope to make a speech for you. I've heard that you'll most likely stand for governor of Illinois."

Henry waited, but Stevenson didn't deny the statement.

"I'll not get into state politics, Adlai, but this president owes you a great debt. You've earned my support. If it's in your future, I'll be one of the first to support you for this job, that is, if you're looking for some real misery."

"Thank you, President Schricker. We'll see. But I do have a favor to ask of you."

"Shoot."

Adlai cleared his throat. "My speech invitation came with a not too subtle request."

Henry nodded. "Politics, as we know, is not too subtle a science. Let's see if your president can handle it."

"Okay. My union friend received word that his nephew, a Marine captured on Corregidor, will soon be rescued from a Yokohama prisoner-of-war camp. When that happens, my union friend wonders if I can help return Sergeant Finch home in a hurry. He's survived, but Red Cross reports Finch is emaciated, weak, but walking."

Henry smiled. "If you will write out Finch's identity details, I'll see what influence a president has with his secretary of war."

From his coat pocket, Adlai pulled an envelope. He smiled and handed it to the president. "Sergeant Finch's data here, sir."

Henry accepted the envelope. "As a Marine sergeant would say, wipe that smile off your face, and we'll get to work writing my radio speech."

CHAPTER 29

TUESDAY AUGUST 14, TOKYO, JAPAN, EMPEROR'S PALACE, AIR RAID SHELTER

THE EMPEROR FIRST SAID HE had listened to arguments for and against accepting the Allies' proclamation. "But my own thoughts have not changed," Hirohito said. "Let me restate them. I have surveyed the conditions prevailing in Japan and in the world at large, and it is my firm belief that a continuation of the war promises nothing but more destruction. The Allies have acknowledged their position in dispatches."

The emperor paused. "In short, I consider their reply to be acceptable."

Delegates bent their heads, shuffled, and shuddered, but did not speak.

"I realize there are those of you who distrust the intentions of the Allies. That is quite natural. But to my mind the Allied reply is evidence of the peaceful and friendly intention of the enemy. The faith and the resolution of this nation as a whole, therefore, are factors of paramount importance."

The emperor paused and took a sip of the green tea on the table beside him. "I appreciate how difficult it will be for the officers and men of the Army and Navy to surrender their arms to the enemy and see their homeland occupied. Indeed, it is difficult for me to issue the order making this necessary and to deliver so many of my trusted servants into the hands of the Allied authorities, by whom they will be accused of being war criminals.

"In spite of these feelings, so difficult to bear, I cannot endure the thought of letting my people suffer any longer. A continuation of the war would bring death to tens, perhaps even hundreds of thousands of persons. The whole nation would be reduced to ashes. Or our seaports flooded. How then could I carry on the wishes of my Imperial ancestors?"

Hirohito's voice began to falter. He gulped to moisten his throat between every sentence. "The decision I have reached is akin to the one forced upon my grandfather, the Emperor Meji. As he endured the unendurable, so shall I, and so must you. It is my desire that you, my ministers of state, accede to my wishes and forthwith accept the Allied reply. In order that the people may know my decision, I request you to prepare at once an Imperial Rescript so that I may broadcast to the nation. Finally, I call upon each and every one of you to exert himself to the utmost so that we may work together in the trying days to come."

The emperor looked up from his manuscript. He saw his ministers weeping. Some of them openly sobbed. He thought, *My time for weeping has come and gone days before.*

WEDNESDAY, AUGUST 15, JAPAN

BEFORE NOON, THE JAPANESE PEOPLE—ISSUED a special ration of electricity—turned on their radios and heard their emperor for the first time. Hirohito had recorded the disc the previous night, just before midnight.

"To our good and loyal subjects, after pondering deeply the general trends of the world and the actual conditions of our empire today, we have decided to affect a settlement of the present situation by resorting to an extraordinary measure. We have ordered our government to communicate to the governments of the United States, Great Britain, China, and the Soviet Union that our empire accepts the provisions of their joint declaration."

The emperor's radio speech concluded, "My subjects, let us carry forward the glory of our national structure, and let us not lag behind in the progress of the world. Submit ye to our will."

WHITE HOUSE, OVAL OFFICE

PRESIDENT HENRY F. SCHRICKER STOOD before the members of the Capitol Press. They had been called to hear the president at seven o'clock. The formal acceptance from Japan had been received by Secretary of State Byrnes at six o'clock. The world's radios had already blared the news, but they all gathered to hear the president read the message aloud. As soon as Henry finished, the Capitol Press reporters ran to their telephones and typewriters.

Maude joined Henry who took her hand and led her out to the balcony. Henry raised his hand and made the 'V for Victory' sign. The street had filled with celebrants. They waved and yelled approval.

CAPITOL PRESS ROOM

HELEN THOMAS TYPED HER MESSAGE into the International Press wire machine.

> *From the moment that President Schricker*
> *announced at 7 p.m. Eastern War Time that the*
> *enemy of the Pacific had agreed to Allied terms, the*
> *world put aside for a time woeful thoughts of the*
> *cost in dead and dollars and celebrated in a wild*
> *frenzy. Formalities meant nothing to people freed of*
> *war at last.*

❦ —— ❦

MAP ROOM

Lieutenant Rigdon read the message he would personally deliver to the Oval Office, or wherever the president was now.

> *A decrypted message from the Navy minister to the Japanese fleet revealed the emperor's decision at the August 14 Imperial Council. "We, who were present, fully realized the extent of his determination and could not hold back the tears which welled up."*

> *Latest report: The war minister committed seppuku, ritual suicide. As did a number of generals and admirals. And the plotters of an unsuccessful coup who wished to continue the war.*

NORTHERN WATERS OF JAPAN, USS *INDIANA*

"Now hear this, your captain speaking. The war is over. The Japanese have surrendered. But, crew of the *Indiana*, don't forget the *Indianapolis*."

MOSCOW, SOVIET EMBASSY

Molotov handed Sato a formal declaration of war that came into effect, this past August 9.

WASHINGTON, D.C., WHITE HOUSE, FIRST LADY'S SITTING ROOM

MAUDE TOOK THE TELEPHONE CALL from 401 South Main Street, Knox, Indiana.

Margaret was bubbling. "Oh, Mom, Mom, I'm so happy. I've got Lewis here at the house. He's reassigned. Will research there. We're headed to D.C. area next week. And the war is over! It's over. And, Mom, can you hear the band? The Knox High School band is outside our house playing *Stars and Stripes Forever*, I think. Who knows? Everybody in Knox is shouting. What's happening at the White House?"

"Pop's standing outside on the south portico waving at what looks like about everybody in Washington. I came in when they told me you were calling. Tell your Lewis I saw some Navy men standing on the roof of a car. Heard one yell, 'We're all civilians, now.'"

WHITE HOUSE, PRESIDENTIAL SUITE

MAUDE HELD UP THE NEWSPAPER for Henry to see. "War's over, Henry. Arthur Krock says so in the *New York Times*. You got top billing: 'President Announces Surrender of Japan.'"

Henry put down his coffee cup and took the folded newspaper the first lady handed him. "But look at the subhead. 'Schricker says MacArthur to receive surrender.' Mac even got ahead of Krock's byline. And Navy beat Army to the front page. 'Naval Academy celebrates V-J Day in Tecumseh Court and beats the Japanese bell until it cracks.'"

THURSDAY, AUGUST 16, WHITE HOUSE

PRESS ASSISTANT MALIA BURCH WAITED her turn. She smoothed down her skirt and sat in a chair by the wall and watched Admiral

Leahy direct traffic into the Oval Office. She enjoyed the times she briefed President Schricker. His jovial greetings made her think of her grandfather in Seattle.

Other assistants had carried reactions from around the world, but she smiled when she thought her summary would be the latest. She would report on Australian press reaction—almost a day ahead, thanks to the dateline time difference.

She had typed a poem written by an Australian father thanking the president for dropping atomic bombs on Japan. He hoped his son would not now have to die in an invasion of the Japanese mainland.

Malia thought, *The president is father of a soldier and a Navy-trained medical corpsman. He will appreciate reading another father's words.*

CHAPTER 30

WHITE HOUSE, OVAL OFFICE

ADLAI WAITED WHILE HENRY LOOKED over the suggested text. Henry took a blue pencil from the desk holder and began to edit. He underlined *the atomic bomb is too dangerous to be let loose in a lawless world.* The underline would help him remember to emphasize the thought and deliver that specific message slower.

He inscribed a large question mark atop *that is why Great Britain and the United States have kept secret its production.*

"Adlai, do we need a sentence that says we do not intend to reveal atomic secrets until we find a means to control the bomb?"

"I understand the sentence sounds negative, Mr. President, but I think it's important that your radio message promises we will safeguard atomic secrets."

"Okay. Understand where you are going. But I think we need a positive reason for our secrecy."

Stevenson nodded. "Give me a minute." Adlai made notes on his legal pad. "How's this? *We must serve as trustees of this new force. Prevent the misuse of our discovered nuclear power. And turn atomic power into a service to all mankind. Not only to protect our countries, but to protect our world from total destruction.*"

The president nodded approval.

⊰——⊱

LONDON, PARLIAMENT, HOUSE OF COMMONS

EAGER TO ANSWER, CHURCHILL ROSE from the bench, waiting for the opposition to exhaust their catcalls. "The decision to use the atomic bomb was made by President Schricker and myself at Potsdam. Yes, we approved the military plans to unchain the dread, pent-up forces."

Winston waited for the Parliament hecklers to exhaust their taunts. "Let me repeat what I've said before. It would have been unacceptable for soldiers to have died in their hundreds of thousands to salve politicians' consciences about using it. It was approved overwhelmingly by the public, and especially by the armed forces, at the time."

His loyal minority that sat behind him yelled, "Hear! Hear!"

The majority responded with more ridicule.

Churchill waited for his detractors to exhaust their taunts. "May I remind the Loyal Opposition that the government's announcement was drafted before the outcome of our election was pronounced? Our words were agreed upon by both, now–Prime Minister Atlee and myself."

A chorus of "hah-hah-hah" resounded from Labour Party delegates.

Churchill sniffed at his tormentors, then continued. "I repeat words that I drafted, and the prime minister approved. The revelations of the secrets of nature, long mercifully withheld from Man, should arouse the most solemn reflections in the mind and conscience of every human being capable of comprehension. We must indeed pray that these awful agencies will be made to conduce to peace among nations and that instead of wreaking measureless havoc upon the entire globe they may become a perennial fountain of world prosperity."

Churchill paused.

"Blather!" came a yell from a backbencher.

Churchill responded, "Blather? Blather? How would you have decided? Would you have chosen NOT to drop even a second atomic bomb to secure Japanese submission? Would you have sacrificed another million Americans and a quarter of a million British lives?"

Churchill waited for his Conservative members to yell, "No! No! No!"

"Let us not forget. Let not the world forget. The bomb brought peace, but men alone can keep the peace, and henceforward they will keep it under penalties which threaten the survival not only of civilization but of humanity itself."

WHITE HOUSE, OVAL OFFICE

"SECRETARY STIMSON, WOULD YOU LOOK over this draft Adlai Stevenson helped me put together?"

The secretary of war held the typed copy of the radio script. "Reads well. You've condensed all of the main points."

"Thank you. I've not forgotten how you condensed our nuclear ambitions into a few paragraphs."

"Yes, Mr. President, I well remember when I brought you my written overview of the Manhattan Project. I'm still surprised Franklin hadn't briefed you before he died."

Henry nodded. "My thought then, and now, although President Roosevelt did hint of a 'great secret' when we lunched outside the White House. However, that was during his reelection campaign. Seems like that election, as a Hoosier farmer would say, is moons away."

"Maybe that's a blessing, Mr. President. You don't have to apologize for Great Britain and the United States hiding the atomic secret. Or spending $2 billion of taxpayers' money."

Henry didn't smile. "But future generations will probably argue over what we decided. Did we have to drop an atomic bomb? I think the question should be, if the Hiroshima demolition didn't bring the Japanese to surrender, did we have to flood them with a tsunami?" Will history agree with our projection of how many would have died if we had to invade the Japanese mainland?"

The question was meant to be rhetorical and Stimson picked up on that fact. The ultimate decision, especially the second explosion, would always be recorded as the decisive word from President Henry F. Schricker.

Stimson held the draft in one hand, raised fingers in the other hand as he enumerated. "We will let historians appraise the fine points you give us: one, we will be guardians of this new weapon, two, not only will we protect our country, but we will protect our world from total destruction, three, we will turn atomic power to solving worldwide problems, and four, the paragraph about future medical advancement should receive universal approval. I particularly like the reference to Madame Curie and the subsequent invention of x-ray. That's a universal use the Europeans will applaud. But I think penicillin helped us survive this war."

"Thanks. But give credit to Adlai for that allusion. Although, in his clever way, he told me not to expect to receive the Nobel Peace Prize for dropping a bomb on Hiroshima."

Stimson grinned. "Sometimes, Adlai's a little too witty. Hear he's already planning to run for Governor of Illinois. He's another Democrat this old Republican could stomach in line after Henry Frederick Schricker."

Henry chuckled. "Actually, I'm asking for a political favor that will help me repay Adlai for the speech writing help he gave me."

Stimson held up his hands to surrender. "Don't make the favor too tough. But immediate. I'm counting the weeks to retirement which have turned to days. What's your request?"

"Adlai wants to favor an Illinois politician by bringing his nephew home from a Japanese prisoner-of-war Yokohama shipyard. That's where Marine Sergeant Finch has been since we surrendered Corregidor."

Stimson chuckled. "Not the first, 'get my boy home' request I've heard."

"Maybe I'm asking too much?"

"Maybe not. For the next few days, General Douglas MacArthur still works for me. Or I work for him. I'm a bit of a coward. Leaving the general for you to fire, Henry. Will take a strong president."

Henry raised an eyebrow.

Stimson grinned. "And, you say, he was a marine on Corregidor. That's somebody Doug owes a big debt to."

Henry thought, *I can hear the gears meshing in Stimson's head.*

The secretary of war smiled. "I think I've got an answer. The Joint Chiefs are sending those generals and admirals who planned our invasion of Japan to fly over Kyushu. Want them to see the Kyushu fortifications we have unearthed. Then the brass will land in Tokyo, go to the surrender signing aboard the USS *Indiana*. I will suggest that we have a service representative, freed from Japanese captivity, watch the surrender signing. And, of course, Mr. President, fly the sergeant back home with our statesmen, generals, and admirals."

Henry sucked in his cheeks and wiped the smile off his face. He remembered, *I was once an Indiana state militia captain serving under Henry Stimson, then secretary of war—the man who impressed President Schricker as much as he had impressed two former President Roosevelts.*

CHAPTER 31

MONDAY, AUGUST 27, YOKOHAMA BAY, PRISONER-OF-WAR CAMP

LEE STRAINED TO LIFT HIS arm and salute the Navy lieutenant.

"At ease, Sergeant Finch. Oh my goodness, we should be saluting you. Let's get you and your buddy Gregg, aboard our hospital ship. Get you some new clothing before you fly back to the States."

Lee smiled and limped behind Gregg's wheelchair as they walked down the dock.

The lieutenant pointed at the unfinished hull. "Look at that hull you might have been working on. It's almost on its side. What happened?"

Lee ran his tongue across his teeth. "Tsunami got it. Water rose. Some hull rivets must have leaked. Bad workmanship. Took on too much water."

And I lived to see it, Lee thought.

TUESDAY, AUGUST 28, WASHINGTON, D.C., WHITE HOUSE, OVAL OFFICE

HENRY READ HARRY HOPKINS'S RESIGNATION letter. "*The time has come when I must take a rest.*"

"Admiral Leahy, I think your president needs to award the Distinguished Service Medal to Hopkins. Cite his exceptional ability for welding the Allies together during World War II.

"And when we get through the formal stuff, I'll rib Harry a little about his visit to Knox last year. Get him to tell me what he told Franklin. I don't know what Hopkins counseled that we would have done differently. You can be sure, history will second guess us.

"Admiral Leahy, please to show General Donovan in."

Henry noticed that the general had an array of medals on his uniform. Before Henry could extend his hand, Donovan braced and saluted. Henry returned the salute and signaled the general to take a seat in front of his desk. Leahy said Donovan had asked for an hour's conference, but Leahy arranged only 20 minutes. *Whatever Bill gave as an excuse for my limited time was fine.*

"Mr. President, I understand your busy schedule, and I have compiled a list to summarize the work my operatives performed. I omitted two sources of intelligence because I thought better for your ears only, and to protect those sources."

Henry nodded his understanding.

"As Navy Intelligence has told you, they not only broke the Japanese code and intercepted diplomatic messages, but also had a source close to their emperor in his palace. At the same time, my office was furnished information from an agent who had worked for both the Russians and the Japanese. Her espionage predated Pearl Harbor. She told us that the Japanese had planned to invade and take Soviet territory if the German invasion of Russia succeeded, and that Japan and Russia had agreed on a neutrality pact, but didn't really trust each other. When the Russians began to push the Nazis back, Japanese army military officials agreed with their navy and their *nanshin-ron* or 'southward advance,' a revised strategy that would lead to Pearl Harbor."

The general paused and waited for the president to react.

Henry didn't respond, but thought, *Some say when the United States limited oil shipments to Japan, the Japanese invaded China and surrounding territories to secure petroleum, and they went to war with the United States. I'll let the historians try to figure out the reasons.*

Donovan continued, "Mr. President, what we have learned from our Japanese operative would have saved many people in San Diego if the war had continued through next month."

This Wild Bill story sounds ominous.

"Our operative learned of this planned assault after the emperor surrendered. He had access to Unit 731, their biological and chemical warfare unit. He even told us the code name and date: Operation Cherry Blossom in the Night. It was scheduled for next month, September 22 to drop what he called a plague bomb on San Diego."

The general leaned toward the president's desk and raised a finger for emphasis. "A submarine aircraft carrier, the Japanese Navy's last creation, was huge. It carried a single airplane on its deck. When the submarine neared San Diego, they would launch a Kamikaze pilot, who would fly from the surfaced submarine and drop their plague bomb on the city."

The general looked for the president's reaction. Henry put his fingers together and waited.

"We think, Mr. President, the Japanese thought this suicide plague attack would cause us to rethink any invasion of the Japanese home islands."

Henry nodded twice. *And would have justified our use of a nuclear weapon.*

Donovan leaned forward. "I hope you agree with me that we need to keep operatives my team have recruited on duty around the world." And, by the way, Mr. President, you will recall I left you information about our OSS project in China. On the day we bombed Hiroshima, our OSS frogmen operatives exploded and destroyed the railroad bridge over the Yellow River in China."

Before Henry could commend the operation, Donovan continued, "And, Mr. President, I'm seeking clearance from the Office of War Information to publish the story, written by one of my staff, in the *Saturday Evening Post*. Maybe you could help us get clearance."

Henry put both hands atop his desk and thought, *How much should I tell him? We haven't announced yet that the Office of War Information will cease to function next month on September 15.*

Donovan didn't wait for the president to answer. "As we have seen, Mr. President, it's important that we augment military intelligence with in-their-midst information—and actions—from our agents. You can be sure, the Communists didn't fire their agents when the shooting stopped."

The door to Leahy's office opened. The admiral coughed lightly. "Excuse me, Mr. President, your next scheduled appointment has arrived."

"Thank you, Admiral Leahy."

To General Donovan, Henry said, "I'm grateful for your counsel, and of course, your great service helping us win the war. I will think much about your information. Thank you for coming today."

THURSDAY, AUGUST 30, YOKOHAMA, JAPAN

GENERAL MACARTHUR PULLED HIS CORNCOB pipe out and pointed at the officer standing in front of his desk. "Captain Metcalf, I think you made a good suggestion. Establishing headquarters in Yokohama keeps us near, but far enough away from the Emperor's Palace that Hirohito will save some face. Of course, the tsunami that our president claims he created has temporarily made Tokyo waterfront locations untenable. Yokohama provides a more usable seaport. You need to know that Ike and I both opposed employing a nuclear bomb. Makes war too barbaric. And now that our secondhand president has reduced radiation terror to a tsunami, we need to elect a president who would never envision using that weapon.

"But, I digress. Thank you, captain, for your counsel on Japanese customs and rituals."

Captain Metcalf said, "You're welcome, sir. And your idea of General Wainwright, imprisoned after Corregidor fell, to attend the signing Sunday, makes a symbolic statement the Japanese militarists will understand. Operations told me an enlisted man—captured on Corregidor when the island fell—will be on the *Indiana*. Also symbolic because he was freed from the Japanese prisoner-of-war camp near this harbor."

MacArthur took another pull on his pipe. "Captain Metcalf, if that was your idea, outstanding. Fortifies our promise to return."

"Thank you, sir, but Sergeant Finch's attendance was a request from the White House. I think a Chicago politician wants him back soon. A war hero to help in the gubernatorial election. Orders say fly him back with the invasion planners General Marshall is sending."

The general frowned and put his pipe in the ashtray. "Thanks, Captain Metcalf. That will be all for now."

WHITE HOUSE, OVAL OFFICE

"Bill, I knew there was an accounting coming. Back home, the insurance company usually made sure the bank got a report on the damage to property where we had loaned money. But this report is different. Really hurts."

"Same here, Mr. President."

"Thank you, Admiral Leahy. I'll read before the next appointment."

Henry reflected. *Now I feel like Old Abe Lincoln walked in, put a hand on my shoulder, and looked at our tally sheet:*

Deaths, 50 million people

Soviet Union, 13 million combatants, 7 million civilians

Germany, 3.2 million soldiers, 3 million civilians

Britain and Commonwealth, 484,482

Japan, 1 million military, 2 million civilian

Jews, 6 million

United States, 291,557 battle deaths, 113,842 non-hostile.

The 32nd President of the United States read the tally sheet again. *Well, Abe, we have suffered the fewest casualties among the major nations. Expect you remember exact numbers from your tally sheet. How many died when we fought each other? I remember reading somewhere around 350,000.*

FRIDAY, AUGUST 31, WHITE HOUSE, OVAL OFFICE

HENRY SHOOK HANDS WITH THE younger man, about his same five foot, eight inches tall. He noticed the thick lenses of his glasses of the Science Editor. "Mr. Laurence, thank you for coming. Also, Mr. Laurence, I want to thank you for your news release work on the Manhattan Project. And the fine notes that General Grove had you write in preparation for our atomic bomb announcements."

"Thank you, Mr. President. And how gracious of your wife to tour Florence through the White House."

Henry smiled. "Well if I can speak off-the-record to the *New York Times?*"

Henry's smile turned into a grin. "What I should have qualified that off-the-record is in regards to my wife Maude as White House tour guide. Maude has also arranged a birthday lunch to celebrate my birthday. I'm told by my informants to act surprised."

Bill smiled. "Yes, sir. I appreciate your delimiter, sir. I know that in the early part of this century, you were an editor and publisher before you were a politician."

Henry grinned. "And I know that William Laurence was born in Lithuania. So was my good Knox, Indiana friend, Israel Mishkovsky. We're a land of immigrants. I also know how you, your publisher, and managing editor at the *New York Times* kept secret what many scientists told you about the Nazis working on heavy water and possibly a nuclear explosive. And I'm told that you knew Einstein had approached President Roosevelt with his concern about the Nazis experiments with nuclear fission."

Laurence nodded. "Yes, Mr. President. You might say what we didn't print, in the true sense, was an explosion going on in the minds of some great scientists."

"There's a book here, isn't there, Mr. Laurence?"

"Yes, Mr. President, I have already edited some of my reports into a manuscript. I have a publisher waiting who is most encouraging. He likes my mythological reference to Prometheus and Zeus and agrees with my conclusion. And, I think, with yours."

Henry smiled. Maude and Margaret had made him keep a diary with a future publication in mind. "Would you like to share your conclusion with me off-the-record, of course?"

"As you have already concluded, Mr. President, in your speech to the United Nations, reconstruction has commenced. Agricultural production is climbing up in spite of shortages of fertilizer and machinery. Industry and commerce are struggling out of the rubble. The revival, with all its distressing shortcomings, has been far better than I foresaw from my own observations among just liberated people in Italy, Europe, and England during the war."

Henry leaned back in his chair. "And what do you conclude, Mr. Laurence?"

"I conclude nations can no longer settle their differences with wars. No person should ever have to make the decisions that have been thrust on you, President Schricker."

Henry nodded several times. "I appreciate your kind words. There is an argument for a just war that I have read. I presume you may have read some of the philosophy of Reinhold Niebuhr."

Laurence nodded. "I have. His scope is very broad. What did you have in mind, Mr. President?"

"I had in mind his quotation, written in the 1930s. He said it wasn't possible to disavow war absolutely without disavowing the job of establishing justice."

Laurence bowed his head to Henry. "Yes, Mr. President, that's one of the dilemmas I raise in drafts I have written. In my book, I want to show how difficult it is to employ war as a means of destroying tyranny, preserving justice, especially now that our development of nuclear weapons could destroy our civilization. We must serve as trustees of this new force. Prevent the misuse of our discovered nuclear weapon. And turn atomic power into a service to all mankind."

Henry extended his hand. Laurence clasped it.

"Mr. Laurence, if you want, I would be honored to write a foreword to your book when you publish."

"Thank you, sir."

Henry acknowledged the knock on the door.

Admiral Leahy opened and announced, "Mr. President, Mr. Laurence, your ladies have returned from their tour and await you in the dining area."

As they walked down the hall, Henry explained that Laurence was expected to go ahead and join his wife and Maude. "I'm told to wait, because there may be a Broadway chorus to sing something more than *Happy Birthday*."

Laurence thanked Henry and entered ahead.

When Henry entered, the Broadway chorus broke into song. *You'll Never Walk Alone* rang true and Henry felt the lyrics to his very soul.

SATURDAY, SEPTEMBER 1, WHITE HOUSE, OVAL OFFICE

MATTHEW CONNELLY PULLED HIS CHAIR close to the president's desk and poised his pad, ready for dictation.

Henry began the work of the day. "Matthew, we want to write Mrs. Roosevelt that we are going to put her column in the Congressional Record. I want to add a personal note and signature, so forget the presidential underline. Please bring me the typed letter. Monday, I will call Eleanor and ask her to lead the delegation to its first meeting at the United Nations General Assembly in London."

Henry looked at the newspaper in his hand before starting the dictation. "'Are we going to censure General Marshall today, even if he didn't send explicit enough directions to General Short in Pearl Harbor in 1941, and forget the magnificent record which he has made during the past four years? You wrote a sentence the world needs to read after both of us are gone."

The president adjusted the reading glasses on his nose:

> *"If we had been clamoring for preparedness as a nation, we would not have allowed certain writers and papers and radio speakers to hurl the epithet of warmonger at the many people who warned us in the years before Pearl Harbor that war might be coming. Secretary Stimson's diary shows that President Roosevelt warned that the Japanese might attack on a certain day."*

Henry handed the newspaper to Connelly. "Here's my copy. See where I've underlined what I just read to you." Then he continued his dictation. "'Eleanor, you were so omniscient when you wrote

'Recriminations will not bring back our dead. Instead of recriminations, it would be safer and wiser if we determined in the future never again to be a flabby and ill-prepared people.'

"Last sentence. 'God Blessed America when he gave us Eleanor Roosevelt.' Sign it Henry."

Henry leaned back in his chair. "Old girl is right on, Matthew, her very last sentence dings the propagandists, writers, and speakers who kept us unaware of danger are as, she writes, 'dangerous to our peace efforts as they were to our war efforts.'"

Peace efforts, Henry thought. *We've got to lower taxes, reduce the bureaucracy, feed our enemies, restore moral standard, and keep some potentate from getting the atomic bomb. Franklin won the war; he left me to win the peace.*

⟞——⟝

SUNDAY, SEPTEMBER 2, YOKAHAMA BAY, USS *INDIANA*

A SAILOR HELPED LEE GET up. Sergeant Finch held one hand on the launch gunwale and shuffled to the lowered stairs. Another sailor grabbed an arm and helped Lee climb the USS *Indiana* metal gangway. Lee saluted the officer, turned, and saluted the flag that had flown over the Capitol on December 7, 1941.

Lee thought, *I'm a Marine who hasn't been on a ship for over four years. I weighed 185 pounds then. And the girl next door said I was "even more handsome" when I wore my dress blue and red uniform.*

A khaki-clad Marine officer moved to Lee's shoulder. The colonel put a hand under one of Lee's emaciated arms and moved him to the rear as the Americans formed rank.

"The general told me to look after you, Sergeant Finch. See that you got on the plane tonight."

Lee raised his eyebrows and dropped his jaw, which caused the colonel to smile. "Wondering why you're here, aren't you, Finch? Not only do you represent our prisoners of war, the ones who survived, but you've got somebody at the White House telling us to look after you."

Thank Uncle Granville, Lee thought. *Bet he cashed in some of his political chips with the Illinois labor bosses when the family heard I was freed. Second time my uncle has rescued me. Got me out of trouble once before. Then suggested I join his old Semper Fi buddies who would make a man out of me. They did. Maybe they could put me back together again.*

Lee leaned against the nearest gun turret. His new khakis scratched. Stiff cloth made his knees itch. *I'm ready to change to my old corduroy fishing pants, put on my wool shirt and old hat, shove the boat into the water, and see if there are any old Fox River fish still waiting for me.*

Sergeant Finch leaned against the metal and listened to the officer's whispered comments.

"A boatswain mate told me they counted over 200 ships anchored here. From what I see, Mac's 'flack' counting all our landing vessels as well as battleships."

"Yeah. Maybe he's counting the frigate that Commodore Perry sailed in here in the 1850s."

"Don't see any carriers."

"Boatswain said they're outside, because they're launching the fly-over planes."

While they whispered across him, Lee watched the destroyer tie up on the starboard side and extend a gangway to the *Indiana*.

A sergeant standing in front of Lee whispered, "That's the *Buchannan*, she's bringing all our brass."

"'Tention."

Men on each side of him braced. Damn if he would, even if he could.

Lee watched the braid come aboard. Three generals and three admirals led. A couple of young lieutenants brought up the rear. *Probably in college when we surrendered at Corregidor,* Lee thought.

The colonel whispered they were the officers who had helped plan the invasion. "Thank God, we never needed an invasion."

Then the Japanese military—eyes straight ahead, chins raised high—marched to the other side of the deck.

Lee recognized the emaciated general who had led the Allies' brass. *That's General Wainwright, forced to surrender Bataan and Corregidor. Like me, he's been a prisoner since we surrendered.*

Here comes MacArthur. The general, as always, even in the tunnel where they met at Corregidor, stood erect with his face frozen. Thank goodness, all the Americans wore open-collar khakis.

Mac, of course, wore full uniform with medals across his chest. His pants looked like cardboard, the legs had been pressed so firmly. *The New Emperor of Japan,* Lee thought. *He's back to rule here just as he ruled in the Philippines.*

Over the colonel's shoulder, Lee watched the Japanese then MacArthur sign the surrender.

When MacArthur started his speech, Lee remembered the measured Corregidor tone that told him he needed a shave. The general continued his oration, but Lee tuned him out.

Lee flinched when he heard the roar, louder than the Japanese planes that flew over his Corregidor gun emplacement. When he had counted at least 400 Navy and Air Force planes passing overhead, Lee smiled. *Mac's staying out here, but I'm going home.*

AUTHOR BIO

DICK ELAM BEGAN WRITING AT the age of 14, earning his first byline for an Abilene Reporter-News article on the city golf tournament. The lanky Texan was 17 years old, Editor of his high school newspaper, working part time at the Abilene Reporter-News when he heard the bells ringing on the newspaper's Associated Press Printer. The Flash bulletin read the U.S. dropped the second atomic bomb on Nagasaki.

Attending college at the University of Texas at Austin, Elam was elected to the position of Editor of the Daily Texan, the institution's daily newspaper. Dick's life was never dull. He worked as a reporter, a TV station manager, a sailboat racing skipper, a cruising skipper, a Naval Reservist, an oilfield pilot, a political consultant, a university professor, and acrylic artist.

Dick Elam discovered FDR's overture to Henry Schricker when he summered in Knox, Indiana. He was only six blocks from the Schricker house that's now a museum. Dr. Elam, Professor Emeritus, researched Schricker's biography and World War II books in the town's Schricker Library. He read all of Schricker's 1990's newspapers on microfilm.

He found that Schricker played organ at his Lutheran church and discovered Schricker's married daughter christened the USS *Indiana* battleship. He talked to Indiana people who remembered the Schrickers. Those memories are reconstructed in the narrative.

The posthumous publication of *Main Street President* reflects his love of history and story-telling and his special delight in surprising his readers.

Dick Elam Books dickelambooks@gmail.com